SEPTEMBER THOMAS

Fan the Flame

The Elemental Gods Book Two

First edition

ISBN: 978-1-7342545-1-8

Editing by Fiona McLaren
Cover art by Natasha MacKenzie

This book was professionally typeset on Reedsy.
Find out more at reedsy.com

To David,
For seeing the beauty in the mystical

Chapter 1

"Give me your passion, give me that fire. I know it's in there somewhere!"

The bullwhip of thorns snapped at my chest, but I smoothly blocked it with my rapier. The vines twined around the blade instead, the ice stained red in the setting sun, as Rose ripped it from my hands. She reared back to strike again, a viper crouching in the grass, but I was already in motion, the world swinging upside down, my hand balancing my full weight as I cartwheeled. My arm shot out, a newly-created dagger arrowing from my palm past the flutter that was her translucent wings.

Her whip coiled around my ankle. I allowed it to pull me up and in as the pixie nimbly dodged my follow-up attack. My back bowed, my teeth bared in a snarl, as I arched over the pixie, a spray of tiny arrows fanning from my hands. She cursed as three lodged deep in her shoulders, the whip unwinding from my leg as she swiped at the trickle of blood on her cheek, an injury inflicted by a fourth.

"Give me more, Zara, yeah? Make me burn."

I couldn't do that.

My ankles screamed when I hit the ground, but I brushed the pain aside, arms thrust wide, sweeping high, palms flat as they molded a smooth pane of protective, glassy ice. Poison barbs hit it and tumbled uselessly to the ground. The pixie blurred as the wall liquified,

1

waterfalling to the earth. I barely felt the spray as I splashed through it, charging at her again, twin katanas of ice raised and angled.

Green skin flashed as she parried my thrusts with elegant flicks of her whip. I released the blades again, shifting into a smooth slide-tackle that wiped her off her feet. A rumble of laughter tumbled from her as she fell, shoulders curling as she hit the ground and rolled. Her wings caught the wind and she flipped to her feet as I tossed her favorite weapon into the shade of a pine tree.

Her chest heaved, straining against the dozens of leather straps that crisscrossed her chest in a blend of beauty and armor. I braced, fingers curled, knees bent, knowing what was coming. She shook her head, sweat spraying from the ends of the dozens of braids hanging from one side of her scalp, then reached to free the double-edged blade strapped to her back.

"Is that all you got?" she crowed. "Where's your imagination? Or did you cut that out of you like you did everything else that made you interesting?"

Passion. Imagination.

Words I'd once spoken with reverence; words that had once driven my entire existence.

Words I wished I could burn along with the rest of my past.

The katanas in my palms melted away. I wished for the familiar tingles of adrenaline and challenge to curl like smoke in my chest, to fill me like wildfire. Instead, I found a layer of ice seven feet deep and equally numb.

"You want imagination?" I asked, barely hearing my own words.

Her lip curled. She spun her weapon, the bluish-gray metal blurring. "Hit me."

So I did.

Torrents of water from four directions smacked into her. The blast should have sent her flying, but it was everywhere, all around her,

2

engulfing her in a bubble of frothy liquid. Inky eyes burned with frustration as she floated here, one hand braced against the icy rim, but I held firm, barely blinking as she twitched. One minute passed, then two. Panic replaced her frustration as she thrashed, smacking the wall again and again. Tiny bubbles spilled from her parted lips. From this angle, the double rows of her shark teeth were visible.

Only when she went lax did I release my grip.

Rose smacked the ground in a crumple of limbs and leather, sputtering as she sucked in bellyfuls of air. The suffocating layer of ice beneath my skin barely trembled at the sight of her misery, of her intensity. Rather than linger on the emotion, I approached.

"You elf," she wheezed. I held out a hand which she smacked away and rolled to her back. "You really were gonna kill me, yeah?"

"I considered it." I crossed my arms as I hovered over her. "But if you had died, that would have made holding my victory over your head for the rest of your life difficult, if not impossible."

Her midnight eyes flicked between my aquamarine ones, her brain ticking a million miles a second. The shaved half of her emerald scalp was already starting to dry. When I wondered if I'd actually gone too far, a brilliant smile split her face. She laughed, the sound as smooth and rich as aged whiskey. Her palm smacked the grass.

"If I didn't know better, I'd say you were heartless," she finally worked out between gales. "But since you've got a heart of a pixie, that would be a mite bit hypocritical."

We looked nothing alike, acted nothing alike, yet Rose had declared me her sister-at-heart less than twenty-four hours after crushing the forces of our shared enemy at the lake. The Order, a religion once sworn to protect me and three other teenage Gods of unfathomable power, did nothing but try to kill us.

The pixie had played a key role in getting me into the position to defeat the general of their armed forces along with a chunk of his army.

She now claimed her spot was at my side as an unofficial bodyguard. At only sixteen, she already commanded her own brigade of pixies originating from a commune tucked deep in Australia's Northern Territory.

The pixie banged the sides of her hands together, fingers curling in a sign I recognized as an all-clear. The half dozen, war-mongering, killing-machines she lovingly called her sisters slipped from the shadows into the grove. They, too, wore leather and clasped an eclectic array of weapons—everything from butterfly swords and poison barbs to hand-guns and weighty crossbows.

"Your defenses are perfect," Rose said, unashamed and unapologetic in her defeat. "There's not much more I can teach you. Even your grasp on water is incredibly advanced, yeah?"

She fished a hunk of willow bark the size of a box of gum from her back pocket. Before taking a seat at her side, I snapped my fingers, drying the lake-water from our skin and clothing. Her shoulders slumped when she bit down on the bark, absorbing its powerful healing effects. I would offer to heal her, a key secondary trait of my water magic, but she'd only refuse.

Pixies respected scars.

Pain only makes you stronger, she'd chanted at me more times than I could remember. *Use emotion to your advantage*, was another one she threw in my face at least three times a day. Judging by the angle of her left eyebrow, she was thinking it right now. I shrugged and draped my arms over my raised knees, my hands hanging limply.

"Not today," I cautioned. "Leave it alone."

She sucked hard on the bark one last time before tucking it away. Her tone was bland as she scrubbed at the cut on her face. "I wasn't going to say anything."

"That's what I thought."

"But you really need to break out your fire."

4

I closed my eyes against the dusky light, grinding my teeth. I refused to touch the magic granted to me four weeks ago, the magic represented on the outside curve of my arm as the black outline of a flickering flame. It lined up perfectly beside the matching, cresting wave with which I'd been born.

That wasn't to say I wasn't fully aware of the heat and smoke of the fire magic prowling my veins like a hungry tiger. As tempting as it was to tap into that power, I also remembered how I'd acquired the magic by nearly dying at the hands of the man who led the Order himself. Geoffrey was yet another person who should have been on my side, yet resolutely was not.

I repressed a shiver. The one time I'd tried to use that magic after the battle by the lake, I'd nearly burned a cabin to the ground. Fire magic was prickly, unpredictable, and wild. I preferred the easy give and take of the water I'd come to master.

I adjusted again, ignoring the stiff muscles and twinges of pain that never seemed to fully heal. "I'm not discussing this with you."

"You're not discussing it with anyone." Rose toyed with one of her braids.

"And that's my call." I winced at the snap in my tone. "I mean—"

"I know what you mean." She swatted at my arm. "But you also need to know it's difficult to watch. You're a shadow of—"

The cry of a hawk pierced the skies, thankfully cutting off the end of that sentence. The six-foot wingspan of the majestic bird was black against the purple of dusk. It released another shriek, wings pulling in for a dive. Rose and I were used to the display, but the other pixies clustered, silver glinting between their hands in the casual exchange of bets.

The arrow that was the bird of prey gained speed, its body growing larger as it angled for the clearing among the greenery of oaks and pines. Its breast brushed a branch, shaking the leaves as it speared the foliage. When it appeared it would crash land, its wings flared wide. It morphed and the shadow of a human touched the ground. Undaunted, the boy tossed back his shoulder-length hair and snatched up a bag strapped to his ankle. More silver exchanged hands as the pixies muttered, their long, dragonfly wings fluttering in the breeze.

"Nearly brained yourself that time, yeah? Maybe next time don't cut it so close," Rose called, pulling me to my feet with her. Standing, she was about a foot shorter than my five-and-a-half feet.

"I had complete command of the situation," the God of Air retorted in his usual arrogant way as he cinched the ties at his waist. He left his feet and chest bare. "The Thunderbird beat some measure of control into my poor, fragmented body."

Rose circled him, sniffing like a dog. "It appears you're in one piece."

"Little do you know." Joseph slid his glasses up his nose, blinking owlishly behind the thick lenses. "One more day of training and It might have done me in. No one will be more thankful than me to finally board Ryder's likely ill-acquired airplane."

Rose chuckled as she snatched up her whip from the shadows. "As long as it gets us to Egypt in one piece, I'll be happy," she said, winding its length around her hips.

"Speaking of Egypt," Joseph trailed off as he surveyed the clearing, full lips quirking when he spotted me, "there she is, our First and almighty savior. How blessed we are to stand in her brilliance." I shot him a glare as he crossed the grove in three quick steps. He pulled my stiff body against his in a hug that was less a greeting and more a check of the day's bruises. He smelled like sunshine and sweat. When he assured himself I was, in fact, in one piece, he batted me away.

"Never have I been so ready to leave these woods," Joseph proclaimed with a heavy sigh. I shook my head and snagged my long braid of silvery hair, pulling it over my shoulder to run the tufted end across my collarbone. I was used to his stilted and overly formal speech. He'd grown up around books, with very little human interaction. "Thank the stars you finally felt the bond of our long-lost sibling. I wasn't jesting about the bird breaking me down."

Over the past four weeks, we'd thrived in relative peace. By all accounts, the Order had gone back to whatever it was it normally did following the battle that resulted in the deaths of two men who ran it. We hadn't heard so much as heard a whisper of retaliation. That had given me and Joseph time to train as I worked to figure out where the Gods of Earth and Fire might be hiding. As the First of Four, it was my birthright to track them down and bring them to heel. For some reason, according to archaic rules crafted by ancient fey and their Gods thousands of years ago, the four of us were needed to stop an impending apocalypse.

However, no matter how much I'd poured over the stupid, foldable map one of the pixies had snitched from Finn, the kelpie tasked with making sure my decisions didn't get too reckless, I couldn't sense my remaining two counterparts. That had changed last week when a thin, golden thread flared in Egypt. Joseph had wasted no time telling me that's where we would likely find the God of Earth since the Lost City was apparently located somewhere in its vast deserts.

My pulse fluttered at the thought of leaving this secluded peace in northern Wisconsin, of venturing into the world of uncertainty once more. This was the closest I'd felt to safety since I'd learned that magic wasn't only a buzz word on a television show. I wasn't sure I was ready to release its reins, yet.

"We should probably get back to the village," I said, bypassing everything I wanted to say, everything I knew *he* wanted me to say. Joseph's face fell, and I swallowed, tucking away the whisper of guilt. "I bet our goodbye party will start soon. I know you hate being late." Like quicksilver, his grin returned, and I swatted his arm before he could hook it around my shoulders.

"You know me too well." He hooked his thumbs in his pockets as he wandered over to the girls. "Besides, I'm starving."

The pixies chorused their agreement as they gathered their things, their dark skin turning their bodies to little more than shadows against the night. Stars twinkled overhead as they ambled in a cluster toward the edge of the grove.

When she realized I wasn't following, Rose stopped. "Come on, yeah? You did well today. Might as well celebrate a little before everything changes." Her Australian accent was thicker tonight as if she were truly ready to let loose and exchange her weapons and armor for liquor and dresses.

"I won't be long." I flicked my thumb over my shoulder at the lake. "I need a minute to myself." The pixie ran her hands over the twist of vines and thorns at her waist, caught between her dedication to my safety and her desire to take a night off.

"I promise, I'll be right behind you. I'll even start a fire if I need help," I joked. Her brow furrowed, but, after another pass of her hands, her head dipped.

"Five minutes," she warned. "Any longer and I'm coming back for you."

I offered a silent salute, then turned to the water so I wouldn't have to see her leave. In the dark, it was difficult to make out much in the reflection of the glassy surface. It reminded me of a different body of fresh water, one where I'd first learned to embrace myself and my magic. Except this time, I could feel the heartbeats of fish rippling against the current and the subtle drag of weeds across the muddy bottom.

I waited, still as stone, listening to the bugs trill and chirp, until I couldn't sense the presence of my friends any longer. For the first time in weeks, I was alone. My fingers laced together and I swayed on my feet, my pulse thudding faster as the enormity of what was happening finally sank in. The sweat froze on my skin.

I was going to dive right back into the insanity that was my destiny. I was going out into the broad, cruel world and see what awaited me there. Despite our precautions, I was a God, and I would be recognized. I was one of the four beings who brought magic back to the world, after all. And once I was out in the open, the Order would be forced to recognize my presence—likely by attacking again. And that was merely the recognition of one organization.

Then there was the entire *world* to think about.

The survival of humans and fey alike was on my shoulders.

Mine.

For the first time, I acknowledged I was *afraid* of what might happen, *afraid* of who I might become along the way. I feared that I might not have the answers, that my abilities might not be enough.

The sheet of numbness coating my soul cracked against the wild, incessant pounding of my terror, of my self-doubt, of my deepest insecurities. My hands trembled as I stared down at the water. I clenched them tight, but that only made my arms shake. My jaw ached around my clenched teeth.

I didn't want to face the Order again, didn't want to become the "savior" that so many people needed me to be. I was just a seventeen-year-old girl caught up in a whole lot of crazy.

Heat flared in my belly, chased by a fistful of ice, and that first crack in my soul splintered, smaller fractures radiating across the surface. With each fracture, came a fresh memory, a foreign emotion restrained for far too long. The swamp of it threatened to suck me under as it thrashed and boiled inside of me. My fire magic leaped at the chaos, the red strangling the blue of water.

I remembered Geoffrey's outstretched hands, the flash of dragonfire bursting from his palms. I shuddered, recalling the agony of my skin igniting, smelling my burning hair and flesh. The bitterness of wanting

9

to die had been so consuming it seemed incredible I hadn't succumbed.

Another fracture, another inferno—this one also caused by the Order and its helicopter whirring over my childhood house, dropping ignition fluid on the roof. My parents had been trapped inside.

The cracks spread quickly now, a torrent of memories racing along with them.

Nearly drowning beneath another starlit sky.

Standing on a spiral of water overlooking a city of steel and glass.

The pulsating beat of friendship and truth in the heat of a sweaty nightclub.

My chest heaved as I clawed at my clothes, tearing at my skin. Another splintering fracture, this one yawning wide, its depths unrealized: a pair of brown eyes, vacant in death, stared at me from behind my eyelids. My best friend. Another person I'd failed in my short life, another casualty of my living nightmare.

I couldn't do this. I couldn't go out there again.

Just because I'd killed Geoffrey and his blood-thirsty minions didn't mean the organization that had repeatedly tried to wipe me off the face of the planet would stop in its mission now.

I staggered back, choking on panic and fear.

I needed to get out of here.

I needed to run.

But when I tried to fall back, my knees locked. The hairline fractures of my soul froze, then retreated, the cracks smoothing into glossy panes of glass. The bits and pieces I had left of myself curling together, eager to retreat into the numbness.

I tried to move again, take one more step, but couldn't. Instead, to my horror, my hands raised of their own volition, a familiar dagger of ice forming in the cup of my palm. A dagger I wasn't creating. I couldn't breathe as I raised the blade to my throat, the point leveled at the hollow above my sternum. I stared down the sheen of ice into the blackness of the forest beyond.

"If you're truly this weak," whispered a voice in my head, one I'd only heard a handful of times before, "then why does death frighten you so?"

Chapter 2

"It would be so easy to end it all, right here, right now," the disembodied voice spoke again. The sound rippled through me like wind through tree branches. "I'd even be willing to help you along."

I swallowed and my throat nicked the blade. Aside from blinking and breathing, I was trapped. A hostage in my own body. An owl hooted from across the lake, unknowing and uncaring of my predicament.

"But I'm sensing resistance." Lips like leaves brushed the shell of my ear. "As much as you want to run, part of you still holds back, am I right?"

I closed my eyes, wondering if it were possible for blood to skitter like goosebumps. This wasn't the first time this woman had snatched control of my body, but it was the first time her presence truly frightened me. As easily as water flowing over rocks, she'd slipped in and snatched control of my body, all without me knowing she was there.

As if she heard my thoughts—which she very well could be—she said, "It's not me you should fear. Reserve that useless emotion for yourself."

I opened my eyes, the tiny hairs on the back of my neck rising, nostrils flaring at the shadowy figure crouched before me. It was the first time I'd seen her in any sort of substantial shape. Until now she'd always lurked as an unwanted voice whispering in my ear, offering both snide commentary and biting advice in equal doses.

The woman—if she could be considered that—appeared more ghost than human: her body tangled in shadowy webs, her limbs spun of flowers and vines, the hand gripping the blade at my neck a mere twist of branches and bark. The moonlight brushing her face offered impressions of cheekbones and a slim jawline. Against the subtlety of her form, the bright glow of her violet eyes sent chills down my spine. She was enjoying this, enjoying my panic, my helplessness, my lack of control.

"Good girl. I knew you'd face me," she cooed. Her tongue cradled her c's and s's, adding a hissing quality to her languid speech. "I knew I didn't choose a coward."

Ribbons of darkness flowed over her shoulders as she chuckled, her face tipped toward the sky. For all her amusement, her grip on the knife remained hard as stone and equally immovable. "Nothing to say for yourself?"

I stared down the length of ice, my lips pressed firmly together. She rolled her shoulders and, after a few moments that stretched thick as molasses, edged the knife back a half-inch with another playful chuckle.

"Who are you?" I whispered, the words an echo of another time, another conversation with someone else who'd held me captive within my own thoughts.

The evening breeze blew the stale scent of standing water over us.

Like Geoffrey had maintained his silence all those weeks ago, she, too, failed to fill the yawning gap of our conversation. I wet my lips and tried again, holding her gaze with fierce determination. "What do you want with me?"

She lifted a branch of a finger to the area around her face where a mouth might be. "Such interesting phrasing. 'With me.' Not 'from me' or 'to do to me.' How fascinating you'd choose the phrase most accurate to my desires." She wound a curl of midnight and smoke around the same finger in concentrated thought. "I want to revel in your accomplishments *with* you. I want you to reach your true potential. I want you to prove you're hardly as useless as your many predecessors."

The last sentence cracked like ice underfoot. I wanted to flinch, but couldn't.

"I'm sorry, that may have been too harsh." She didn't sound sorry. She certainly didn't look sorry as she crowded my space, our faces nearly touching. "I see many great things for you, Zara. I see someone full of potential. I see someone worthy of the lessons I've taught you."

My jaw ticked before I locked it into place.

It was my first voluntary movement. Her control was slipping.

"You're wondering *'what lessons?'* It's written on your face, plain as your nose." She dragged the flat of the blade along the underside of my jaw. I sensed movement along my periphery but found myself caught in the prison of her gaze.

"Everything you know is because of me," she purred. "Did you truly think you could master water so easily? With so little training? It takes years to learn the patience necessary to understand the complexity that is magic and even more time to *understand* how to wield it in any sort of effective form. The fact you've made it this far, with no grasp of what being a God means let alone knowing how to use that to your advantage, is purely based on my willingness to share information—to allow you to think that you were learning it all on your own."

My heart squeezed and I barely held back a gasp. From the very beginning when I'd offered myself up to my magic, I'd thought it had embraced me as a God and found me worthy. I'd wrapped myself in the cadence of silvery voices that made up my magic, voices that always seemed to have the right answers, voices that were always eager to assist. Those voices that were laced with underlying laughter I now recognized.

It had been *her* this entire time.

A pinprick of a spider jumped from the edge of her finger to the bridge of my nose. I attempted to bring forth the veil of numbness I'd crafted to protect myself, but what I found instead was a mere figment of that icy barrier.

"Now, now. Don't be so hard on yourself, though it is a quality I admire," she sighed. "It's the spirit of a fighter, of someone who won't give up even when the going gets rough. It takes courage to face your mistakes, to analyze them, and to then set them aside—your lesson learned." The blade twisted against my pulse. "It's why, of all the minds in the world, I picked yours. Yours held a certain... *appeal*."

"You still haven't said what you want," I growled, pleased with my boldness.

She gripped my hair, ripping at the strands so silver they were nearly white, and dragged my head back as she loomed above me. "I want you to continue with your quest."

"You want me to find the God of Earth," I clarified.

"I want you to be the strong, capable individual I slated you to be. Is that so difficult?" She dropped the blade and relinquished her control over my body, though she kept me locked in her embrace. The branches of her chest stabbed painfully into my ribs.

"What do you get out of this?" I asked.

"The continuation of my lineage." Her eyes burned into mine.

Purple eyes.

The ones from *The Word*.

"You're Kaleal." The Original God of Water.

"It took you long enough," she hissed, the thorns of her fingertips dug grooves into my scalp. "You finish your mission, you find the other Gods, you save the world from itself, and I'll leave you be—magic,

15

friends, and all."

"Just like that?"

"Deals don't get much simpler, do they?"

"I'm not a fool," I snarled. There was no way a God as ancient and as cunning as she would be satisfied with such a trivial desire. Kaleal smirked haughtily and released my hair. When she cocked her head, I heard the call, too: Rose hollering my name with marked exasperation.

The God's eyes roved over me as her figure blurred, melding with the moonlight.

"No you're not," she purred, "which is why you'll take the deal."

She dissipated in a blur of cobwebs and leaves.

I hovered there, my hand flattened against my chest, relief flooding my veins with each heavy thud of my heart. It wasn't that I doubted her existence, but more that I'd begun to question my own. Rose called my name again, her voice louder this time.

I found my voice and yelled back, amazed at how calm I sounded. In direct contradiction, my movements were disjointed and painful when I strode forward to find the pixie. It was as if my brain were trying to remember how arms and legs worked.

The more I walked, the more I seethed. I resented how easily Kaleal had stolen my body for herself. I never wanted to feel that utter loss of control again. My mere existence was barely my own as it was. At the very least, I deserved my body for myself, but until I found a way to get rid of Kaleal for good, she wouldn't hesitate to take back that control again if she found it necessary.

However, I didn't know how to exorcise her from my mind.

I also wasn't sure what she was: a memory, a splintered piece of her soul, a ghost?

I needed more information.

The answer dawned on me when I spotted Rose ahead, hands braced on her hips. I carefully stepped over a small tree blocking my path.

Maybe the information I needed could be found at a temple of the Gods.

One of the two temples left.

I sighed, shaking my head. For now, it appeared Kaleal would get exactly what she wanted.

Chapter 3

Rose escorted me back to the cabin we shared, worry-lines fanning from her eyes despite the stream of sarcastic commentary flowing from her mouth. I knew how I looked: aquamarine eyes wide, hair tangled, skin scratched, and feverish. It was very different from the too-calm, too-quiet, too-carefully *controlled* zombie she'd forced to partake in human interaction over the past month.

For the first time in weeks, I'd truly sunk back into my own skin, dragged from the depths of the dark depression that had folded me in. I wanted to talk to Rose, wanted to tell her about what was going on, explain what had changed. I wanted her to know about Kaleal.

Yet every single one of the half dozen times I opened my mouth, nothing came out. The words with their sharp nails and biting teeth refused to claw their way out of my throat. Instead, they swirled in a pool of sap in my chest: trapped.

"Are you ok?" Rose finally asked, holding open the door to the cabin. It was one of several circling the outskirts of camp. "You seem quiet, even for you."

I thought of Kaleal's whispery voice, the spidery hands that clutched my arms, the chill of the blade against my throat, but a thin membrane smoothed over my airway when I opened my mouth. I settled for nodding. "I'm fine."

A corner of her mouth lifted but her eyes remained somber. "You sure about that?"

"Yeah, go on to the party." I waved at the door, heading to the bathroom. "I'll shower real quick, change into something else, and meet you there." I shut myself in the tiny room and slumped against the door with a sign.

I'd prefer you keep me a secret, for now, Kaleal whispered in my head. My neck snapped back and I saw my reflection in the small, oval mirror over the sink. Lurking in my shadow, I could make out the tendrils of wispy hair and the curl of claws on my shoulder.

They already know you're inside me, I replied, curling and uncurling my fists. *You revealed yourself to Finn and Ryder before, remember?*

True, but they don't really know who I am or that I've returned, do they?

Rather than respond, I slipped into the shower and turned on the spray as hot as it would go, attempting to drown out the thoughts that weren't my own beneath the pounding torrent. It seemed to work, because the God kept quiet as I dressed, though I could feel her lurking in the back of my mind like an unwanted house guest.

I didn't want to go to the party, especially right now. What I *wanted* to do was wrap myself in the icy cloak of numbness that had blunted reality for all these weeks and go back to bed. But I had a feeling that when I'd shattered, I'd also shattered the façade, and it wasn't coming back. Besides, Joseph's friends and family had gone to a lot of effort keeping us hidden from the Order. I owed them an appearance tonight. It wasn't like I had any money to pay them for their trouble.

The soles of my worn, black Chucks squeaked on the wooden floors as I exited the bathroom. Joseph's aunt had found them for me at a second-hand store after catching me staring enviously at the green high-tops one of the boys wore around the camp. Combined with boot-cut, dark-washed jeans, a clean blue t-shirt, and a forest green jacket, she'd nailed my style.

Too bad I didn't feel like that girl anymore.

Around my neck on a simple chain, I'd strung two silver rings shaped in the forms of my water brand. They were two of three things my temple had managed to shepherd out when they'd saved me from the Order's onslaught. I used to wear them all the time, but they seemed to channel the heat of my fire magic, turning wicked hot. When I'd shaken the hands of one of Joseph's cousins, the metal had burned her and I'd removed the rings then and there.

I shook my head at the memory and tucked the jewelry beneath my shirt where they belonged. I shouldn't even possess fire magic. Gods were only granted control over one of the four elements, and all four Gods were needed to save the world from whatever apocalyptic scenario was threatening existence as we knew it. Sometimes it was drought, other times famine, or things even more complex. In this instance, Joseph and I were pretty sure that stopping nuclear warfare was on our plate.

I tamped down the reddish magic nipping at my fingertips, wishing I understood why I had it and not air or earth magic. I'd nearly burned alive a month ago, but something had unfurled within me when I'd been sure I'd meet my maker. That something had not only saved me, but somehow unlocked the gift of flame that I'd never wanted. A gift I stubbornly refused to use, no matter how tempting it was.

I tossed a few things into my pockets and glanced around the cabin. Eight bunk beds with metal frames lined opposite walls of the cabin. It lacked both windows and decoration. I loved it and I'd miss the simplicity. But I needed to find the other Gods, I needed to save the world, and I needed to get control of my own body back.

I snapped off the overhead light and exited. When the sun had set, it sucked the warmth of the day with it. The chill of fall this far north was unrelenting, but I barely felt it thanks to my combined magics. I dragged my hand through my hair and moved in the direction of the bonfire through the trees. A twig snapped. My skin prickled. The sound of nightlife that normally saturated the woods was lacking, the silence expectant.

I gripped the hilt of the dagger concealed inside my jacket and scanned the darkness with careful deliberation. Magic hummed, ready to transform at will, but that wasn't necessary, not tonight. I breathed in through my nose, out through my mouth.

"I know you're there."

A human-shaped shadow detached from the trunk of a tree. "I'd only just arrived when you came out," Ryder said.

"Sure." I forced myself to release the knife, the third gift from the Water Temple, and held out a hand, my palm flat. He cocked an eyebrow. "That's why you were lurking like a creeper."

"I take offense to that terminology."

"How would you classify it? Stalker?"

"More like casual observer," he said. His golden eyes glowed as he shrugged off my order and bridged the gap between us. His long, calloused fingers slid across mine in a sensual way that spoke of familiarity I wasn't comfortable with. I tugged him toward the fire. "I was coming to check on you. It's rare for you and those damnable pixies to be separated for any length of time."

Despite his words, Ryder and Rose were kindred spirits. If I weren't as confident in my standing in either of their lives, their casual rapport might have made me jealous. I already struggled with my budding feelings for the cocky, quirky prince of darkness; I certainly didn't have the time or the energy to worry about his emotions for anyone else.

He stopped and tugged me closer, walking us backward until my spine pressed against the slender trunk of a birch tree. The corner of his mouth tipped up, crinkling the thumbprint of his dimple, and he swept his hand along my jawline, tipping my face toward his.

No, I definitely wasn't concerned about his feelings for anyone else.

Not when he was so patently transparent about his emotions toward me.

The hard length of his chest pressed against mine and he lowered his head until our noses brushed. His eyes, the amber-rimmed coins of gold I was secretly obsessed with, glittered knowingly as he brushed my cheek, smoothing my hair behind my ear.

"I've wanted to talk to you all day," he whispered against my lips. My heart hitched. In my chest, smoke and flame unfurled as I allowed myself to sink into the decadence of his touch, his presence. I shuddered when his hand curled around the indent of my waist, drawing me closer.

"This doesn't feel like talking." I slid my hands up his chest, enjoying the steel of hard muscles wrapped in his shirt.

"Bodies can talk." He nipped at my lower lip and grinned when I gasped. My skin trembled as sparks ignited and swirled. "Besides, it's impossible to remember what I was going to say when…" He groaned when I fisted the lazy spikes of his choppy, dark hair and tugged. The incubus rocked against me. The fire inside me flared hotter.

"When what?" I asked, barely aware of what I was saying as I stared at his lips.

"When I can finally see *you* again."

His words confused me, but I didn't have time to ponder them before his lips crashed against mine. My thoughts washed away in the flood that was *him*. Ryder's hands gripping my waist were the only things grounding me as I wound myself around him, pulling us impossibly closer. A waterfall of blood and heat rushed in my ears when he pulled away, adjusting the angle of our faces, our lips fitting like puzzle pieces. My pulse skipped when he shuddered against me.

I reveled in the seemingly endless pull of magic he drew from my lips, enthralled in my own ability to give him the power he needed to survive.

Panting, he dragged my hair back and my moan of protest transformed when he brushed butterfly kisses along my jaw. "For weeks I've searched for you," he whispered, words so soft I wasn't sure they were meant for my ears. My spine arched, my head tipping against the tree as I closed my eyes. "For weeks you've hidden. But now you're back."

I curled my hands around the biceps bracketing me in. The light scent of cinnamon and smoke dusted the air around us. I encouraged him in closer, groaning when his teeth found the fluttering pulse in my neck. I gasped when he bit down softly. I wanted more. No, I *needed* more.

"My glowstick is finally back."

His thumbs pressed against the hollow in my throat, his fingers fanning out on either side of my neck, and I froze. Everything luxurious and rich and wonderful inside me went cold at the touch. Somehow, someway, it felt so similar to the kiss of a blade against that very flesh. Flesh I'd healed with a thought. A face of cobwebs and hands of twigs flashed across my vision.

"Get away," I gasped, my hands twisting into claws as I lashed against him. The incubus immediately pulled back, golden eyes narrowed and face twisted with concern.

I slid to the ground, curling around myself as I fought against a torrent of confusion and panic. That one touch had shattered my shock, and I was abruptly forced to confront the blinding reality that someone else had stripped away my control no longer than an hour ago. Not only that, but there was nothing I could do about it. My body was no longer completely my own.

The hurricane that was my understanding of that simple fact roared in my mind, rendering me deaf as I rocked back and forth, choking on harsh gasps.

In my periphery, Ryder carefully lowered himself to my level.

"Zara." My name registered. The noun was spoken patiently as if it wasn't the first time or even the twelfth time he had tried to get my attention.

"Zara, what happened?"

Slowly, I lifted my head, scrubbing at the brittle ice beneath my cheeks. The incubus crouched maybe twenty feet away, his body coiled and prepared to spring as he scanned the forest.

"That can't happen again," I said. My throat felt raw as if I'd been screaming.

"What can't happen again?" His careful words, the softness woven through them, infuriated me. The last thing I needed from him right now was his concern and his pity.

"This." I waved a hand uselessly between us. "Us. There is no us. There can't be."

"Why not?" He settled back on his heels and steepled his hands beneath his chin.

"Because I'm not the girl you met at the club, Ryder." I stood, searching for the words that would push him away, keep him from delving deeper, to prevent him from figuring out how scarred and confused and broken I truly was. I couldn't stand to face his revulsion when he uncovered the real me.

"That girl, she's gone. Your glowstick isn't coming back." I threw his words at him, wanting to make him hurt without really understanding why. "I can't be anything special to you, because I'm not."

"I think that's for me to decide." His tone was gravelly, yet restrained. "Why don't you tell me what happened here, instead? Because that?" He pointed at the base of the birch where I'd fallen to pieces. "That wasn't ok. You're not ok." I wanted to sob and scream in equal measure, but I squared my shoulders instead. "Something I did caused that. I want to know what, because I never want to cause you that kind of

24

pain ever again."

It took me a few tries to find my voice. It was so tempting to cave in, to lean on someone else for once, but I couldn't. I wasn't ready for that. I wasn't sure who I was anymore—even without the issue of Kaleal to contend with.

"Leave me alone, Ryder," I said, the words stiff. "Forget that ever happened."

"Don't you dare insult me by saying that." The skin on his face thinned, revealing the hint of blackness that was the demon he kept tightly restrained. He seemed to catch himself as he made to advance on me, his fingers curling into his palms. "As if I'd ever forget causing pain to the one girl who makes me feel something real for the first time in decades."

He sucked in air but cut me off before I could fire off a retort.

"I know what you're doing. I know that you're pushing people away. I know that you're trying to bury the girl you used to be, trying to destroy her joy and vibrancy because you don't think you deserve to be her anymore." He reached out like he wanted to shake me, but pulled back again with a grimace.

"You've been hit hard. You've been knocked down. You've lost people you never thought you could lose—in some of the worst ways imaginable." His eyes softened and I hunched against it, hating how transparent I was to him. "And I understand that—*we* understand that. All of us, your friends. We really do. But, Zara, you can suffer and grieve and change, and still be that girl. You *are* my glowstick."

I flinched at his term of endearment, craving it despite having tossed it at him like a piece of cheap confetti.

"I see through this person you're pretending to be, this numb creature that you've allowed to reside in your skin. I wasn't joking when I said that I see *you* shining through. You are ready to let her out, whether you realize it or not." He straightened to his full height. "I won't push you any harder tonight, because Gods I can't stand to hurt you again. But be prepared, because tomorrow I'm coming for you."

Chapter 4

"So you spit in his Cheerios, huh?" Joseph asked.

I stopped sawing at the lemon-pepper chicken breast. "Is that something people say?"

"I'm attempting colloquialisms." The God of Air slid onto the bench beside me. He held bowl in one hand and a single shortbread cookie in the other. "I take it I forayed too far?"

"You forayed something, that's for sure." I dropped my utensils with a clatter, giving up on eating entirely. As delicious as the rosemary red potatoes, grilled chicken, and garlicky green beans smelled, my appetite had vaporized with Ryder's retreating back. I shoved the mess of food an arms-length away and twisted to straddle the bench. "Who are you talking about anyway?"

"That intense, brooding cluster of shadows over there." He cracked his cookie in half and waved one piece vaguely in the direction of the massive bonfire. "If I'm correct, and you know I am, Ryder's in a snit because of something you did or said."

I squinted over the flickering flames until I found the incubus leaning against the wall of the main cabin that housed the kitchen and dining hall. His arms were crossed, his face turned in my direction. Tension practically tinted the air black around him.

"I may know something of it," I said.

Joseph snorted and shoved the remainder of the cookie in his face.

He wiped crumbs from the front of his white t-shirt. "I figured parties weren't your scene, but you seem glum even for you." He snared a potato, sniffed it, and slipped it between his straight, white teeth. "Penny for your thoughts?"

I pulled a finger gun at him. "Now that one I do know."

He returned a grin that didn't match his dark, probing eyes. My fellow God was a brand of intensity to which I wasn't accustomed. He approached life like a science project: logical and understandable once dissected and cataloged. I attributed it to his isolated upbringing.

Joseph was about four years older than me, a peculiarity among Gods who were typically born at the same time. However, the Order had killed the original child meant to be the new God of Air, and that had left the element running hot and free, searching for the perfect conduit. For some reason, the element found what it sought in a small boy crouching beside a totem pole as his grandfather carefully chiseled the sharp beak of the Thunderbird that would top it.

It struck Joseph with a bolt of lightning, fusing its energy to his very blood, simultaneously killing his grandfather in the blast. Joseph's grandmother recognized the brand on his arm—a gust of wind with an arrow beneath it—and took great pains to hide him from civilization.

She feared the reaction of both the other people in their town and the wrath of the Order if she was found harboring an illegal God. So his family kept him tucked away at a nearby camp that had formerly been used for Boy Scout retreats. They raised him in secret, keeping him entertained with a steady diet of books.

The camp where he'd spent the majority of his life was the same camp that harbored us now.

I shoved some hair behind my ear and leaned on my elbow. "Can we set aside the whole Ryder thing for a minute?"

"Gladly." He eyed my mostly uneaten plate of food, then crammed some vegetables into his mouth. "As long as you say something, I don't particularly care what it is."

"I have reservations about leaving."

"So do I," he said around some beans. "I think nearly everyone here does."

"The Order is going to come for us." I drank some water. The pixies were attempting some kind of synchronized dance beside the fire where the radio blared alternative rock, but every time they got into position, one of them would collapse on the ground in a fit of drunken hysterics. Ever the leader, Rose would pull the offending fey to her feet and start the whole fiasco over again. "I'm pretty sure it wants us dead, even without Geoffrey at the helm. Whatever happens, it will get bloody."

"So let them come," Joseph said. "I'd rather deal with them head-on than continue this waiting game. I've been waiting for them my entire life. The Thunderbird promised to watch my family here, so I have very little to lose by leaving."

"Yeah." I plucked at a string dangling from my sleeve. His straightforward sentiments struck me somewhere deep. I was running low on people who cared about me, people I'd give anything to protect. In fact, everyone I had left was in this clearing. Nearly everyone, I amended, scanning the dozen or so members of Joseph's family for a familiar lanky figure. My stomach twisted when I couldn't find Finn.

"Listen." Joseph's hard tone drew my attention. The smooth planes of his face settled into stubborn lines as he clasped my hand between his. He and Rose were the only ones who touched me anymore. Well, and apparently Ryder. "Whatever happens is meant to happen. All we can do is deal with it as best we can. And let me tell you, there isn't a more well-equipped bunch of rag-tag heroes out there."

He spun a small tornado on his empty plate as if that proved something.

"I might not know what the rest of the world looks like, but I'm the best Jeopardy contestant who never played." He settled back on the bench. "Rose is the nastiest blend of anger and spice I've ever seen. Her war-party over there is ready to drink the blood of their enemies.

"Finn—" Joseph's head angled when I opened my mouth. I dutifully closed it. "Finn is a crackerjack box of strategy and tactics. I've talked to him. I'd put money on that. Ryder, the ritzy entrepreneur he is, has connections that would scare even the most heavily armed mob boss. Not to mention, he's dangerously protective of anything to do with you.

"And you—" He jabbed my sternum and I rubbed the ache away. "You are the biggest surprise of all. You, Zara, God of Water, you can achieve almost anything you put your mind to."

His tongue traced his lower lip, eyes lowered and unfocused as he gathered his thoughts. "Geoffrey wanted you dead because he knew that you were capable of changing the world. How about we prove him right?"

My heart swelled two sizes in my chest. Sunshine rays that felt a little like hope filtered through my ribs. In a move reminiscent of the girl I'd proclaimed dead a half hour ago, I threw myself at Joseph, wrapping him up in an octopus hug. A rumble of laughter shook his chest when I gave no indication of letting go. His broad hand spanned my back, shoulder blade to shoulder blade.

"Thank you," I whispered. "Who needs colloquialisms when you always say the right things, anyway?"

Chapter 5

Rose talked me into drinking one beer.

Ok, maybe it was more like two.

The alcohol combined with the lack of food loosened me up while simultaneously soothing the jagged edges of my pain. I told myself that was also the only reason I didn't run screaming back to the fire when I found Finn sitting on the stoop outside my cabin.

However, I did hover at the edge of the clearing, the toe of my right foot on the ground with the heel raised. Inhale. Exhale. Finn had been my touchstone from the beginning. My Great Beast, the Kraken, had ordered the kelpie to teach me about magic and guide me on my journey. In the week we'd spent together fighting off the Order and piecing together the mystery that was both my past and future, we'd become friends.

Well, friends until he'd revealed a deep-seated secret about himself that had warped our easy dynamic. We'd barely looked at each other, let alone talked over these past few weeks, but I guessed that changed tonight. I advanced on Finn, sensing his relief even though nothing about his demeanor changed. His slender arms were spread wide, fingers curled around the lip of the top step. His shaggy, dark hair fanned across his forehead, green eyes glittering warily as he waited.

I dropped beside him as far over on the step as I could be, leaving a good two feet of space between our bodies. I hugged my knees to my chest and rested my chin on one bony kneecap. Overhead, the blur of a bat squeaked sharply as it scouted for dinner. The weight of exhaustion settled on my shoulders as seconds of silence turned into minutes.

"Hey," Finn said, staring intently at the broken bough of an oak tree.

"Four weeks of silence and that's your opening line?" I snapped. Maybe my feelings weren't so conflicted after all.

"I *have* tried to talk to you. You're the one who shuts me out." Finn's knuckles swished as he brushed them together. It reminded me of another illuminating conversation between us, where we'd perched on the side of a cliff, waves tugging at our toes. "I've also visited every night since we arrived. And every single night, a member of your horde of bodyguards chases me away. I guess they're too hopped up on booze to worry for once."

I released my legs and extended them so the edges of the stairs dug into my jeans. I subconsciously scrubbed at the hollow of my throat, the same spot Ryder had so innocently brushed earlier.

It was true. I had asked the pixies to keep my guardian away from our cabin. I'd tried to expel him from camp, but the incubus had put his foot down, declaring Finn a member of our team whether I wanted him there or not.

Now that I could finally see beyond my own inner torment, I realized Ryder was right in keeping him with us. I still felt for Finn, even if I didn't quite trust him anymore.

"I needed time," I said slowly. The kelpie's metal bracelets jangled as he turned. "I wasn't ready to deal with it. Any of it." Gathering my strength, I faced him straight on, raising my inner shields high against the memories that threatened.

"Finn, you confessed to betraying your entire temple, to allowing the Order to sweep in and ransack the Palace of Oceans seventeen years ago. You said you failed to do your job, and that cost hundreds of people and fey their lives." I was shouting, the words ripped from the bloody hole in my chest that he had caused. "You admitted that you ran away, rather than help save *me*, save the God that you swore to protect to your dying day." I jabbed at the cresting wave that cut across his neck and underside of his jaw. He flinched, his body curling in on itself as his eyes rippled with pain, tenderly touching the mark as if it burned.

But I wasn't done.

"You were my... I thought you were my friend," I gasped. "I thought you were the one person I could count on when my world was falling down around me, and then you hit me with that sledgehammer right as we were heading into war. I didn't have time to deal with any of that. Instead, I killed Geoffrey. I killed his second in command, and I destroyed dozens of soldiers." My voice broke. "And I nearly died, too."

My hands were shaking again. I wanted to stop. I wanted to run, but I couldn't. Not anymore. These were words that had gone too long unsaid, words crying to be let out. "I lost myself that day. I lost my grip on reality, on everything that made me, *me*. I'd lost too much, too fast: my parents, my best friend, my team, my home, my entire future. All of it. And then... I lost you, too."

My voice shook, barely higher than a whisper, as I finally faced the reality I'd denied.

Finn grunted in pain.

In a movement too fast for me to follow, he wrapped himself around me, his strong arms pulling me against him, my face tucked in his shoulder as he buried his nose in my hair. I slammed my hands against his chest and sides, fighting him, fighting what he'd done to me, what we'd done to each other, but he bore the brunt of it without protest.

After what felt like hours, I finally stopped, my fingers curled in his shirt, drained. This time when I pushed against him, he pulled back, mossy eyes damp.

"At first, I couldn't process anything that had happened." I wiped my nose on my shirt. "Doing that felt too much like accepting that it was real, that everything about my life had changed. So I didn't." I touched my chest. "But today I woke up, and for the first time in a long time, I'm remembering not only the people that I've lost but the parts of *myself* that I've lost, too. And I don't know if those are parts I'm ever getting back... but I want to."

Finn's eyes widened, hope peeking out at the corners. Though he'd pulled back, he still gripped the hook of my elbow. Part of me I wanted to throttle was surprised to find I didn't want him to let me go. He drew a deep breath and tugged on the silver hoop looped through his eyebrow.

"I was once betrayed by someone I loved deeply," he said pensively. "I thought I knew him. I thought I knew his soul. But when I realized what he'd done and what his decisions had cost me, I broke. Then I spent seventeen years in hibernation to avoid dealing with both how I felt about him and about what I'd done to the people who were counting on me."

Leaves crunched and we both swiveled as a rabbit crept from beneath a bush, its long ears raised and alert.

"Zara, I'm done letting down the people I care about." His grip on my arm tightened. "You might not think the best of me right now, but I'm still your friend. Even if you decide at the end of all this... that you can't forgive me for what I've done... if you decide that I'm not someone you want in your life anymore, know that I will still be there for you, no matter what."

He swallowed, his brow furrowing then clearing. "I messed up. A lot. That's a weight I will bear for the rest of my life. But I hope you'll give me the chance to prove that I've changed, that I'm a better version of what I was."

I stared into the dark, my thoughts quiet for once.

I surprised us both when I reached for him as he stood, and tugged him back down.

"I'm not ready to forgive you yet," I said. "But I don't think I'm angry anymore."

It was the truth.

Finn admitted to changing. Maybe I was, too.

"Will you stay here a little longer?" I asked. "And sit with me? Before things get crazy again?"

His eyes flicked between mine. "I think I can do that."

We didn't touch again, but neither did we sit apart, floating in this strange newness of companionable silence. As I leaned against the railing with my arms pressed tight against me, I realized that gaping wound in my chest—the one that refused to heal—was lined with stitches.

Chapter 6

When I finally went inside after spending an hour with Finn, I didn't sleep.

I, instead, closed my eyes and rolled so I faced the wall when the pixies stumbled back to our cabin, smiling at their loud shushes in an attempt to cover their drunken giggles. Beds creaked as the girls fell into them followed by the thuds of boots hitting the floor.

The hair on the back of my neck prickled, fully aware that Rose hovered by the edge of my mattress like she did every night. And, like every other night, she lightly traced a rune for protection on my shoulder, right beneath my elemental brands, before slipping into her own bed across from mine.

An hour passed.

Then another slipped by.

Once I was convinced the pixies were well and truly asleep, I slipped from beneath the covers fully dressed. I dropped my feet into my shoes, not bothering to lace them, and slipped my packed bag over my shoulder. I didn't have much, but I had more than I did when the Order blew up my house.

"*Promedis ad.*" Rose's quiet warning froze me at the open door, my hand on the knob. It was pixie slang for '*at your ready*,' a motto the horde slung at each other all the time. Of course she wasn't asleep. Of course she knew I was up to something. I'd never slipped by her before, her awareness of me bordering on uncanny. I bet she'd known Finn was waiting earlier, too.

I shook my head but pulled my magic to my fingertips all the same as I closed the door. I tested my abilities as I crossed the compound, sensing signatures of people nearby using the water magic. Nearly everyone was tucked behind thick walls, asleep in their beds. Everyone except for three.

Ryder's bed was empty in the cabin he shared with Finn. I scanned the skies, knowing he got as little sleep as I did, but I didn't want to run into him as I skirted past the coals from the bonfire. Beside the main structure was a fourth and smaller cabin with one occupant who was busily moving around. I rapped on the door, the sound like gunshots in the night. Joseph's easy smile greeted me when he opened it.

"I'd wondered if you'd grace my doorstep."

"And skip our last study session? Hardly." I shouldered past him and dropped to my usual spot on the edge of his twin bed. He hovered in the doorway scanning the grove, then stepped back.

"No escort tonight?" he asked as he settled into his desk chair, the one with a broken back support and a ripped seat cushion. "I thought you weren't able to ditch your shadows."

"You're actually not the first person to say that tonight." I smoothed a hand over the blue, patchwork quilt. It was a gorgeous piece that Joseph had mentioned being passed down several generations. When his parents had died in a car crash when he was five, he'd inherited it.

Joseph kicked his heels on his desk and leaned back, the chair groaning in protest. "Do tell."

"Finn and Ryder both said something," I said. "But that's not why I came by tonight."

"You'd rather study instead?" He waved a hand at the four walls filled with books. Hundreds upon hundreds of spines, some etched with titles in elegant scripts while others lacked any telling features

37

whatsoever, begged to be read.

Shortly after arriving, I'd inventoried his selection, marveling over the fact that one wall was devoted entirely to material about the Gods. Everything from myths and legends to recent copies of *The Word*—a text devoted to the teachings of the original Gods. There were even binders filled with news clippings including the fall of the temples to Geoffrey's rise to pictures of my grand entrance in Kansas City.

Like me, Joseph hadn't been raised in a temple. The City Among the Clouds was razed in the same series of attacks that destroyed mine, yet he knew so much about our world and its magic that he might as well have been raised in a temple. He put my distinct lack of education to shame, but he'd eagerly worked to rectify that by putting titles in my hands and quizzing me on what I'd learned.

"Anyone home in that head of yours?" Joseph teased. He nudged his glasses up, his almond-shaped eyes dark behind the lenses. The frames immediately slid down and stopped at the hitch in his nose where he'd broken it twice.

"Do you remember when I asked you to teach me what you knew?" I asked. My fingers twined in the rope holding the top of my bag together, the course material pricking at my skin as the contents inside burned to be released.

He cleared his throat. "I asked you what you hoped to find."

"Do you remember my answer?"

Joseph's feet slid off the desk with a thump. "The truth."

I unraveled the knot and dipped into the bag. The metal case at the top burned as I pulled it out, as if unwilling to part from me. In the shadows at the back of my mind and in the core of my belly, darkness uncurled. Kaleal's ghostly fingers clenched tight around the base of my spine, warning me against what I was about to do. With effort, I pushed her back and held out the box, relief sweeping over me when he took it.

38

He didn't say anything at first, taking in the ornate script carefully chiseled in the lid. He slowly peeled it open and removed the artifact tucked inside. With an intrigued sniff he eagerly traced the cover of the book.

"How do you have this?" he whispered, lifting one page by its gold-dusted edge. I could practically see through the paper it was so thin. "I didn't think there were any left outside of Order headquarters."

"Finn found it for me." I closed my eyes against the words, remembering how much the kelpie had done for me, remembering the extent of what he'd done to protect me, to bring me to this place. "I don't know how he knew where to find an original copy of *The Word*, but he assures me it's real."

His eyes shimmered when he finally looked up from its beauty. "You realize that this might carry information that human eyes haven't seen for thousands and thousands of years? We already know the Order changes things from print to print." He lifted a different copy of *The Word* from his desk and shook it. "This copy from two-hundred years ago has discrepancies from the newer versions from this past decade. It's… I can't even imagine how much has changed from the original text over time."

He reverently rubbed the title. "And you're giving it to me?"

"Yes." My jaw worked around the word, not realizing until now how difficult it was to actually part with so special of a gift. But I had to, I needed answers about our history. Specifically, I needed answers about Kaleal, and the text I'd given him was supposedly an account right from their mouths.

Joseph took in every expression that crossed my face, his frown growing.

"It's written in a dead fey language," I said with a shrug. "If anyone can crack the code, it's you."

"I'm honored in your faith in me, but Zara…" He waited for me to look up from my clenched hands. "I'm only borrowing this. Ok? And the second I have it figured out, it's yours again."

I nodded, not trusting my voice as he rushed to pack it with his other things. I'd talked him out of bringing any of his books with him, telling him that he needed to experience the world and stop hiding behind paper and ink. Turns out he'd bring one. Possibly the most valuable one of all.

"Before I dig into it though, what do you hope to find?"

One of his favorite questions, one rife with curiosity.

I longed to tell him about Kaleal, to pick his brain and see if he knew anything about other Gods being possessed before. I wanted to ask him to help me figure out how to beat her, but the tightness in my throat made that impossible.

"I'll know it when I see it," I hedged.

Chapter 7

A bag smacked my shins and I shielded my eyes against shards of sunshine splintering the foggy dawn haze. Past the pixie with her hands braced on her hips, the totem poles keeping silent watch over our campground loomed high over the pine trees.

"Was that necessary?" I asked Rose, bleary with sleep.

"You didn't sleep at all, yeah?" she drawled, jabbing my thigh with the point of her boot.

"I plead the fifth."

"You're lucky we're still in the States and that still applies." She flopped beside me, her back to the airplane that had touched down in the grassy plain about an hour ago. "Did you get your *situation* resolved, at least?"

I grunted, returning to the newer copy of *The Word* open in my lap. I'd dog-eared the pages about Kaleal a few hours ago while waiting at the rendezvous point, then had fallen asleep while meticulously picking through the passages. "Which situation are we talking about here?"

"There's more than one situation, now? Busy girl." She whistled through her teeth as Finn crested the hill. He rubbed his knee as he scanned the clearing, his gaze lingering on Joseph who was slouched on the steps leading into the private aircraft, pouring over the book I'd given him.

I rolled the sleeves of my black and white flannel shirt to my elbows. "I'll cop to two."

The pixie smacked my shoulder. "You keep telling yourself that, yeah?"

A rusty laugh slipped out of me, and she answered it with one of her own. Ryder shot me a look from where he chatted up the blue-haired pilot beside Joseph. A couple of duffel bags crowded the ground at his feet. Even thirty yards away it was impossible to miss the heat in his golden irises.

"That boy there makes at least six *situations,*" Rose said out of the corner of her mouth as we stood. I closed the book, giving up on it until we were thirty-five thousand feet in the air. The pixie flashed a few hand signs to her half dozen mates who silently surrounded us as we congregated around the door.

Ryder nodded to the pilot who lifted a hand to all of us before stepping inside.

"Who's he?" Rose asked, palming a knife.

"You can call him Steve." Ryder mussed his purple-tinted locks with a rough hand. The pixies chortled. "He's been my personal pilot for the better part of the decade, and I trust him explicitly. He's helped me on a number of jobs. He's also helped clean up my messes. Steve is very well acquainted with what happens to those who break my trust."

The incubus flashed his teeth, and again I wondered exactly what kind of life Ryder led before he'd roped himself into my impossible mission.

Joseph leaned into me. "Remember what I said about that mob boss thing?"

I gnawed on a thumbnail, eyes narrowed.

"This plane is one from my private collection," he continued, ignoring us all. Collection. As in more than one. My eyes narrowed so tightly they bordered on closing. My head was starting to hurt.

"I've personally checked it over and can assure you it hasn't been tampered with in any way, shape, or form. The Order doesn't even know these planes exist. We have plenty of fuel and won't need to stop anywhere else before arriving in Cairo." He clapped his hands once. "Any questions?"

"Who's hosting us again?" piped up one of the pixies who had a pinched quality to her face that spoke of too much stress and not enough sleep.

We'd run through all this a few days ago—but apparently, someone hadn't been listening.

Ryder preened. "Thanks to my vast and wondrous connections, I've tracked down a group of fey who are rogue from the Order. They swear their allegiances to the God of Earth, and they want that being restored. Make no mistake, that's the *only* reason they're helping us. Be on your guard. Do not think of them as allies, because they aren't."

He paused to let that sink in.

"These fey are called nero, a very powerful lineage with roots in sand magic. Not only are they powerful, but they're connected, and they use those connections to stay hidden. Very little is known about what they can do, only that you would rather not see them do it." Ryder tucked his hands in his slacks with a half-hearted shrug.

"We can still take 'em," Rose called, tapping the whip of thorns wrapped around her waist as her horde cheered. "Strength of will trumps magic." She gave me a long look and amended, "—most of the time."

Ryder mounted the first step of the plane, gesturing for everyone to quiet down. "I'm getting to the best part. These fey are some of the few who can locate the Lost City, otherwise known as the Earth Temple. Without them, there's no finding the missing God. Without that God, we can't stop nuclear destruction. So please play nice."

"Why's it called the Lost Temple?" the same pixie as earlier asked.

"Because it's just that," Ryder said, his tone taking on the spooky quality of a ghost story narrator. I half expected him to wiggle his fingers mysteriously. "Lost."

"The Lost City can only be found by those who've been there before," Joseph chimed in, ignoring Ryder's irritated huff. "It was difficult enough to find before the attacks on the temples, and it all but faded from existence in the aftermath. So we'll need to win them over."

The incubus threw his arms wide. "Absolutely. Any other questions? No? Then find a seat, we're on a tight schedule." He disappeared into the relative darkness of the plane. Finn and the pixies followed while I waited with the God of Air. He waved cheerily at his family members who'd clustered at the edge of the clearing, before mounting the stairs.

"It's ok to admit that you'll miss them," I said, patting his back. "I miss them and I barely know them. You've never *not* been around them."

The air conditioning sent his hair fanning out behind him, and he wrapped an arm around my waist when I joined him inside.

"Not true," he said and tweaked my nose. "I had an overnight camping trip about six years ago. I left them then."

I snorted. "Hardly the same thing and you know it."

"Oh, it was pretty traumatizing I'll have you know. Didn't sleep a wink. Cried into my pillow. It was awful. The other boys taunted me for years afterward." He mock-shuddered and turned to toss his bag in the overhead rack.

Taking advantage of his distraction, I snatched a seat beside a window. As I situated my stuff between my leg and the shell of the plane, Joseph took his seat beside me. When I turned to ask him about his early thoughts regarding *The Word*, I jerked when I found Ryder's lazy grin leering back at me.

"You're not Joseph," I said.

"Nothing gets by you, does it?" Ryder squeezed my knee. The man

44

in question remained in the aisle, awkward in his height. He blinked and took the spot directly behind me.

"I didn't think you'd complain, considering I'm the better looking of us. Not to mention the strongest, the one with more career options and financial—ow." The incubus yelped as Joseph smacked him over the head. He scoffed, "That was unnecessary. And rude. Plus, you hit like a girl." Joseph squawked and Ryder caught his hand as he drew back for another swat. "Slap me again and you lose it," he threatened. Joseph gritted his teeth when Ryder squeezed.

Finn clicked his tongue as he sank into the plush seat beside Joseph. "Now children, how about we try to get along before mommy's driven to drink."

"Wait, who's mommy in this twisted scenario?" I asked. "I'm not volunteering."

"But if you're mommy, that means I can be daddy," Ryder snarked, his smile stretching impossibly wide as his hand found my knee again. This time I swatted him, refusing to acknowledge the weird fluttering in my chest. "Though you can call me that anytime you want, *honey*."

I folded my arms. "You're gross."

The incubus pressed his twined hands to his chest, swooning. "Save that talk for later, dearest."

I peered between the seats at my Godly comrade and rolled my eyes when Joseph clutched his hands in a mockery of Ryder, falling back with his tongue dangling out the corner of his mouth. My grin faded when two fingers gripped my chin and forced my head back to the instigator himself. Ryder's eyes flashed from my eyes to my lips. My cheeks heated.

"Why are you here right now, anyway?" I grumbled, tugging on his wrist.

"The answer should be obvious."

"Well, it isn't."

"Remember what I told you yesterday?" he asked. My jaw locked and he stroked the throbbing muscles, leaning in close enough for our lips to brush as he whispered, "I wasn't kidding. And yes, that means I'm perfectly content being your seatmate for the whole twenty-hour flight, even if you pretend to hate me." He kissed my forehead, satisfaction radiating from every pore.

"Want me to kick his ass?" Rose called from the front of the plane. She'd made herself at home in the flight attendant spot to better keep an eye on the cabin. The remaining pixies were scattered in the back, bodies sprawled across the aisles. One even lay backward on her seat, legs crossed and propped against the backrest. I seriously considered Rose's offer for a good three seconds before signing a negative.

"I'd like to see you try, pixie brat," Ryder taunted, fingers drumming a beat on his leg. "I'd have you pinned on the ground before you so much as laid a finger on me."

The pixie bared her double-rows of teeth, black-stained eyes narrowing. "My thorns have been begging for a taste of your blood you—"

"Please fasten your seat belts." Steve's nasal voice came from the speakers overhead. "We're preparing for takeoff."

Rose made a crude gesture at the ceiling but dutifully fastened the belt around her hips. I reached for mine, and nearly grabbed Ryder's arm instead. He took care sliding the black vinyl around my hips, making sure each of his fingers brushed against the skin exposed by my shirt that had hiked up at some point.

Sparks danced and my mouth went dry when he pressed his lips beneath my ear. "Safety first, glowstick."

He chuckled when I tried shoving him away with all my strength. I caught Finn's eye over the seat, but couldn't gauge the weariness of his expression. The plane started moving and Joseph opened the book with another huff. Finn did a double-take when he spotted it.

"He'll crack the code," I explained and he nodded. I still wasn't comfortable with the kelpie, not like I used to be, but the heavy weight of resentment that I'd harbored for weeks had dissipated overnight.

"Up for a game of I Spy? Or maybe tic-tac-toe?" Ryder thrust a notebook and a purple pen in my face. I sighed as Finn barely disguised his half-grin. "It'll be difficult playing the license plate game from up here, but if you're down I'll give it my best go."

I snatched the book and tossed it to the floor. "Are you seriously going to sit here this entire trip?"

"Absolutely. You and I, we have a long story to tell." The palm of his hand curled around my cheek as his fingers brushed hair from my forehead. I leaned into the touch despite myself. "And this is only the beginning."

Chapter 8

Water deep as my ankles sluiced over my boots, yet my feet remained dry.

I turned a slow circle, the ripped hem of my lacy dress dragging across the surface of the water, the ripples fanning outward in the small room. More water trickled down the gray stone walls stacked twice my height and dripped from the ceiling. Aside from the pool that never seemed to get higher, no matter how much water rained down, the room itself was empty.

My fingers twitched and a whip of liquid wound itself into my palm.

"What a morose little chamber." Kaleal's voice came from behind me. It didn't surprise me that she'd found me here. She'd probably hovered behind me every night when I finally fell asleep, clicking her tongue in disgust at my inability to deal with my emotions. "Why you chose to lock yourself in here is beyond me. There are far more interesting rooms in this vast mind of yours."

I pulled the whip through my hands, the water molding to my whims. The ancient God slouched against the wall, her body little more than mist wrapped in a human shape. Yet, even in the shadows, her purple eyes glowed: intelligent and wicked. Tendrils of liquid dripped from my ragged braid, soaking my back.

Despite her words, she knew why I'd tucked myself behind these walls, why I'd curled in on myself in the pool of water, staring at my reflection, willing myself to remain flat and blank every night. Outside this room, my mind was a riot of emotion, of memories.

Beyond that door carved into the wall beside Kaleal was a world of fire. That door had vanished the first night. Now it was back, open a crack, further evidence that I'd truly shattered my defenses.

"Why are you here, Kaleal?" I asked, my voice echoing.

"Because you willed me here."

"We both know that isn't true." I curled the end of the whip around my wrist and snipped the length, leaving a crude bracelet behind.

"Are you so sure?" The pool remained flat as she stepped away from the wall. The streaming ribbons of her blue robe hung elegantly from her watery shoulders. "Maybe you're apprehensive about burning this place to the ground. Maybe you're ready to take hold of your role in this life once again, but you need a little push. Maybe you know I'm the one who can do that for you."

She wasn't exactly wrong.

I narrowed my eyes, waiting for her to reach me. Despite her lack of shape, we were the same height, roughly the same build. I reached for her before I knew what I was doing, and her eyes danced. "Just say you're ready, and I'll do the rest."

I wrenched my arm back, wrestling control back with it. I didn't need her. I didn't need that extra push. Part of me knew that giving her even the smallest inch would mean sacrificing an inch of myself. Right now, I desperately needed to get *myself* back—not peddle it away.

"No."

In four impossibly long steps, I was at the door. My fingers curved around the crystal knob, and I turned for one last look. Kaleal lingered in the center of the room, her back to me. I tugged the door harder, the heat outside warming my back. Sweat trickled down my neck.

"What are you waiting for?" the God taunted. "You want yourself back, don't you?"

Damn her.

I flung the door wide. The heat hit me first, a punch that nearly knocked me to my knees. But I stood firm as the flames devoured me whole, vaporizing my dress and burning my hair. Despite the intensity of the fire licking at my heels, swiping its claws along my skin, it felt as pleasant as the water I swaddled myself in day in and out. It licked up my arms and seared down my legs: a phoenix reborn. A gown of feathery golds and reds and oranges rippled down my body. My silvery braid, once limp and ragged, now hung sleek and long enough to brush my hip.

Purple eyes scoured me, seared me.

I extended my arm, an imitation of her manipulation earlier. "As fun as this was, Kaleal, I'm taking the reins."

I snapped and the dreary room of water went up in a roaring fireball. I closed the door, knowing the ghost of the ancient God had already taken her leave. I turned, finding myself at the end of a hallway. On one side was a forest of smoldering embers. The other was a smooth, rippling lake. Both extended farther than I could see. As I walked, a trail of flames followed me. I didn't know where I was heading, but I sensed it was somewhere important.

I halted when the flames and water formed a cul-de-sac. At the far end of the circle, where flame and water met, was a door. It was charred and ragged with splinters. A handle of obsidian appeared when I reached forward. Wariness curled in my gut, but I couldn't stop myself, my movements dreamlike as I pulled it back.

I was met with a bridge of glass. On either side and straight ahead loomed a vast, starless darkness. Standing on the bridge, at the edge of the haze that concealed the other end, was a man I'd never wanted to see again.

He wore a well-fitted suit, the jacket buttons undone. His dress shirt was blue, his thin tie a strip of gold. He leaned forward on a tarnished, silver cane. Despite the distance between us, the mottled skin on the backs of his hands was stark in the pale firelight. It matched the burns curling around his jaw, reaching fingers into his hair. The effect twisted the Xs already carved in his sunken, somber cheeks. Across his forehead, four symbols burned lightning white in the middle, rimmed with a bleak darkness reminiscent of a well that had long run dry.

"Geoffrey."

His fingers flexed.

"It can't be you. You're dead," I stuttered, my mind reeling. I stank of nervous sweat. "You died. I killed you by the lake."

"Funny how people sometimes don't stay dead."

Like me. How I was presumed dead for seventeen years. How I'd seemingly risen from the grave, reborn, when I'd discovered the Kraken.

I stumbled forward, trying to get a clearer read on his face. But where they had always run hot with emotion before, his eyes remained cold and elusive. I opened my mouth, but he beat me to the punch. "I wondered when you'd find me."

"I didn't know there was anything of you to find," I breathed.

"I never wanted you dead, Zara." His bi-colored eyes glimmered. "That was Toren and my mistake in trusting him. Then again, you never believed me. You never gave me a chance, and that was also my mistake."

Hatred.

Pure, unrelenting hatred stained his expression.

He released the cane, swinging it back like a bat. I didn't wait to see what he might be capable of doing. With a shriek, I slapped my glowing brands, forcing my mind to rip back from this hellish sleep. As my body faded, a torrent of flame licking at the heels of my ghost, I heard him say, "This time, I'll make sure you stay dead."

Chapter 9

"He's back." I choked on a scream, my voice rough with horror and sleep. "He's back."

Gray light nearly blinded me, and I jerked so hard I cracked my forehead. Someone cursed and arms snaked around me, but I threw out an elbow and bone met bone with a snap. The resistance vanished and I was free, gloriously free. I whipped around, tucking my back into the corner, knives of ice frosting my fingers, and blinked through the confusion.

Ryder cupped his nose, blood dripping from the spaces between his fingers. He swore colorfully in a multitude of languages.

"Oh, for crikes sake, let me," Rose hollered, baring her teeth as she tumbled into the fray and nearly fell into his lap. She forced his head back and knocked his hands away. His incited cussing heated when she twisted his nose in a vice to stem the bleeding.

I felt like I was still in a dream, but the steam rising from the backs of my hands and warming my icy digits wasn't a hallucination. Neither was the bracelet of clear water I couldn't evaporate. I gasped in amazement. I'd done it. I'd actually done it. I'd freed myself of my self-imposed shackles and unleashed the full extent of my fire magic. And if I'd unleashed my magic, there was no way Geoffrey was merely a dream.

"Seriously, what did you expect to happen grabbing her when she was half-awake, yeah?" Rose laughed as she accepted a tissue from her lieutenant, a pretty brunette named Briar. "I have half a mind to clock you myself, ya oaf."

Ryder's response was muffled as she pressed her hand to his mouth. "Hush now, let me fix this before you end up with a black eye. Not like you don't deserve one."

A violent flash of movement at the edge of my periphery caught my attention.

"—now that's how you block." Through the gaps in the seat, Joseph mimed smacking Finn in the face with his elbow, but before he made contact, short, sharp gasps of laughter shook him so hard he folded in two. The kelpie regarded him calmly, mirth dancing in his eyes.

Finn caught my stare and tilted his head. I slipped my palms under the open flaps of my flannel shirt, hugging myself tightly until I felt a little more like myself again. Their laughter was dampening the horrifying quality of the reality of our situation.

Geoffrey was back.

But maybe... maybe that wasn't a bad thing.

"He's not dead. Not even a little," I said once they'd calmed down a bit. Joseph tugged his lips in concentration, motioning for me to continue. And Ryder—Ryder appeared downright murderous despite the fluffy, raspberry-colored towel he pressed to his nose. Smoke curled from his nostrils and his irises swirled.

"Who's not dead?" Rose glanced between us, wiping blood off her hands using a wet wipe she'd procured from one of her pockets. "And how exactly do you know that?"

"Geoffrey. The Hand of the Gods. The head of the Order, you know, the guy who's supposed to protect us but only seems to want all of us dead." I flexed my hands in my lap, the twin magics warring with one another sparked irritably beneath my skin. "I believe you briefly met him four weeks ago."

53

"The wanker who tried to kill you? The one you drowned after he blasted you?" The pixie stood and popped a hip against the backrest of a chair. One dusky emerald hand fell against her whip.

"The one and only." I pondered his burns. Had he done that to himself when he'd launched that fireball at me? Had I somehow done that? I'd thought I'd thrown him before I'd gained my fire magic, but… everything was so hazy in those final few moments.

"And you… what, dream about him? That's kind of creepy."

"We share a mental plane," I said, stretching my legs. That's what Joseph called it anyway, another term he'd derived from one of his many, many texts. I'd confided in him not long after arriving in camp. He'd ripped through his reading material like it was nothing, wanting to know if he, too, shared the plane, but came up with an inconclusive answer.

"Uh huh." And that was why I'd avoided bringing up the topic with the pixie. She was all about what she could see with her eyes and feel with her hands. Even her very magic by birth was rooted firmly in reality: primarily the ability to fly and create weapons out of handy materials. Going beyond the physical and delving into artificial concepts like dream-walking, was a stretch for her.

She peered at her black-clawed fingers. "Forgive me if I have a difficult time believing that not only is someone you hit with that much power still alive, but you're also the only one who can connect with him that way."

I went to run my fingers through my hair but stopped when I encountered the thick twists of a braid instead. It was a familiar braid, one that was as beautiful as it was intricate. Ryder rocked his head back and forth when I narrowed my eyes at him. The intensity of his anger had faded.

"Well, he did visit me now," I growled. "We had a lovely little chat, him and I. Mostly affirming that both of us were, in fact, very much alive and very pissed off."

I fiddled with my bracelet. It surprised me, the relief I felt knowing he was alive. I'd thought I'd wanted him dead, wanted him cast to the underworld forever where he couldn't touch me or anyone I loved ever again. But the guilt I'd felt thinking I'd killed him... I didn't want to be a murderer, even if I'd destroyed the lives of others to protect my own.

"He doesn't know where you are?" Finn asked, reaching out to touch my shoulder, but stopping as he remembered himself. Ryder glanced between us, a coy smile forming on his lips.

I thought it over. "Not that I can tell."

Joseph removed his glasses and rubbed his temples. "Do you think you can keep it that way? Because if he is back, and I assume he's taking the helm of the Order once again, I imagine he's going to do anything in his power to stop us from accomplishing our mission."

I can teach you to block him if you wish. Kaleal's whisper was little more than a touch of wind through the cherry blossoms of my mind.

"Yes," I said, answering them both. "I can keep him out."

"Right, then." Rose clapped her hands together brusquely. "We'll leave you to that, and I'll worry about dealing with him when he's within reach of my whip."

As always, I appreciated her matter-of-fact way of looking at the world, but I doubted it would be so simple. If I'd learned anything, it was that the Order was both well-equipped and relentless.

Finn scoffed as she made her way to the front of the plane. "Are you sure you're ok?"

"I will be."

"We're making our final descent into Cairo," Steve droned overhead.

"Good." Finn did clutch my shoulder now. I was strangely ok with that. "Because you have a whole new battle in front of you."

Chapter 10

"Y ou remind me of an ancient queen preparing to address her unruly council," Ryder said, hands shoved in his pockets as he looked me up and down. I squared my shoulders, wiggling my eyebrows saucily at the incubus who'd sneaked up as I peered out a window to the tarmac below.

"A queen who chooses denim and high tops over silk and stilettos sounds like my kind of gal." I dug my fingers into the thighs of my dark-washed jeans. In the spirit of packing lightly, I decided against bringing my single dress. Instead, I opted for dark colors that set off the jewel-tone of my eyes, the metallic gleam of my hair.

"Exactly." The incubus tucked an unruly strand back into place, smiling softly as he traced the pattern he'd created as I slept. "You look beautiful."

I ignored the quiver in my stomach at his touch, glanced at Finn who tugged at the tight collar of his aqua dress shirt, and resumed my vigil at the window. Rose and her pixies had fanned out, checking for security risks. Only at her signal would the rest of us would deplane.

"What does the symbol mean?" I asked.

"Pardon?"

"Don't play coy with me. I know you're the one behind my hair."

Ryder sniffed. "Is a man not allowed to have his secrets?"

"You're hardly a man." The crescent that was his smile grew in the reflection of the window. "And no, I'd rather you stop playing around and be straight with me."

The incubus remained silent for so long I wondered if he even would answer.

Finally, he tugged his chin and sighed. "There's so much you don't know about me, glowstick. Come to think of it, I'm not sure if there's a soul on earth who truly knows who I am or the secrets I carry."

"So help me understand you." Despite my misgivings about any romantic involvement with this soulful creature who exuded power and sex as confidently as he walked, I couldn't help being drawn to him. "You want me to want you, you say you're coming for me, that you'll make me yours." My cheeks heated. "You know that isn't going to happen if you don't let me in."

"Is that so? Am I wearing you down already?" His head tipped, mischief flitting across his face. "I must admit, I thought you'd be a tougher nut to crack."

I scuffed the sole of my Chucks on the royal blue carpet. "I'd hardly call this cracking."

"How about a trade?"

I wanted to scrub at my face but I had actually applied cosmetics for once, and doubted I'd have time to fix them before Rose called us down. Come to think of the pixie, she was taking a long time scouring the situation. I frowned and peered down again.

Since we weren't ready to announce our fey presence to the world, Rose had shifted back into her human guise. The unshaven half of her head was still heavy with tiny braids and her dark skin nearly matched the straps of leather armor criss-crossing her back. Her hand hovered over the whip hooked around her hips.

"A trade?"

"Quid pro quo. Tit for tat. An exchange."

"You wanted an excuse to say tit."

"Maybe." Ryder's breath warmed the shell of my ear and he gripped my waist. "So? Your answer?"

I met his gaze in the reflection. "One truth for another, they must be of equal value. None of that 'you spill your guts and I tell you my favorite color is orange' nonsense."

"So she has played the game, after all!" He smacked a loud kiss to the side of my head and withdrew triumphantly. "And for the record, my favorite color wouldn't be something so dull as orange. Perhaps tangerine or sherbet, but hardly *orange*."

My head bodyguard swiveled to the plane. Rose traced a large circle on her flattened palm followed by several taps at the cardinal directions. A few more complex gestures followed.

"Rose says it's clear, but to be on guard," I called out to the boys. Joseph shoved his glasses up his nose. He'd changed into a thin, green hooded sweatshirt that set off the warm gold in his hazel eyes. "The nero are here, but she thinks something is off. I think believe leader is waiting for us to come out first."

I flicked my braid over my shoulder and sucked in a large gulp of air. "Here goes nothing."

Joseph strode forward to take his spot at my side but hesitated when Ryder stepped between us, a finger lifted apologetically.

"I get bored easily, too easily," the incubus told me. "I distribute investments and collect businesses because it amuses me. Name a trade and I've got my fingers in at least several connected pies. Money is of little interest to me, and perhaps that's why I've got so much of it." He slipped something in my pocket. Its weight settled against my hip. "Despite all that, I've never considered myself to be a particularly charitable man until I met you, until you wrapped me up in this harebrained scheme of yours. And I'd gladly let it all burn to the ground if it helped you get what you want."

Ryder squeezed my arm, nudged Joseph into place, and fell back alongside Finn who muttered something to him. Ryder offered him a silken smile, sliding his hands in his black slacks as if he hadn't scattered truths at my feet like glittery beads.

I forced my thoughts to come together when I exchanged a look with the God of Air.

"Let's go," he said with some amusement.

Shoulders thrown back, spine elongated, face set in hard lines, I felt prepared for anything as I stepped on the platform leading to the runway. At the foot of the stairs gathered a dozen or so beings I didn't recognize. The pixies remained around the periphery in strategic locations. At my side, Joseph restrained the wind that would have otherwise tugged at our clothing and hair.

Once our feet were firmly on the ground, I acknowledged the delegation with a small nod but kept my hands folded. I could taste the potency of the nero's power, the tang of it clung like allspice to my tongue. The fey themselves were spectacular, garbed in flowing clothing of bright colors with small chips of jade centered on their foreheads. The women wore flowing dresses paired with gladiator sandals strapped up to their knees. The men donned loose pants and shirts that opened in a deep vee to the middle of their chests, revealing dark tendrils of tattoos snaking across their coppery skin. A dozen matching bronze eyes hungrily drank us in.

A woman in a dress of deep violet and a silver hoop through her septum stepped forward, her movements nimble. She bent in a slight bow, though she kept her eyes fixed on my face.

"We appreciate you coming all this way to meet with us, Gods of Water and Air." Her thick accent was decadent. "We understand you've had quite the journey already. We're honored you chose to meet with us."

"The appreciation is all ours," I replied, "for not only being so willing to meet with us on short notice, but also discuss the possibility of assisting us in the search for the God of Earth."

Her lips flattened. "Of course. We swear allegiance to the Lost City, and we're all too eager to see our God returned to his rightful spot."

My gaze swept over the other nero. Despite her claim, not one of them boasted the broad calligraphy sweeps of a three-peaked mountain brand on their necks—a classic, magical symbol of true allegiance. I didn't dare look at Finn and the cresting wave on his throat. Something else about what she'd said struck me wrong, but when I tried to puzzle it out, the nero shifted, parting in two, even lines. The woman, too, stepped aside.

If they hadn't moved, I might not have noticed the man who'd slipped in among their welcoming brigade. Even now, I had a difficult time remembering if he'd been there to begin with. He didn't so much as glance at the nero as he walked up the line, hands hanging casually at his side. Hair a few shades lighter than an oil slick framed a decidedly ordinary face, with its wisp of a nose, smooth copper skin, and oval eyes. Up close, he had about three inches on me. His lips were pressed in a thin, white line as he surveyed Joseph, his jaw set in soft lines that hinted at boredom.

The most remarkable thing about him was how incredibly unre-markable he was.

Whoever he was, he wasn't a nero. Where they bristled with the heat of sand and sun, I wasn't getting a magical signature from him whatsoever.

"You must be exhausted after such a long trip," the man said, his voice as bland as the rest of him. He still hadn't so much as looked at me. "Forgive me for the delay in escort. If you'd follow me, we'll be on our way."

Ryder's frown intensified and Finn swished his knuckles together once before he locked his hands tight. Since Joseph seemed disinclined to speak, given he was busy trying to crack the puzzle that was this newcomer, I bravely stepped up. "Where exactly are we going?"

"*Temple de Sable.*" *The Temple of Sand.* The French flowed off his tongue like wine. He glanced at the pixies who'd drawn closer. "My house, per se. An oasis in the desert."

"And you would be…"

He briefly glanced at the sky. "Phenex." He blinked and finally met my eyes. The immense punch of power he'd concealed crashed into and *through* me. My head buzzed as my twin bands of fire and water roared forward. No, he wasn't a nero. He was something more. Something much, much more. "Phenex Allard."

I know you. Kaleal's ghostly voice was a surprise. So was her strength when she surged forward, nudging me so we shared my eyes. I flinched at the raw hunger in her tone, realizing how incredibly lonely it must have been for her, trapped all this time.

I know you, she repeated.

Phenex's lips parted, his bland disinterest flickering into shock before he shored it up. But I'd caught it, the razor's edge of intelligence lurking beneath the surface, the hint of something dangerous prowling beneath his skin.

He offered his hand, steady as a surgeon. "And you, Zara Ramone of the Water Temple, require no introduction."

I reached for it at the same time Ryder jerked in my periphery.

"No!" My head rang at the sharp syllable, unsure if I'd heard it out loud or in my head, because Kaleal wrenched control of my body away, stopping the movement before our palms brushed. A corner of Phenex's eye twitched, that wicked cunning he'd so cleverly masked rising to the top like crème as he stared intently, his chest barely moving.

"Forgive me," I heard myself say. Over Phenex's shoulder, the nero shifted. Hell, even my own friends seemed shocked. "I'm recovering from an illness and wouldn't want to pass it along."

Kaleal released me back into my own skin, the reverse of a snake shedding its scales.

"Of course." He blinked. "Your concern for my health is commendable, though I assure you I can't remember the last time I fell ill." He lifted the hand he still had yet to pull back, the one that looked as normal and boring as my own, and twitched his middle and index fingers. The engines of a handful of jeeps behind him fired up.

He seemed to shake himself loose and scanned our small pack of players. "If you'd please accept my offer of transportation, we'll have you at *Temple de Sable* in no time at all." Phenex spun on his heel, making for the vehicle at the head of the line, the nero followed without comment.

Numbly, I gestured at my friends, feeling trapped in both the situation and my own skin. Joseph clung to my side like saran wrap, his hand grazing the small of my back as he increased the pressure of the air around me until I could breathe again.

Two thoughts circled my head in a loop:

What was Phenex and *who* was he to Kaleal?

Chapter 11

I f Phenex considered his place a house, my imagination faltered at his definition of a castle.

It started with the towering, wrought iron gates that swung wide to grant the jeeps access to a winding road of crushed quartz. I hadn't expected to find a forest in the desert, but inside the black bars rose trees carved of rich onyx and gold-veined marble. The road snaked for half a mile before opening to a wide lawn with thick, blue-green grass.

"Is that a peacock?" Rose asked, pointing at the cluster of opulent birds. "Seriously?"

"That's what caught your attention?" Ryder asked as we passed through a pair of gates with knife-bladed suns etched on their surfaces. Men in gold uniforms peered down on us from the top of the limestone walls, spears close at hand. "And not, oh, I don't know, the *palace*?"

I pressed against the window. Gold-red walls towered hundreds of feet in the air. In strategic places, towers were capped with white domes and twisting spires. Dozens of deep-set windows cut into the stone glittered in the mid-afternoon light. The grounds were as expansive as they were vibrant, teeming with flowers and short trees I didn't recognize. A fountain in the shape of a pelican spilled an endless stream of water from its mouth into a pool. Fine sand covered the multitude of paths crisscrossing the lawn.

Finn whistled through his teeth as we slipped from the vehicle. Ryder—unfazed by the hour-long drive that ended here on the outskirts of Cairo—gazed up at the monstrosity with thinly-veiled hostility. The pixies didn't waste any time fanning out around us, hands resting on their weapons as they scanned for danger.

"I forget how magnificent it is until I see it through an outsider's eyes," Phenex said.

"Forgive me, but I don't see how that's remotely possible." I glanced at the man who'd sidled up as my I eagerly devoured the sight of *Temple de Sable*. "I believe you know exactly how this looks."

His mouth twitched, but he didn't turn to the trio of balconies hung with vines to which I pointed. Instead, his attention fixed on the band around my wrist.

"I may have had a hand in the finishing touches," he conceded.

"If your intent was to dazzle, I'd say you pulled it off."

"Certainly." He raised his voice, calling out to Finn who was rummaging through the vehicles. "You can leave your bags, someone will take care of those." The kelpie scoffed and waved off one of the nero who approached while slipping the strap of a maroon backpack over his shoulder. Joseph stood from where he crouched beside the pool, examining a large, green hunter beetle as it scaled a thick blade of grass.

"Bast here will help you to your rooms." Phenex gestured to the woman in purple who'd greeted us at the airport. Her head lowered in acknowledgement, face pointed flat at her feet. "She will help you in any way you require during your stay. All you must do is ask."

"I'd like to survey the grounds with a member of your security," Rose piped up. "My girls and I would like to get a lay of the land."

"As thorough as you are beautiful," Phenex said. Rose frowned and stroked her whip, but didn't unwind it as Phenex slipped a hand into his pocket, emerging with a cell phone so thin I wondered how it didn't bend. He continued in that neutral, unaffected way as he tapped a few buttons on the screen. "There are a few rules I ask you to respect. First, don't leave the grounds without permission. Please understand, this is for your safety. The nero tend to shoot first and ask questions later. The property backs up to a river that feeds the Nile, so we do get the occasional intruder."

I kept one ear tuned in to *what* he was saying but focused more on *how* he said it.

At the airport, he'd come across as bland, nondescript. His clothing was made of quality fabrics, but nothing about them was particularly memorable or fashionable. He limited his hand gestures, but the ones he did make were elegant and poised. His Middle Eastern accent came out strongest with his vowels, but he spoke cleanly and clearly, without room for misinterpretation. Even the way he stood was authoritative while not stiff or standoffish.

Everything about him was carefully crafted. Too well crafted.

Kaleal, are you there? I mentally asked, probing the back of my mind for the wisps of the being I'd come to recognize. *You've been quiet since the airport.*

Nothing.

Annoyance simmered and I rolled my neck before I did something foolish, like tear through my mind, pulling it apart in search of her.

"...you must be exhausted, so please take a few hours to get situated before supper. We'll discuss your situation and how I can be of assistance." Phenex gave a short nod. However, when I took a step to join my friends, his arm shot out, blocking me.

My hands came up. "What—?"

"Except for you, Water God." He dropped his arm, a sly smile touching his lips. "You and I have other matters to address."

Though my heart thundered, I slipped right into fight-mode. In training, Rose favored sneak attacks, and I'd come to expect them. I

65

darted backward, the familiar grips of my icy daggers formed in my palms and I crossed the translucent blades with a clang. I'd styled them after another dagger, one strapped to my thigh if worse came to worse.

In my periphery, Joseph surged forward, unleashing his favored arrows of air at the creature standing tall and straight before me. Phenex didn't so much as flinch when they exploded in bright pops of yellow against an invisible barrier. My insides clenched and I lowered my center of gravity while simultaneously reaching for more water to play with.

My eyes narrowed when I hit the invisible barrier that had deflected my friend.

"I see you've discovered the true extent of my reach," Phenex said. He remained as calm and steady as if we stood in the center of a ballroom, glasses of champagne in hand. "I imagine you're having a difficult time tapping into that wonderful water magic of yours. I'm told it's profoundly difficult when there isn't a source within reach."

It was true. He'd somehow cut me off from the pool, and there wasn't enough moisture in the air to fill an eyedropper. Red strands of fire magic seared my palms, but without a spark or a flame or anything within a few hundred feet, it, too, was useless.

"What are you?" I hissed through my teeth.

"That's a very good question." He lifted a hand. White sand swirled in a ball before his chest. Behind him, a shaggy, black horse dripping with kelp and gore reared back and struck the invisible barrier. The sound of Finn's backward hooves didn't permeate the thickness of the bulb. "You first."

"Me first what?" Icy sweat trickled down my neck as I adjusted my grip. What was Phenex waiting for?

"Who are you?" The ball in his hand grew bigger, the sand swirling faster.

"You know who I am." I edged first to my left, then the right, gauging the distance. "You said I needed no introduction."

"And I, as I so rarely am anymore, was incorrect." He straightened, hunger apparent on his face. "You said you knew me. I want to know how."

My skin pebbled and a rush of vertigo threatened to knock my feet out from under me. No way in stars had Kaleal said that out loud. No way. My back hit the curved wall of his barricade. I used it to steady myself, blinking back black waves of surprise and confusion.

"What if I told you I don't know how I know you." I shoved my magic outward as I moved again, searching for a crack, a weakness, anything to give me the upper hand.

The ball of sand rained to the ground. "I'd say you're either lying, which would be a pity because I resent liars, or you're growing more curious by the moment. If it's the latter, then color me intrigued."

Sand crunched under my shoes and before I could recover from my mistake, the ground collapsed beneath me. My shriek was buried in the cocoon created by the sandy path I'd unwittingly crossed, and it squeezed me impossibly tighter. I gasped, agony rippling through me as my bones compressed, threatening to break a hundred different ways.

I clawed at the sand with one hand and stabbed furiously at it with the dagger with the other, desperation giving strength to my thrusts. Tiny grains filled my mouth and nose as I struggled to breathe. It wouldn't be long before I ran out of air. Something popped in my right side, a rib likely cracking, and I shuddered out a yell, wondering if this darkness pressing against me would be the end. Desperation surged and the tip of my dagger slipped through an opening.

Blissful, beautiful light filtered through and I scrambled for it, getting an arm through the opening when it snapped tight around it. My legs went weak when the darkness swept in once more. I was out of ideas.

Another rib popped and tears pricked at my eyes, absorbed by the sand before they could fall. There was nothing I could do but accept the pain.

As suddenly as he'd attacked, Phenex released me.

My body smacked the ground and I spilled to my hands and knees, coughing up sand and gulping greedily at the oxygen. My ribs burned with every heaving gasp, but I didn't care. I was alive.

"I'll ask you again, *Zara*." Phenex spoke my name like a taunt. His slender shadow spilled across the backs of my hands and I realized how close he'd gotten. "Who are you, and what are you concealing?"

I looked up, shaking with fatigue, one eye closed in a squint as I peered at his profile. I'd tried to see his magic before, but he'd blocked it somehow, clutching its signature in an ironclad grip. Now though, through the lens of my Iridescence—my ability to see and analyze magic—I realized he was easily the most powerful being I'd ever encountered—aside from myself and Joseph. Bright strands of gold shot with brown so dark it was nearly black whipped around him, his whispery figure so much like Kaleal's in its lack of true shape.

Whatever he was, it wasn't remotely human.

"Yes, you really are more trouble than you're worth, aren't you?" His flawless calm was starting to piss me off. "No matter how you know me, I suppose. You're hardly talented enough to defend against me for long. Maybe you should give up now, because you're only extending the inevitable."

Over his shoulder, Ryder had shifted to his demon form. Long, veined bat wings flapped as he pounded at the barrier, his mouth wide in what I could only imagine were yells. Beyond him gathered a congregation of nero, their eyes glowing yellow. Something about them...

The sand shifted beneath my knees again, dragging me backward. I let out a short yell of my own. On either side of me rose thick walls of sand. As they snapped together, I reacted, reaching for the only source of water left to me, a source I'd sworn I'd never use.

The walls exploded, showering me in sand. Phenex stumbled, clutching his chest as he choked, clawing at his skin, nails digging bloody grooves. I raised my clenched hand, ripping harder at the very blood coursing through his veins, driving him to his knees as I advanced.

"You think me powerless, Phenex," I said. Violence burned in his eyes as he curled in on himself, snarling angrily. I smiled wide, the expression ugly. "And you've got tricks, but I'm done being pushed around by men who think they're more powerful than me, who think they're better than me."

Like Geoffrey.

In my mind's eye, I could see the ball of flame rushing toward me.

"Release me now," I ordered, shaking the vision aside, "and I'll consider not leaving you a dry husk of skin and bones."

"Alright, alright." With effort, Phenex fought my hold and lifted his hand in a placating manner. When I was sure he'd drop the shield separating me from my friends, he vanished. I blinked as my insides went deathly cold in horror.

"Nice try." His voice came from behind me and I snapped around as a fist cracked my cheek. I stumbled, but even as I reclaimed my fighter's stance, I couldn't believe what I was seeing. Three Phenexs standing side by side grinned broadly back at me, savoring my confusion. The three forms roared with pure magic: no blood, no organs, nothing human about them.

The beginnings of true fear flickered in my belly.

"I must say I'm impressed with that little trick of yours." The three Phenexs spoke as one. I flinched and closed my eyes against the stereo effect. When I opened them again, he'd multiplied. Nine of him surrounded me now, nine matching versions all closing in. Behind them loomed a growing wall of sand. I scrambled for a plan, anything to save me, but came up blank.

My skin felt icy, my limbs disjointed. Even my head was lighter than normal, my vision foggy with panic. This was really, really bad.

Phenex was still talking, "—never had a chance."

I spun in a slow circle, nearly tripping over nothing as my breathing went shallow.

"You want to know what I am, Zara?" The bass of his voice pounded my ears over and over again, louder than standing beside the speakers at a rock concert. "I suppose I can let you in on that little secret since you won't be around long enough to speak of it to anyone."

Motion across from me caught my attention. Ryder. He was doing something strange with his fingers, cupping them and flipping his thumb first straight up, then flattening it, over and over again.

A wall of sand rose high, but I barely saw it, grasping instead at the answer to Ryder's gesture that loomed past my fingertips.

"I'm a djinn. The last djinn alive, in fact. You want to know how I know that?" Phenex laughed, the sound reverberating against the walls of the barrier, hammering me like hail. "I killed my siblings and devoured their magic. Every. Last. One of them."

The incubus patted his pocket and made that gesture again, then pressed his palm to the barrier. Understanding ignited an inferno in my core. My hand shot to my own pocket. On the plane, the incubus had given me something. My fingers closed around a cold, metal rectangle the size of a matchbook.

Heat swept under, across, over my skin.

I had fire.

"Any last words, little God?" One of the Phenexs raised his hand.

I assumed he was the real one.

The bright red of my fire magic blazed hotter and hotter, so blinding in its intensity I'd worry about it consuming me alive if I wasn't so certain I could control it. I shook now not with fear or pain, but with excited energy as I raised the lighter high, flipping the top back as if I'd done so a million times before. My thumb braced on the tiny textured wheel as the djinn squinted at it.

"As if you care," I said.

The wheel rolled.

A sliver of a flame emerged, and my magic caught it, erupting like a room filled with gasoline. Everything inside the djinn's barricade went up in flames, hot and bright, and gloriously *mine*. I poured my energy into the brilliance, allowing to burn hotter and hotter, the flames barely touching me. It wanted to do this, it wanted to breathe. It sizzled and soared and raged, delighting in its free reign.

The bubble of Phenex's magic burst, flames bursting forth like a breached dam. Sweat dripped from my forehead, my spine going rigid as I ripped my power back, denying the inferno its life force. The magic screamed in protest but sucked back beneath my skin.

Before the smoke cleared, an arm snaked around my back, clutching me immobile. A thin, silver blade pressed against my throat and I froze, afraid I'd slice my own throat by swallowing. Everything in me protested, my skin quivering at the contact.

Phenex cupped the back of my head, his fingers digging into my scalp forcefully, directing my face upward. My lip curled. He was remarkably unaffected by the force of my power. His skin was untouched. Even the white collar framing his throat was barely singed.

His lips parted and my world narrowed. Nothing penetrated the bubble encapsulating us. A nuclear warhead could detonate beside me and I wouldn't notice.

"I'm honored to have the privilege of teaching you a very valuable lesson, Zara." The fingers digging into my hair relaxed, but he had me so ensnared I was beyond considering escape. "The simplest attack is the most effective."

His thumb traced a line along the column of my throat.

"So vulnerable, so breakable," he mused. The pressure of the blade returned and wetness dripped down my skin. "Even a God can be damaged. Don't forget that."

He released me, though in my stunned state I could barely move. The djinn folded the blade of his knife into its handle and presented it to me with a flourish. My rigor mortis broke and I took it numbly. The silver and pearl were warm from his body heat.

"What's this for?" I asked.

He straightened from his subtle bow, one that felt more sincere than mocking. He flicked the fingers on his left hand, dispelling the barrier he'd seamlessly recreated around us. The rest of the world filtered through, and I flinched at the rush of noise.

"You surprise me," he said dryly. "I'd forgotten what that was like."

Chapter 12

Knuckles rapped against the door as I unwound a towel from my long hair.

I raised an eyebrow at Briar stationed in the corner of my room cleaning a wicked set of elongated throwing stars. She nodded without looking up from her work, giving me the all clear from the pixie stationed out in the hallway.

"Come in," I called. Someday I'd understand the telepathic bond between the pixies—after I figured out my own mental irregularities anyway. Like how Kaleal had sunk so deep inside me I couldn't find or hear her. She had no right to leave me in limbo like this. I could use her help since it seemed we were stuck at Phenex's palace for the time being.

Finn was the number one advocate for leaving straightaway. I was a close second, but Ryder argued that if we left, we'd lose what could be our only shot at getting across the desert. He'd won over Joseph, who seemed to think the Order was on to us, and the pixies were dying for a fight if it came down to it... so here we were: residing in enemy territory at *Temple de Sable*.

I tossed the towel away as the door to my rooms opened. Finn strode through. He whistled low and slow, taking in the four-poster bed draped in wispy purple and blue fabrics and its thick, black comforter was shot with pinpricks of white. To the side was a sitting area with chairs upholstered in silk; the vanity was really a wall of gold and mirrors with a ledge. Briar straddled the back of a gilded chair in the corner there, her back to the reflection. She claimed all the glass creeped her out.

"Fancy," he drawled, an arrogant lilt to his tone. "It's like I don't know you anymore, now that you're big-time and all." He spun a slow circle in the center of the room before disappearing into the equally, and unnecessarily, elaborate en suite. Seriously, no one needed a Jacuzzi tub the size of a backyard swimming pool in their bathroom.

The kelpie's voice was muffled through the wall. "It's so strange knowing someone who's someone. Try not to forget about us little guys, would you?"

Briar snorted as she tucked the spiked points of one star around the rimmed center, forming something that looked like a thick, black button which she promptly pinned to her bandolier. She selected another star from a tray and restarted the polishing process.

"I take it your digs aren't as nice?" I asked, toeing on my Converse.

"Hardly." He emerged in the doorway between the two rooms and leaned against the trim, one boot propped on the other. I blinked and tilted my head. The kelpie's clothing was more punk than I remembered it being when we'd met. His black jeans were tight, his leather jacket scarred. He pushed at his messily-styled hair with a gloved hand. Finn had always favored jangly, metal bracelets. Judging by the sounds he made when he moved, he'd apparently added to the collection.

"The bedroom—if you can call it that—is an oversize closet with two cots and a trunk," he added.

"Two cots?"

"Yeah. I'm sharing with—"

"—his favorite dark horse BFF." Ryder swaggered into the room that suddenly felt much smaller. In imitation of Finn, he, too, whistled, though he never looked away from me. "And while he's lying through his teeth about our room, I prefer what I'm finding in yours much, much more."

I had a funny feeling he and Finn were referring to two very different things.

Briar cleared her throat before the moment could stretch into awkwardness. The chair creaked when she unfolded her four-and-a-half-foot frame. "Zara, if you don't mind I'll take off and check on my sisters." She made a point of looking at the three of us in turn. "I pity anyone who tries to launch an attack with the three of you in here."

I waved her off and waited for the door to close before raising a finger in protest. "Before you start—"

"Do you have a death wish?" Ryder asked mildly. "Because I'm starting to think so."

"I didn't ask him to trap me." I slipped off the bed, my arms folding defensively.

"When a djinn makes you his target, the correct response is to run. You do *not* engage." Our eyes met in the mirrors Ryder stood before, his hands hooked behind his back. "You especially do not give him further reason to take interest in you."

"And who do you think you are?" I demanded. My fire magic ignited, hot and heady as if I hadn't depleted it a mere two hours ago. "I didn't know he was a djinn for one, and two, *he* attacked *me*. My choices were pretty limited."

"You could have run."

"I'm not that fast."

"You could have died," he hissed, spinning around.

"If I hadn't engaged, I would have died alone and defenseless."

The incubus snarled, black-tipped claws sprouted from his fingertips. "Why don't you have more faith in us? In *me*? I'm more than capable of—"

75

"I think he means to say—" Finn interrupted, bravely stepping between us as Ryder prepared to charge. "—is he understands what an impossible situation you were in, and we're glad you're ok. You are ok, aren't you?"

I resisted rubbing the slender, two-inch mark on my neck, the one I refused to let my magic heal. As much as Phenex frightened me, and as much as I resented him for what he'd done, I found a strange sort of value in his lesson and wanted it to sink in deep.

"I'm beaten, but not broken." I sank to the bed where I picked up the djinn's gift to me. It was about the size of a Swiss Army knife, the wooden grip inlaid with a pearl so white it nearly glowed.

Rose had examined and cleared it earlier, allowing me to keep it with an addendum that I someday, "stab him in the eye with it, for irony's sake."

I chose my next words carefully, giving voice to the thoughts that frothed like white water rapids. "I don't think he actually wanted to kill me."

Ryder whirled on Finn, smoke billowing from his nostrils, hands clenching and unclenching. If he'd possessed my fire magic, odds were we'd all be burned to a crisp right now. The kelpie nimbly darted out of the way and flung himself on top of the vanity, tugging his eyebrow ring in thought.

"What makes you say that?" Finn asked.

"He had every opportunity to kill me." I sifted through my memories of the battle, wishing for the millionth time that Kaleal would pop her wispy head up and give me some answers.

Oh, Kaleal, where are you hiding you pretentious witch?

I continued, "Right from the get-go, he could have crushed me. I wasn't prepared for his first sand attack and he wrapped me up like a spider with a fly. I had nothing to do with him releasing me. He was pushing me, he wanted something from me."

The butt of the knife smacked the palm of my hand. It was starting to drive me crazy, this inability to talk about the ancient God with my friends. I'd even tried writing a note about her earlier in the bathroom, but my hand turned to stone on my arm. I shifted aside my thoughts of her so that my throat would open.

"I think he sensed the fire magic," I said, semi-truthfully. He'd certainly known something wasn't right about me. "It was a test, all of it. I guess I passed or, yeah, he might have killed me."

Finn's feet swayed and he risked a glance at Ryder who hovered in the corner, seething.

"I think so, too," he said. At Ryder's sharp look, he added, "—once I got past the whole 'nearly watching you get crushed by your enemies again' thing. Jeez, would you calm down already?"

The incubus huffed and started pacing instead.

"Anyway." Finn dragged out the last syllable. "I thought the djinn vanished thousands of years ago. Even at the airport when I sensed the magnitude of his abilities, it didn't occur to me that he could be one. I mean, you're technically stronger than him in terms of power, but djinn are ancient and he's had several dozen millennia to hone his abilities, no offense. Given what I saw, he could have destroyed you, but he really wanted to see what you were made of."

He paused and undid one of three buckles strapped to his thigh. "He was also honed in on *only* you. He definitely sized up Joseph, but you held his attention. I wonder why."

Finn's eyes narrowed and my stomach flipped eagerly. Maybe if he guessed correctly, I could tell him about Kaleal. I needed his brain to work a little faster.

"You should know, he's a soul stealer," Ryder said, and I could have smacked him for breaking the kelpie's chain of thought, "in addition to commanding sand. And that's only a fraction of what he's capable of."

I perked up. "Like what?"

"Since they've been gone so long, most of what we know is myth." Ryder shrugged and ran a hand through his hair. The highlights in his black locks seemed to change on a whim, and today they shimmered with amethyst. "Unbound djinn, meaning they aren't tied to vessels anymore, are practically Gods in their own right with their elemental abilities alone. There are also stories that frame them as tricksters capable of getting into your head and destroying you from the inside out. That's why it's important to not let him touch you. Rumor has it that touching skin grants them access to your mind."

So that's why Kaleal didn't want me shaking his hand. Interesting. I unfolded the knife, angling the blade so it caught the light. "And, like you, they get their power by stealing souls."

Finn hopped off the vanity when Ryder went quiet. "Djinn are cursed creatures. They're bound to answer wishes for their masters. Three wishes per master. But after that third wish... they can rip your soul right from your body. Each soul they collect adds to their base power."

Finn bit his lips. "If he's the last one left, his power would be unparalleled. In some ways, it's pretty incredible that he *didn't* kill you back there."

I folded the knife up and stuck it in my pocket. "How do we combat that?"

Finn's emerald eyes flickered. "With cleverness and a lot of luck."

"Finn." Ryder dropped the kelpie's name like an anvil. He'd calmed considerably, though his stare was an accusation. "You're a bigger asset than you're giving yourself credit for."

"You're one to talk," the kelpie fired off, before he, too, started pacing. Watching the two of them weave around the room was making me dizzy. "Zara, there's something else I haven't told you."

My gut curdled and I tucked my legs beneath me, my small smile fading with his seriousness. I wasn't sure how many more of his secrets

I was prepared to handle, especially if this one was anywhere near as bad as...

"I was an officer in the Water Temple's navy." Finn swallowed, his jaw flexing as his eyes went cloudy with memories. "I was third in command of the temple's defenses, that's why it mattered so much when the Order attacked. People who counted on me were waiting for me to give a command. I never gave it. I lost everything that day. Everything."

It surprised me, the emotion that filled my veins. Anger hit first, but it paled in comparison to the pity and sorrow that rose with it. As upset as I'd been with Finn these past few weeks, I hadn't considered the turmoil he was going through.

Ryder knelt beside me. "In case you aren't picking up on what he's actually saying." His golden gaze searched my face until I finally made eye contact. "Finn is trained in military tactics. And he was a brilliant strategist when he let himself loose. He made a mistake. A lot of people made mistakes that day. But he's an invaluable asset to our team. Let's say that between his brains and my connections, if war is what you're after, you'll have it."

Ryder's absolute faith in me, his devotion to our mission, made my heart swell.

Someone knocked on the door and we looked at it in unison. I nudged Ryder back with my toe and slid off the comforter when Finn rose to answer it. Pitching my voice low, I said to Ryder, "One more question for you."

He quirked a grin. "And that would be?"

"How did you know?" I held up the silver Zippo. "How did you know I was using my fire magic?"

"I didn't." He curled his fingers around mine. "But I wanted you to be prepared whenever you were ready."

Chapter 13

Turned out, it was a nero at the door.

He introduced himself as Tau and had been sent to escort me to dinner. Finn and Ryder attempted to follow, but Tau was firm when he said it was only the Gods who would be dining with Phenex tonight. I put my foot down, though, when he tried to keep Briar from joining me. The nero blinked his almond-shaped eyes and, with veiled disdain, instructed us to follow.

In retaliation, I was positive he took us the longest route through the maze of the palace, moving so quickly we hardly had time to admire the delicate furnishings and paintings. Not once did we see other nero moving about.

I was so struck by our surroundings that I nearly ran into Tau when he stopped suddenly. While I was still reeling, he gestured at Joseph and Rose who lingered beneath a golden archway, bowed, then vanished behind one of the many silken tapestries hanging from the walls. I blinked after him as Briar wandered over to Rose.

"About time you showed up, yeah?" Rose bumped knuckles with her.

Rather than join them, I lifted the tapestry and felt the smooth wall of stone behind it. No edges of a door, no cleverly concealed latch, nothing.

"Something's not right about them," Joseph mused. "They're too subservient. I researched them back at the cabin and found out they're about as warmongering as the pixies. For them to be this docile... it's strange."

"Stereotypical much?" I deadpanned, though I agreed with his assessment. I couldn't put my finger on it, but between their quiet demeanors and lowered gazes, the fey felt off. "Maybe these nero are comfortable here. Maybe there's a whole band of them roaming the deserts, burning villages to the ground, and shooting strangers to make up for it."

I glanced to my left and found myself alone. I sighed. "Would you quit doing that?"

Joseph grinned from the archway. He'd thought he was so clever when he'd figured out he could use his magic to carry his voice wherever he wanted it to go, like some strange version of tin-can telephone. The God of Air could even hear conversations from the other side of the room, though I'd threatened to remove a delicate bit of his anatomy if I ever caught him spying on me.

A golden door engraved with sigils and patterns of the sun groaned, silencing the banter of the pixies. The double doors swung wide beneath the archway, revealing a room more than triple the size of my bedroom. A nero with a round face and long hair bound back with a strip of yellow leather appeared at the entrance. She flicked a hand at the table laden with food. "Please take a seat, Gods of Air, Water. Mr. Allard will be but a moment longer."

Her flinty gaze flicked over the lot of us, her frown deepening when she settled on me. I grinned. Finally, someone who did more than smile and nod.

Rose captured my arm, her extra-digited fingers gripping hard. She'd shifted back into her emerald skin and swirling tribal tattoos at some point, and her braids had swooped forward, obscuring one inky eye. She'd twisted her whip in a loop that hooked around her shoulders and draped down her back in a ribbon of thorns. Like Briar, she'd strapped a sword to her hips with a braided black belt.

"*Promedis ad*," she hissed with force, reiterating the warning with a jab of her finger. "I don't trust any of them, especially after that display in the courtyard." She shook her head. "I understand why we're here, and I understand that he's in charge of the people who are our best shot of you figuring out what you need to do, but don't let him get to you. He's a *valrax* if I've ever seen one."

She looked so serious, so intensely focused, that my own resolve turned to steely focus. I was incredibly lucky to have people like Rose at my side, people as loyal as they were kind. I gripped her forearm in answer, squeezing hard in silent thanks. My other hand twisted a sign that, in my best interpretation, meant close companion—a term of deep respect and comraderie among friends.

"Don't ever change," I said as she gaped. "Besides, if a slimy, gray worm tried to steal me away in the dead of night, I'd rip its beating heart right out of its body, like you showed me."

I ducked into the room with a chuckle. The door closed at my back.

"If your intention was to give her a heart attack, congratulations on a job well done. She's going to talk about nothing else for the next few days, and you know it," Joseph said drolly, examining the spread on the table. It smelled decadent, a wonderful blend of meats and spices that I didn't recognize, but despite my improved mood, my gut still churned. "Though I'd watch for Briar the next time you see her, she's got a mean left hook."

"I'm no threat to her," I murmured, circling the room.

Like seemingly everything else in Phenex's palace, this room, too, was lavish with riches: walls of black-veined green stone, hand-crafted trim pressed with gold-flakes, sparkling windows framed with white drapes of Egyptian cotton. Fey with blue skin and glossy wings peeked out from satiny clouds painted on the ceiling, flirting with us above the table large enough to seat twenty people.

Tonight it was set for three.

"I wish she'd make her move, already." I tipped a chair back on two legs. "As smart as Rose is, she doesn't pick up on nuance very well."

"Patience, grasshopper." Joseph tossed an apple back and forth. "Besides, you're one to talk."

Before I could snap back, a door cleverly concealed within a painting opened across the room. Through it walked the djinn. Given everything else I'd observed, I'd expected more fanfare, but Phenex came alone, his magical signature carefully tucked away. He'd changed from his slate suit into a black one that set off the silver jewelry shimmering in his ears and on his fingers.

"I apologize for my tardiness," he said, sounding thoroughly un-apologetic. "An unexpected matter arose that required my immediate attention." Joseph and I exchanged a look. Two guesses who was the cause of that problem.

"Is everything alright?" Joseph asked.

"Nothing too troublesome." Phenex boldly met my eyes as if daring me to unleash the creature that so intrigued him. I quirked a brow. Good luck with that. "Zara, you appear to have recovered, I'm glad to see. Shock can do strange things to people, yet again you've surprised me with your resilience."

My mouth moved before I could check myself. "Before you go thinking you're something special, you should know I've had some practice with the whole nearly dying thing. It was bound to happen again at some point or another."

He tweaked his cuff links. "Yes, I'd heard an inkling of something along those lines. I'd be delighted to hear those stories sometime. I do love stories." Phenex gestured at the table. "Please, sit. How rude of me, as my honored guests, to keep you standing like this."

Obligingly, Joseph and I took seats opposite one another. Only once we settled in did the djinn take his seat at the head of the table, his movements graceful and calculated. He reached for a plate of flat-bread and said, "We'll be serving ourselves tonight, I hope that's alright."

"Somehow we'll manage," Joseph said with a straight face as he piled food on his plate. "We appreciate you agreeing to meet with us."

"You're most welcome." Phenex frowned. "I could hardly turn down an invitation by the Gods, could I?"

I spooned small piles of everything on my plate, though I had no intention of eating any of it. When my fellow God raised his fork, I kicked him under the table and shook my head. The djinn smirked when Joseph froze.

"It would do me little good to poison you." He took a hearty bite of steamed chicken drenched in a sauce of red and yellow spices. "Though the idea is intriguing." He patted his lips with a cloth napkin. "Do you think so little of me?"

"You attacked me out front of your home with no provocation." I took a sip of water. At least my magic could tell me that was clean and clear. "I wouldn't put much past you."

"That little test?" The djinn chewed some bread dipped in herbed oils. Despite his assurances, Joseph took care to only eat what Phenex had sampled first. "Hardly any cause for true concern. I wanted to see what you were made of. Ask anyone and you'll quickly discover I've exercised similar engagements in the boardroom."

"What line of work are you in?" Joseph asked, lowering his fork.

"A little of this, a little of that," Phenex said. "Like your friend Ryder, I prefer to dabble." His eyes glittered. "Have either of you heard of Senet?"

It took true effort to keep my shock from my face. In terms of name recognition, it was one of the largest, most diversified companies in the world.

"That's yours?" Joseph asked, nodding to himself. "I suppose, given time, I would have put those pieces together. If I recall correctly, you've never been seen in public?"

"Not if I can help it." Phenex popped a last bite of chicken between his lips. "I prefer to maintain my privacy. Speaking of privacy." He glanced my way. "Were you not instructed on where to find the bandages?"

I was enjoying this, I realized, the sharp give and take reminding me of the banter among my teammates before swim meets.

"I wear my badges with honor." I lifted the short, lacy sleeve of my shirt. I'd refused to wear the silky dress the nero had brought to my room, insisting that dressing up would give Phenex too much power. But I had changed into my one nice shirt and opted to leave my jacket behind. "I'm not one to back away from a challenge—no matter who issues it."

The djinn eyed my matching fire and water brands with slow deliberation. A coldness settled over his features and he drank deeply from a crystal goblet containing a thick, red liquid.

"It's interesting that you should bring up challenges," he said as the silence between us stretched a hair too far. "Because a very interesting one was issued yesterday."

Joseph set his fork beside his empty plate and folded his fingers together. "Well, don't leave us in suspense here."

Phenex traced his lower lip. The room trembled as he deliberately peeled away a corner of the restraints binding his magic. "Unlimited wealth and unparalleled status to whoever turns you over to the Order... alive or dead."

My head roared as Joseph roped his magic tightly around him. I recognized the buzz of it as he raised a barrier of hardened air between us and the immediate threat in the room. However, I hovered, suspended in a strange state, staring at my glass with lethal calm. Despite hearing it from Geoffrey himself, despite having warned my friends, part of me still hadn't come to grips with it actually being real. My Hand was back and he wanted me dead.

I also had a funny feeling Phenex missed very little as he watched us with relish, his chin propped on the backs of his bridged fingers. I steeled myself against that expression, the one where the cat ate both the cream and the canary, and motioned at Joseph using the pixie sign to stand down. He glared at me as if I'd lost my damn mind, but retracted his shield.

"Not worried about me, Water God?" Phenex asked. "Despite what you witnessed earlier, you think you can take me?"

"I don't think you've faced a real challenge in a very long time." I leaned forward, seeing my glowing aquamarine eyes reflected in his. "And I think you underestimate how powerful we are. Even djinn are secondary to the Gods, no matter how much power and authority you've stolen."

If Phenex were a snake, his tail would be rattling.

"Besides, you told us yourself that not only do you manage one of the largest and most entrepreneurial powerful organizations in the world, but you've also maintained absolute privacy." I dragged my fingers across the table, scorch marks trailing across the wood. "At the end of the day, an offer of wealth and power wouldn't mean much to you, so I have to imagine that you would have only been willing to kill us or turn us over for your own reasons. Since, to my understanding, you've attempted neither with any true intent, there must be something else you want from us. So tell me, Phenex, what exactly is going on here?"

I curled my fist in my lap, waiting.

"You're correct," Phenex said, leaning back in his chair. "I am disinclined to kill you at the moment." His words hung there, their implication unspoken.

The buzzing in my head returned and with it, the slow uncurling of another presence. About time. I wondered what specifically about this conversation appealed to Kaleal. Phenex frowned, I'd taken too long to respond, but Joseph jumped in.

"If you're not willing to help the Order, are you saying you're willing to help us?"

"And by help 'us' you mean…"

"Find the God of Earth. You and the nero are the only creatures left who know where the Lost Temple is," Joseph said.

Phenex waved him off. "There are others who know where the Earth Temple lies, though it would take you considerable time and resources to uncover them." He ran his thumb over his well-manicured nails. "Regardless, no. I haven't reached a conclusion about assisting you on your quest yet."

I took a sip of water. "Is there anything you'd like to know that may help?"

"Not in particular," Phenex drawled. "There's an edge of danger to this all that the world has been lacking for the past several centuries that I find appealing, but this is a decision I must make of my own accord." He started to rise. "I'll need some time to think it over. Now if you'd please—"

Joseph's eyes widened, his spine straightening. It was an expression I'd seen before, one that signaled some stroke of random brilliance that had crossed his mind. "Before you dismiss us, I have one more point I'd like to make."

Phenex lowered himself back down. I got the impression he hadn't wanted to leave in the first place. For all his bluster, he, too, seemed to enjoy our banter.

"Go ahead."

"You said you like stories, right?"

The djinn's eyes narrowed. "A great deal."

"Then allow me this liberty." Joseph pushed his plate back and rolled his shoulders. I spun a funnel in my glass, trying not to smile.

Joseph was one of the most well-read people I'd ever met. He was also an incredible story-teller, and I'd told him as much after a week of listening to him relay stories to his younger cousins before bed.

I wondered where he was going with this one.

He began:

"In this tale, we focus on one of the ancient Gods, the Originals, the first to feel the clutch of Earth within his fingers. You see, this God was a clever sort. Davarius was curious about the world and how it worked. He loved experimenting.

"But after many decades of this, he grew bored. He'd toyed with all the metals and minerals the world had to offer, he embraced the aid of water and fire. He had used all manner of material to assemble and destroy. But he'd never used his own blood."

Phenex's coy smile slipped.

"Davarius wondered about life, he wondered how it came to be, and he wondered if it could be created beyond the Earth's natural means. As a God, surely he could have a say. It only made sense."

Joseph drained his glass. "He tried infusing his blood into metal and leaves and wood. He drew blood from his arms and legs and feet. Yet nothing happened, until one day, out of sheer frustration, he drove a needle directly into his heart. The act weakened him, and he dropped it. The vial shattered, his blood spattering everywhere. It quickly soaked into the sand.

"As he bent to clean up the mess, dozens of shadows flew from his fingers and shaped themselves into creatures not quite man and not quite shadow. Through his own clumsiness, Davarius had finally succeeded in his attempts at creating life."

Phenex was so riveted on Joseph's tale that his grip on his magic loosened. It flooded the room in waves of golden power.

"Davarius was thrilled with his creations and set about teaching them all he knew. He'd always wanted sons and now he had them.

Forty of them. They soaked up his teachings and learned his values. They gained independence and, as the decades passed, they demanded freedom, because, you see, Davarius wouldn't let them past the temple walls. When he didn't grant their requests, his sons rebelled and some tried to escape. Humans and fey caught in the middle died in the fight for dominance, and the Earth Temple began to splinter."

I eyed the crystal glass clutched in Phenex's white-knuckled hand. I could barely see the rise and fall of his chest.

"Realizing what he had done, what was going to happen, Davarius agreed to a truce. He requested a meeting with his sons, saying he wished to speak with them about how to release them into the world. Elated, his forty sons agreed.

"Davarius said he would allow them out, but he worried for their safety. He told them humans and fey would fear them for they possessed great magic. They had inherited their father's immense control of the desert, for they were made of sand. He told them they needed to be hidden in order to leave. He said they would need a safe place to shelter should anyone learn of their true existence.

"Davarius was clever and had brought forty containers with him: a mixture of pendants and vases and metal boxes. Some were beautiful, others plain, some tall and others fat. He implored his sons to embrace their inner shadows, the life spirit that animated them and gave them free will and thought, and instructed them to use them to hide within the vessels."

Joseph shifted in his chair, leaning forward eagerly. Phenex reciprocated.

"His sons agreed and tucked themselves inside those containers. Once they had disappeared, Davarius, for he was as cunning as he was creative, recited a spell of binding that he'd learned from a witch, a blood oath that could not be broken. The spell sealed his sons inside.

"When they tried to come out, they realized their father's treachery, for they couldn't extend themselves farther than the opening in each container. Davarius said he would stick to their agreement and allow them to leave, but they would need to earn their true freedom. They could only find freedom by granting wishes to those who possessed their vessels. Three wishes to each master. Only their master could set them free by their own free will.

"Enraged, his sons had no choice but to agree. They believed they could find ways to trick their masters into freeing them. But they soon discovered another twist to their captivity: For each master who failed to free them, they were permitted to kill them and absorb their life force.

"And so the djinn was born. And the legends around them grew wild. For the sons knew freedom was elusive, but power was forever. And it was power they sought, biding their time and gaining strength, until, at last, they started to find freedom."

Phenex's glass shattered in his grasp and Joseph smiled. "Phenex, that's all I know of the djinn, but I have a feeling you know how the story ends."

If he hadn't wanted to kill us before, it was clear the djinn wanted to now.

"You've given me much to think about," he spat. "Leave before I make a decision I'll regret."

Chapter 14

Time to think it over by Phenex's definition did not, unfortunately, mean *I'll have a decision by morning*.

Joseph and I discovered that small fact by simultaneous knocks on our doors at 5 a.m. The nero messengers informed us that while we had free reign of the palace, we were not to seek out the djinn directly. I'd only managed to get about an hour of restless sleep before that, so I gave up on the concept entirely and set out to find out more about my not-quite-so-enemy.

"Figures I'd find you here," Ryder said. I lifted a hand in greeting when he dropped beside me. "Though why you aren't spending your time soaking in the Nile is beyond me."

I squeezed my stress ball of water. During my prowls in one of the towers, I'd discovered this eight-feet wide window complete with a wide ledge that begged to be sat upon. After some fiddling, I'd figured out how to slide the glass aside and settled in. I'd spent the past hour watching the activity around the palace.

I pinched the skin between my eyes where my headache pounded.

"I don't understand them," I said, nodding at the nero guards sparring inside the fenced-off courtyard. Phenex's palace was set up similarly to medieval castles. It had a main building that seemed to be his domain, with a smattering of smaller, yet equally gorgeous, buildings that housed the nero. I'd counted a half-dozen courtyards and mini markets from up here but imagined there were likely more tucked away between the houses. "It bothers me."

Ryder propped his shoulder on the frame, his golden eyes fixed on the clashing partners. Some thrust and blocked staffs, while others ran laps. A range not far from away provided plenty of target practice for those with guns.

My team was down there with them, too. Earlier, I'd watched as the pixies had approached, and after a conversation that involved a lot of hand waving the wing flapping, they'd finagled their way into the training grounds. Joseph had joined not long after that.

"Your mind is a fascination of mine," the incubus said. "Please elaborate."

"Why are they here? Why are they tucked away in this little community?" I ran a hand through my hair and teased apart the knots created by the wind. "They're people of the sand, right? Why are they beside the Nile then? And why do they serve Phenex? It's like something I've only ever watched in movies and on television, similar to peasants and serfs serving a king."

"Maybe it's their way of life," Ryder said. "It could also be a security thing. Supposedly this is the last group of them left. They could be like pixies who cluster in small communes. Their philosophies are similar."

"I can understand that," I acquiesced. "Though I can't see fey as strong as they're believed to be willingly subjecting themselves to the whims of someone else, no matter how powerful."

"You've seen Phenex." Ryder leaned back on his palms, his back arching in a supine stretch. "He's not exactly a pushover."

"No, but the Gods were gone for two-thousand years," I reminded him and winced when Rose failed to block a thrust of one of the sand-fey's staffs. "And, as you well know, that means the fey couldn't access their magic during that time. So while he has power, it's human power.

I'm not sure if that would be much of a threat."

"I think you assume a lot," Ryder said. "People have an uncanny ability to adapt to a certain way of living. He also doesn't necessarily need magic to appeal to them. Money and security speak strongly to more than just humans."

I glanced at the incubus and realized he'd taken my hand and rested it on his thigh. The back of it tingled pleasantly where he rubbed a slow circle with his thumb. I decided to let him keep it for now.

"It's more than the logic of their circumstances, though," I said, enjoying our debate. Ryder might be more devilishly handsome than anyone in their right mind should be, but he was also intelligent. I liked that. "Their magic feels... off. It's wrong. They're clearly powerful. I can sense it. But none of them seems to be in possession of it.

"Sure, they use their magic to walk through stone walls and throw sand." One of the smaller nero hurled sandy projectiles at Joseph, who swatted them away with a gust of wind. "But I'm expecting more. They're capable of more, but it's like none of them can *do* it. I don't—" I stopped and pursed my lips, my frustration mounting and my magic heating. "I've sat here for an hour trying to figure out what I'm trying to say, and I still don't know how to say it. But it's wrong. There's something wrong."

Rather than release my hand when the blood reached a boiling point, Ryder tightened his grip and flipped it over so he could massage my palm.

I shuddered and my magic retreated. "What do you think? Am I being crazy?"

"While you may occasionally do crazy things, I'd never actually attribute that adjective to your character." His cheeks tightened as Joseph launched himself up a series of invisible steps crafted of air. He flipped off the end, spinning with a wooden practice sword as he landed in a cluster of nero who immediately launched into attacks.

It was incredible what he was able to do. As much as my thoughts irritated me, I'd enjoyed watching my fellow God test his abilities like this. I'd never had a chance to watch him train back in the States since I had always been wrapped up in my own training.

"If you think or feel that something is wrong, I'm willing to bet it is," Ryder said. "Your magic is tied to all magic, it's the root of it after all. The nero's abilities are some of the closest to yours I've ever seen." I almost groaned in protest when he stopped rubbing my hand, though he still clasped it loosely. "You're smart, you'll figure it out. But please, for my sake and the sake of everyone here, be careful. Phenex may have been toying with you yesterday, but if he's anything like…" He paused, pondering his words, "…other powerful creatures who are used to one way of life, it doesn't take much for him to snap."

"Who are you talking about?" I asked and immediately regretted it when his face tightened with pure, ugly hatred. He caught himself and the expression smoothed into his normal lightheartedness. He dropped my hand and leaned in until our faces were a few inches apart.

"That would be a truth, wouldn't it?" A dimple popped as his grin spread. "And I think you're the one who's overdue spilling some of yours."

His scent wrapped around me, more cinnamon than smoke today, and I inhaled deeply, loving the molten quality of his eyes. I couldn't deny how he affected me, how I couldn't stay away from him no matter how much I wanted to.

"Come on, glowstick," he whispered, moving closer. He traced the healing cut at the base of my throat. "Your eyes are telling me so much, but I need to hear it from your lips." His finger moved drifted upward, caressing my neck.

"I don't know if winning more gold medals at the next Olympics would have been enough for me," I admitted, stunned at voicing the small suspicions that had rattled around in my head for weeks during our team summer trip. Ryder's thumb brushed the underside of my jaw. Our faces drifted closer. "It's what I wanted, and I knew I could do it. It was always the goal, one I'd pushed for my entire life. But I think I knew deep down I was meant for more."

He didn't respond for so long, simply caressing the silky skin beneath my ear, I wondered if he'd even heard me. But when I opened my mouth to repeat it, he said, "That's why you'll figure this out. The nero. Phenex. The end of the world, all of it. Because you know you can."

I closed my eyes when he leaned in, his breath tingly on my lips, but at the last moment, he pulled up and pecked the tip of my nose. My insides turned gooey, and I ducked my head when heat filled my cheeks. This man… he was something else.

Chapter 15

When Ryder warned me to be careful, this was probably the very behavior he meant for me to avoid.

I glanced down the darkened hallway. When I didn't see anyone following me, I rounded another corner and twisted the handle of a doorknob. Ryder had left with a bite of laughter and a bounce in his step after my confession, and I'd resumed slinking around the castle like a cat in need of a new hiding place. After pausing for dinner, which I'd actually sampled today, I was back at it.

My sleuthing paid off when I discovered a secret passageway that led me to these darkened tunnels. It smelled like mold and stale water, and I was only able to see by the flame I sent bouncing ahead.

The door opened, revealing yet another nearly empty room badly in need of bleach and a good scrubbing. The rusted frame for a bed leaned against a wall in one corner, exactly the same as the last four rooms I'd tried. Was this a prison of some sort? Holding cells? I felt Kaleal stir behind my eyes, and while she still wasn't talking to me, the relief I felt knowing she was back surprised me.

I pulled the door closed, noting its silent hinges despite the disrepair of everything else down here, and continued onward, my dejection growing as I uncovered more of the same. When I was ready to turn back and give up entirely, the ground rose sharply and a new door emerged at my left. Unlike the others made of metal, this was wooden.

Across from it was a peg for a torch. The stone above was blackened.

I flattened my hand against the board and tingles raced across my skin.

Something was in there.

I tested the knob, not surprised when it didn't give. "Phenex, what are you keeping in here," I mused to myself as I knelt. The keyhole was large, the decoration ornate. No, this door definitely wasn't like the others. The mystery enticed Kaleal enough to speak.

Push water into the keyhole and freeze it in the shape of the key, she suggested.

Genius, I replied. On my first attempt, I froze the whole lock, but after two more tries, I finally formed the right shape. However, it didn't work, no matter how hard I pulled, tugged, and kicked at the knob.

Kaleal leaned in, crowding the space behind my eyes. *Fire?*

Why not, I said, balling some flames in my hand. This time, when I attempted to move in, the flames went out. I couldn't so much as singe the wood.

It's blocking the magic, Kaleal mused. *But feel that, that sensation of ants crawling under your skin and spiders nibbling at your eyes? That's magic, very powerful magic. We definitely need to get in there.*

What do you think I'm trying to do? I snarled. In frustration, I froze the handle solid, then blasted it with a burst of fire so hot it turned blue. The knob cracked, then shattered. The door swung wide.

Clearly, you weren't trying hard enough, Kaleal chided, her presence lingering as I marched in. What I found made my breath catch.

Gold stretched for what felt like a mile, the treasure illuminated by trenches of orange flames running the lengths of the walls. Coins were stacked taller than me, jewels in glass containers glittered an array of colors more brilliant than any rainbow, and statues of marble and quartz guarded the troves jealously. I paused beside one barrel high as my waist filled with rings and bracelets and necklaces adorned with gems bigger than my thumb. A barrel beside it of equal height was flooded with diamonds big and small. On shelves pounded into the jade walls rested an array of portraits and paintings by artists so famous even I recognized their work.

My magic hummed as I moved down an aisle carved in the middle of the riches. I wanted to touch everything all at once, but couldn't figure out which to settle on first, so I kept walking, each new discovery more glorious than the rest.

Then I stumbled upon a single emerald trapped beneath a bubble of glass.

It wasn't particularly large or rich in color. It lacked any sort of adornment, yet the longer I hovered there, the more its power reverberated through me. I tilted my head, moving so I was nearly on top of it. It reminded me of something. The cut, the color…

"How did you get in here?"

Phenex's silvery voice ripped me from my thoughts. I was in the middle of reaching for the globe, probably to push it aside and hold the gem myself, and I stopped short. I couldn't move, my mind racing…

The sickening sensation of falling backward hit me.

Kaleal smoothly slipped into place.

"Your wards aren't as powerful as you think they are," she chastised, drawing back her—*my*—hand, in no hurry to face the djinn. "It was remarkably easy to get in here. I'd suggest finding a more effective means of protecting your precious collection in the future."

His face was smooth, his eyes bland, but my magic brushed his and I knew he was barely holding himself back from strangling me. The djinn's eyes flicked over her before stopping on her eyes.

"You're back," Phenex said bluntly. "Right when I'd thought I'd imagined it, too."

"The eyes are a bit of a giveaway, aren't they." Kaleal fingered a cloudy, white rock the size of a quarter. "It would be so much easier if that weren't the case."

"Who are you?" His anger tempered as his curiosity grew. This was why he'd allowed me past his barriers and into his home. He'd seen Kaleal and wanted to know what she was.

"Does it matter who I am?"

"It does to me." He plucked a coin from a nearby pedestal and balanced it on the back of his knuckles, sending it dancing across them. "I'm not in the habit of allowing just anyone on my premises."

"How about this," Kaleal said. "You hear me out about why you should help us, and I'll consider revealing my identity."

Dread filled me and I launched myself forward, only to have her throw me back and pin me in place. I had no idea what she was about to say, what she was even thinking, but I had a miserable feeling this wasn't going to end well.

"That seems hardly fair since you already said you know who I am," he drawled. I knew it. He had heard her in my head back at the airport. "But I'm willing to play your game."

"Odds are you're seriously considering trying to take me out and wiping your hands of this whole mess." Kaleal moved to examine a gilded statue of a stallion. "I imagine that's the direction you're leaning because it's by far the easier option. However, doing so will cause problems for you."

"Oh?" He sounded bored.

"For starters, the Order will want to know why you took so long taking action. They likely already know we're here. Maybe not *here* in your delightful home, but they know where we're headed next." She touched a banner of green silk draped across the back of a copper chair. "You claim to be rogue, but only because the Order hasn't minded you much over the past several centuries. They knew you were here, and that was good enough for them. However, there's the simple matter that magic has returned to the world."

"Your point?"

"You now pose a threat, especially since you haven't kissed the hand that feeds you in some time." Kaleal spun to face him, his hand white-knuckled around the coin. No, he definitely wasn't as smooth as he thought was. "They will want to know what you've been up to, and I bet they will probably not like what they find. Not to mention they'll disturb all you have amassed." She motioned at the riches, arms stretched wide. "Least of all what's in this room."

"The Order promised to leave me alone after I last helped them out." His eyes were plates of bronze. "We agreed that I would keep to my part of the world and they would keep to theirs."

"The *Order* promised," she emphasized the noun with sultry sophistication. "But what about Geoffrey? What did he promise? Did he swear to honor that vow?"

"He promised autonomy to anyone who took you out."

"We are talking about the man who first claimed he wiped out the Gods, then tried to take them in peacefully when he realized they were, in fact, still alive, and is now, suddenly, demanding their blood again, right?" Kaleal mused, tapping her jaw.

The first crack in Phenex's carefully guarded exterior appeared. "He has his reasons."

"You're smarter than this." She tsked. "Geoffrey is as unstable as any overly powerful world leader you've ever encountered."

"And you can do better?" The coin was back on his knuckles, but he had yet to continue the fish-like motion.

"If you help us find the Temple, we'll leave you alone." She glanced at the emerald, and I realized we probably wouldn't be figuring out what it meant or what powers it possessed. Not yet anyway. "And we'll remove Geoffrey from his position of influence."

Phenex strode three steps forward, his chest brushing hers as he peered down at her. "And what assurances do I have that you'll follow through," he snarled, his careful veneer thoroughly shattered. "As you've pointed out the failures of others to do so."

"Because you know me, too, Xenith."

The color drained from his face when her tongue twisted around the name, her tone sticky-sweet. His eyes darted back and forth between hers, his magic threatening mine with barbed hostility. But finally, finally, he pulled back.

"We leave in the morning," he said.

Chapter 16

One huge, brown eye framed by long, sandy-colored lashes blinked as I leaned in close. The camel regarded me warily before drawing back its black lips to expose thick, yellowed teeth. A low groan rumbled from its barrel of a chest and I danced back.

"Yeah...I don't think so," I murmured, slashing an x across my chest to ward off evil. Or whatever weird vibes I was picking up here.

Joseph, possessing a far braver soul than my own, actually *stroked* the beast's wiry hair as its belly lunched in something I could only call a belch. My friend threw his head back, sending the hood he'd carefully affixed over his hair flying, baying from the bottom of his lungs. The camel and I exchanged a look.

"Something funny?" I asked.

"I'm imagining you being stuck with this lovely creature for the next two weeks."

"Did I miss a text message?" I shoved my hands in my pockets before remembering I hadn't so much as held a phone since Kansas City. "Are you not coming with us? Because I definitely don't remember agreeing to that."

"Oh, I'm coming." He tossed his bag on the back of the camel Finn had claimed. Now that I thought about it, the two of them seemed to be spending a lot of time together. My eyes narrowed as I glanced from the bags to Joseph to the doors where the kelpie had vanished through. "But I'm not going in this form."

"Can red-tailed hawks survive in the desert?" I asked, tugging at the brown scarf looped around my neck. It itched fiercely and I'd already scratched my skin raw. The rest of my beige clothing was fine, minus the constant sensation of boiling in my skin, but Bast assured me I would be thankful for the layers of shirts and pants and wraps when we got caught in our first sandstorm.

I hadn't bothered to remind her that the person who could stifle such a phenomenon would be riding next to me. Or flying rather.

"I can take more than one form," Joseph said dryly. Across the courtyard, the pixies squabbled over a half dozen other camels. The animal's hair was scratchy, they smelled like dung left in the sun, and they looked awkward. What could there possibly be to argue over? "One of the nero worked with me yesterday until I figured out the roadrunner. It only took about an hour."

Yesterday. When I'd been skulking around Phenex's castle like a rodent—which I still had yet to tell anyone aside from Ryder about. My shoulders hunched and I couldn't meet his eyes. "Listen, about yesterday—"

"It was fun, getting to know them," he continued, either ignoring or not hearing me. "They're fascinating: insanely intelligent, quick on their feet, willing to both educate and be educated." He pushed some of his long hair back behind his ear. "I wish you'd come down. While they didn't ask about you *per se*, they definitely wanted to. I could tell."

"About that—"

"Nope, none of that." He shoulder-bumped me and the hole in my chest filled. "Your guilt is scribbled all across your face. I don't need it nor want it. You have nothing to feel bad about. Because of you, whatever it is you did, we're leaving this morning. The whole point of this deal is to find the God of Earth, after all, even if it means dealing

103

with the djinn himself."

The hair on my neck prickled as hooves clattered on the cobble-stones. I turned as Phenex tugged the reigns of his white horse.

"Are you prepared? We won't wait once dusk falls, even for the Gods," he said, peering down at us. The djinn wore similar attire to the rest of us, only unlike our strict browns and reds, his cloak was a rich shade of lapis lazuli. Behind him, a dozen nero carefully formed two lines on camel-back.

"Did I say 'djinn?'" Joseph mused, rubbing his scruffy chin. "I definitely meant devil."

A chuckle rose in my chest, but I tamped it down and cast a wan smile up at our host. "Do you know the way to the Lost City?"

"Obviously." His tone dripped with derision.

"If you don't like answering stupid questions, you shouldn't ask them." I removed the canteen at my hip and unscrewed the top, taking a sip I didn't need. I was careful to keep my face blank as we scrutinized one another. The djinn's nostrils flared when Kaleal slipped in, momentarily flashing her amethyst glare. Apparently, she also couldn't resist poking the bear.

It was the nero at the front of the line who broke our stand-off. "Sir, Akil needs you to sign off on the supplies. I believe you wanted to check the list personally?"

Phenex's lips curled, though there was no warmth in his smile.

"No offense meant," he said stiffly, his horse shifting restlessly. "I was only under the impression that you and your *fellow God* considered speed of utmost importance."

He wasn't referring to Joseph.

I inclined my head, wondering if he knew that the others still didn't know about my secret.

The head of another camel rose on my left and perched behind its hump was Ryder, lean and lethal as always in his black attire. He'd also escaped the drab browns, it seemed. The whisper of darkness in my chest that was Kaleal clutched tight, warning me to take care with my answer here. She couldn't risk rising to the top.

"I appreciate your attentiveness," I replied as Joseph frowned, his arms coming up around his chest. "Please consider us always prepared moving forward."

"Anything for the Gods," Phenex growled, and the surge of power building between us settled. Kaleal relaxed her grip. With another hard look of warning, he kicked the sides of his horse and galloped to the entrance of his palace. The nero hesitated a moment too long, the one at the head of the line with the face wrapped completely in fabric stared straight at me, before they, too, followed.

"What was that about?" Ryder asked, sliding off his camel. He reached for the rope hanging from the reins of my beast.

"Oh, nothing," I said. Joseph still had yet to turn away, something about his stare seemed familiar—like how he got pouring over his new copy of *The Word*, or when we stuck our heads together back at the cabin, discussing ways that the Gods could help solve the nuclear crisis.

"What?" I asked, my shoulders hunching. "Why are you looking at me like that?"

The breeze tousled his hair and his eyes tightened. "No reason."

"It's like I've walked into the middle of three different conversations happening at once," Ryder grumbled, finishing the complicated knot he'd formed, effectively tying my camel to the caravan. Joseph whistled tunelessly as he snatched his hood off the ground and walked away. "But since apparently none of you want to talk about the nothingness that is definitely not nothing… how about you tell me what you got up to yesterday? I have a funny feeling you ignored my dire warnings."

His arms looped my shoulders in a brief hug, then he helped me find the long loop of leather that was supposed to be a stirrup.

"What makes you feel that?" I huffed, pulling myself on top of the creature. I sensed its too-large eyes rolling back at me as it chewed slowly on something. What could it be eating? Rocks? Sand? There wasn't anything out here. I narrowed my eyes, my legs feeling too tight around its massive middle. Ryder's rumbling laugh made me jump.

"You should make nice with your transportation, glowstick," he said, squeezing my calf. "You can trust it, unlike a certain djinn we both know."

"Are you comparing Phenex to a camel?" I pondered that mental image, then shook the thought away. "I don't trust him either. But we don't have a choice in the matter, do we?"

I was getting good at spitting.

No matter how much I kept my mouth sealed and my scarves pulled high, sand somehow found its way into my mouth. Then again, fine grains of the stuff had worked into every wrinkle and enlarged pore of my body.

Surprise, surprise, the desert was filled with the stuff, and it was about as irritating as the scenery was boring. My body clock was also completely messed up from the reversed sleeping schedule. At Phenex's demand, we rode at night and slept during the day. Both were uncomfortable, but at least the heat of the sun while traveling wasn't compounded on top of all my other complaints.

I squeezed the reins, wishing I had something to do besides think about how much my muscles ached. I'd never ridden so much as a horse before, and I never would have guessed how stiff I'd get in the saddle. I swore the tension knotting the backs of my thighs drove right to the bone, jarring me with each step the stupid camel took.

And no, we still hadn't *made nice*.

"You know, when I imagined leaving home for some grand adventure, I never thought I'd end up somewhere so... lackluster," Joseph said beside me. He'd gotten tired of running after the first day and snatched up one of the spare camels the nero had brought along as if anticipating his change of mind.

"Can we not talk about the landscape?" I asked, scratching behind my ear. Sand gritted under my nail. "I'll go crazy if I think about it anymore."

"What do you suggest, then? The weather?" He motioned at the sea of shimmering lights spilling across the black lagoon that was the evening sky. The desert did have one thing going for it, I supposed. His glib question got me thinking, though.

"I wouldn't mind talking about magic," I said, twisting in my saddle.

His eyebrows winged up over his yellow bandanna. "What about magic?"

"Your magic. I understand fire and water and the restrictions associated with both." I could only work with what was within the reach of my powers. The exact distance wasn't entirely clear to me, but it seemed that the stronger I got, the wider that boundary got. "But what about air?"

"What exactly about air?"

"How do you do that—" I slapped my palms together and twisted them "—you know, make those pane things? The flat panels that you stand on? I don't understand it."

His eyes danced as he nudged his camel closer. "Good question. It took a bit to figure out. The Thunderbird gave me the idea and made it sound easy, but it's not." He dropped his reins, motioning with his hands. "See, I had to figure out how to draw the molecules of the air together. Oxygen works best for whatever reason, I'm still figuring that one out." He twisted what I assumed was air in his grip in an excited demonstration. "Anyway, by condensing the oxygen into a super-tight layer, I was able to make a surface strong enough to bear my weight. See?"

I nodded, tapping the pane he held up with my nail. It was fascinating, seeing how his mind interpreted the world, figuring out how his magic fit within it. Using science to determine how things worked seemed incredible, especially to someone like me who simply fumbled around with my abilities until I got it to do what I needed it to do.

"What's interesting, though, is if you think about the availability of oxygen," Joseph continued, his tempo increasing. "Because we could get into a sticky spot if I tried to make a panel like that in a small room. Obviously, I'm not creating oxygen so much as I am stealing it from around me..."

As he chattered, reaching for more magic to show me more technical aspects of his abilities, I realized the cobwebs littering my mind had cleared and the ache in my legs didn't feel so bad.

Chapter 17

I t took three days for dehydration to set in.

I tried to summon moisture to my mouth but couldn't. Thirst was too tame a word for the driving desire to *drink,* the feeling that coated my mouth and esophagus, making it difficult to swallow and sometimes breathe. It was a sensation that spread like dandelion roots until it was all I thought about.

At least I'd positioned my camel in front of the pack animals hefting our supplies of food and water today. After spending most of the day yesterday positioned right behind the bloated sacks of water, I'd about died from want. Our group was comprised of several dozen individuals, and rationing was essential.

I'd never realized until now how much water I consumed in a given day, how much water I took in through sheer osmosis. Turns out, there was a reason I wanted to swim for a living, a reason my temple was beneath the waves of the North Sea.

I tugged my bandanna higher on my nose so only my eyes peered out over the sweat-stained material. It wasn't so much to keep the sand out. No, I'd given up that fight the second night. But the scarves and bandannas *did* allow me to hide.

At dusk, I'd woken with the rest of the camp and discovered my inner wells of water magic dry. I'd panicked, casting my senses far and wide, searching for any sign of life, but aside from a few cacti and some scattered desert animals, there was nothing. I'd never considered what it would be like, not being around water, and the lack of connection left me thoroughly shaken.

Fire magic had filled the void, but without the water to counter the searing heat, I was burning up from the inside out. I'd made the mistake of removing my leather gloves a few hours ago, and found the skin on the backs of my hands cracked, my fingers thinner than usual. It didn't hurt exactly, and I was beginning to find a balance within myself. But between tasting ash whenever I inhaled and the constant tug of thirst, it took all I had to not turn back.

Don't let him find out, Kaleal warned. Even her presence was softer, lighter, as if she were struggling to hold her form. *He can't find out you're weakened.*

How stupid do you think I am? I whined tiredly. *Besides, in all your eons of lurking, waiting for your next prey, surely you know how to fix this problem.*

The Water God has never come first, she reminded me drolly. I didn't like how quiet she was, her voice textured with static. *And none of them were foolish enough to head into a desert.*

I am here because you pushed me. I stalked into the recesses of my mind, into the shadows where she lurked, my stomach swooping when I found only wisps of her fiery power. I crouched down, pleading. *Tell me what to do. Please.*

Survive, she whispered. *And keep pushing your boundaries. You'll find water sometime. Until then, I'm going to hunker down for a bit. The lack of magic is... taxing.*

And she vanished, flicking me outside my mind once again—where Joseph's keen gaze was fixed upon me, his brows drawn tight with questions. Unnerved, and wondering if he was somehow starting to figure out my unwanted secrets, I looked toward the front of the line where Phenex rode. My jaw tightened.

Out here, in the heart of the desert and heat of the sand, the djinn was more at ease than he'd ever seemed back at his palace. How I'd ever thought him bland and boring was beyond me, because now he practically glowed with energy and enthusiasm. His braided, black hair was sleeker, his skin dark and lush, his seat on his horse prouder.

He fit in this territory.

And I did not.

My head was spinning when he spun his horse around, knowing he was searching for me. He'd stopped his annoying banter and had taken to staring like the rest of them. As a group we were quieter and calmer, having little to discuss in general, but I'd carefully extricated myself from any and all conversation, not wanting anyone to guess what was wrong with me.

He held up his gloved hand. In one practiced motion, the nero halted the camels.

"We'll set up camp here." The djinn pointed at an outcropping of rocks that looked like a hand reaching high into the sky. Beyond it, a thin ribbon of red cut the horizon.

Finn swung down beside me when we finally reached the rocks. Like the days prior, the nero immediately went to work setting up tents and laying out cooking supplies. Not wanting to be a burden on anyone, I'd learned how to prepare my own tent on the first night, and accepted the equipment with a murmur of thanks.

"How are you holding up?" the kelpie asked, accepting his own bundle. He'd removed his hat and pulled his thick facial covering down. Fine wrinkles branched crookedly from the corners of his eyes and fine, dark hairs scattered across his cheeks and jaw. In all my weeks of knowing him, I'd seen him frantic and stressed, jovial and joking. But I'd never seen him *exhausted*.

"I'm fine," I answered shortly, dropping to my knees and fumbling with the materials. I removed the longest of the tent poles and soon found my rhythm. The scent of roasting meat teased my nose and my stomach growled.

"You're lying."

I looked up sharply. "What makes you say that?"

"Because I'm not fine." He licked his chapped lips to emphasize that fact. "And I'm the only other water elemental of our lovely little party here."

I didn't argue.

The kelpie sighed, holding our stare for another solid ten seconds. "Why do you think I didn't travel in my second form? It's too draining." Come to think of it, I had wondered that. I felt foolish for not having thought of him suffering similarly earlier.

I opened my mouth to respond, but he couldn't see it behind my bandanna.

"I know you're miserable. If I feel this awful…" He swallowed heavily, glancing over my shoulder where the pack camels were staked. I recognized the longing, one thick with a need that couldn't be fulfilled. "I can only imagine how you, the person who commands it all, must feel."

I'd given up on my tent. While the poles were still in my hands, they were little more than weights holding my arms down. My mind was racing.

"Zara, you don't need to be so proud. You aren't alone in this; you don't need to isolate yourself." His green eyes glimmered. "We won't think you're weak because you're human.

"I know that you need time to figure things out between us, but I need to be honest with you, too. And it hurts me, Zara." He splayed his hands wide across his chest. "It hurts me that you won't trust me… or anyone for that matter. Someday I hope you realize that you don't need to bear all that weight by yourself."

I'd barely processed his words and had reached up to pull down the bandanna, stupefied by his confession, when he turned and walked toward the fire around which the pixies and nero gathered.

He didn't look back.

Chapter 18

"So this is where you've been hiding," I said, sizing up Kaleal's shadowy figure with her back resting against the iron door. Flames that gave no heat bracketed one side and a dry, cracked lakebed framed the other. The ancient God didn't so much as glance my way as she stared out over the barren wasteland.

"I'd think you'd be more grateful," she responded. "I'm here for your sake, anyway."

My gown of ash brushed against my ankles. Today there was no fire licking my heels, no dresses of lit gasoline. Part of me missed the riot of color and feeling. I hesitated, then slid down beside her, our legs extended and splayed like forgotten dolls in a child's room.

"I'll bite. Why are you hanging out here?" I folded my hands in my lap.

The shadowy features of her face didn't so much as twitch. "Close your eyes."

I obliged, not sensing any hostility or manipulation coming from her. For a minute there was nothing aside from the beating of my heart, the steady rise and fall of my chest, the blissful silence I couldn't find in my everyday life. Then I twitched, goosebumps skirting my arms, what I'd heard too quick to interpret.

It came again.

Three sharp raps vibrating the door against my back. I stiffened as it seemed to morph in my mind's eye, pulsing and heating and moving like a living, breathing thing. The raps came again, someone on the other side asking for entrance into my mind. The obsidian knob jiggled.

I scrambled to my feet, arms raised, fists clenched, waiting for the door to swing wide. Kaleal didn't so much as cross an ankle.

"He's not the pushiest Hand I've ever encountered," she said, eyeing her shadowy curls of fingers as if checking for chipped polish, "but he's still fairly effective at pressing each and every button marking my frustration."

I wished I could see her face to get a gauge on what she was, what she thought, what she felt. I wondered at her state of being, half-human and half... poltergeist? How lonely she must be, trapped in there all the time. I almost couldn't blame her for taking control of my body occasionally, even to break some of the monotony of her existence.

Three more raps against the iron door, but this time I didn't start. I toyed with the slender bracelet of water around my wrist. I wondered why Kaleal returned here, tucked in the back of my mind. Why wouldn't she stay out there? In the real world? It was clear that she was capable, but I didn't know her true strength. Maybe... maybe she couldn't.

Not yet, anyway.

I shivered at the thought.

"He stops by once an hour, though not always at the same time," Kaleal said, oblivious to the dark turn of my inner ponderings. She stared down the length of the hall. When I'd last walked it, my path had been clear. But now several openings branched outward, offering additional avenues into my head. I wondered if I traversed them if I would or could get lost.

"Don't fear, Zara, it's locked for now," Kaleal said, calling me back to this particular spot, this particular reality. I flattened against the door, my ear pressed to the metal as the raps seemed to hammer against my head. Geoffrey. He was there. I could sense him.

And if I was aware of his presence...

A rumble of icy laughter.

Then a whisper, "You can run..."

He didn't finish the sentence, he didn't need to.

"The Fates messed up when they chose him, didn't they?" Kaleal pondered, though I barely heard her as I lingered, breath barely touching my lips, wondering who, between the creature trapped at my side and the other barred against me, was more dangerous.

Chapter 19

My encounter with Kaleal had me second-guessing everything. It wasn't that I didn't trust the ancient God, but I still hadn't unearthed her motives, whereas Geoffrey's desires were clear cut. Even though Kaleal apparently wanted to bring him down, I had to remember that didn't necessarily make her my ally.

To handle the challenges both beings presented, I needed to swallow some of my pride and make things right with someone who, for as long as I'd been with him anyway, had stood by my side and supported my decisions. Also, as one who'd been on the receiving end of Kaleal's awful manipulation, Finn, I figured, stood a better chance of figuring out what was going on in my head than anyone else.

Not talking about her was eating me alive.

I untied my camel from the train and, with a twitch of the reins, moved the beast up the line. I'd rehearsed my words so many times they were practically etched on my tongue. Despite knowing that, strategy had never been my strong suit, so this was new territory for me.

I nudged my way between two other camels who grunted at the inconvenience.

"Hey, guys," I said, quieter than I'd intended.

Ryder flashed his signature grin, his eyes shaded by the brim of his wide hat. Finn remained stoic, his back stiff.

I tugged my scarf down and allowed my hood to fall back, revealing my face for the first time in days. The braid I'd carefully wrapped in a ball at the back of my head felt frayed, my cheeks overheated, and my head light, but I persisted.

"Ryder, I'd like to confess another truth," I said.

His gold eyes glimmered. "You never have to ask permission, you know."

"In this case I do," I said. His grin faded and his eyes glowed hotter. "Because this truth isn't for you."

His gaze skirted past my shoulder. "Alright."

I caught the kelpie glancing at me from the corner of his eye. "Finn, I've operated on my own for most of my life. You met my parents; you saw what they were like. They loved me, but they kept me at arm's length." My throat closed up at the thought of them, of the painful way I'd lost them, but I swallowed past the lump.

"I've only ever known a world where weakness represents an opportunity for someone to knock you down, to steal your accomplishments, to push you out of history books." I tugged at the fingers of my gloves, sliding the soft material down my hands. "You've seen me at my weakest, and you never judged me for that. So I guess I felt it was time for you to see me at my strongest... because I hate when people I respect see me as anything less than what I aim to be."

I gritted my teeth, forcing my spine to fuse, my head to turn, my eyes to meet and hold his. "I'll try harder to trust you, to put my faith in you. In Ryder and Rose and Joseph and whoever else might come along, too. But this isn't easy for me, so I may need you to help me figure out how to do that."

"Z—"

I shook my head, though his nickname for me warmed something in my chest, but I needed to get this out. "You were right. I am hurting.

It does hurt being away from water. I can't cool down no matter how much I try." I bit my lip and carefully raised my hand, exposing the blistered fingertips. Horror limned his features as he grabbed it, careful to avoid the injuries. "The fire has a mind of its own, and I think I need the water to balance it out. I'm figuring it out, but it's taking some time."

He protested when I tugged my hand away and pulled my glove back on.

"You want me to open up, and I'm going to try, but…" I tilted my head at the front of the line where a figure on a white horse had shifted sideways to monitor us. "But while I may eventually be ok with you seeing me weak, I'll be damned if he gets to see that part of my soul." I hesitated, then extended my hand, pinkie out. A promise. Everything inside me trembled as I waited for Finn to speak.

Fierce, green eyes burned into mine, hot and wide on his pale face. Before he had a chance to snag my finger with his own, to deliver his verdict, another man shouted my name.

"Zara, please join me at the front of the caravan," Phenex called, his voice cold as a winter wind. The command stunned me. In four days, he'd barely spoken a word. Around us, the nero watched, eyes hard and dark as they parted the long rows of camels. I glanced at Ryder, who shrugged, and carefully made my way to the front.

Whatever flippant thing I'd thought to say to the djinn fled when my attention snagged on the bright lights flickering ahead. They weren't stars like I'd thought from the middle of the pack. Red magic snapped to attention, falling into line for the first time in days. No, this was something more earthly, more tangible.

"It's fire." The words dripped from my lips like the water I so craved. "Very good."

I swung around. "I thought you said few knew these trails?"

"Few do." He scrutinized me and I remembered I'd forgotten my bandanna. Too late now, I could only hope I didn't look as ill as I felt. "Fortunately, I recognize this particular caravan."

Music plucked from a stringed instrument drifted across the sand. I shivered beneath my many layers of clothes. Phenex clucked the flat of his tongue against the roof of his mouth, and our animals surged forward. He rode uncomfortably close, our legs nearly brushing.

"I wanted you to be the first to meet some of my most highly skilled employees." He waved a hand at the bulky tents and picket lines. "Should you wish to make your presence known, you're certainly welcome. No doubt, their scouts have spotted us by now."

Make my presence... "You want me to use my magic? To disturb them?"

"If it pleases you," he said dryly. Shouts sounded from the camp and a number of forms clustered around the bonfire rose to gather weapons and mount horses. "I figured you'd want the option. It may help smooth things over."

"Are you high?"

"I'll take that as a no." He hummed. The shouts stopped when a wave of sand rose ahead of us. "What a pity. I do appreciate a good spectacle."

Rose appeared at my elbow, whip in hand and wings whirring furiously as the nearest horse galloped close. Her inky eyes narrowed as she asked, "Who are these *nero*?"

"Phenex claims to know them," I said, stoking the flames in my belly higher as the first rider stopped short of the djinn. "And he's apparently all about spectacles."

"Sounds like someone else I know." She grinned, surveying the closest man who had dyed, scarlet hair. His hard gaze met mine unapologetically, then returned to Phenex.

"I didn't think you ever left your castle," the man said by way of greeting. "And with such a large group to boot."

Behind him, two riders with long guns pulled up, faces grim. All three swirled with the sand magic I'd grown accustomed to, though I hadn't seen any nero address the djinn so casually before.

"I was expecting you a week ago," Phenex drawled, leaning against his pommel.

"Problems happen, issues arise. You know how it goes at the Lost City." The stranger's accent was warm and full-bodied like honey. Though unlike honey, it lacked all sweetness. "I've done the best with what I was given. It's why you trust me, right?"

"Careful, Maat," Phenex said. "Mind yourself in front of our guests."

"Sure thing, boss." He kept his gaze fixed on me, one brow raised, and I drew up tall in the saddle. He sneered and I noticed a scar ran the length of his nose. The hand he'd casually draped across his thigh shifted to the butt of his revolver. In my periphery, Rose raised her whip, but I signaled for her to wait.

"Did I do something to you?" I asked.

"Hard to say, since I don't even know who you are."

"Zara ring any bells?"

His horse huffed and danced, bringing Maat's other side into my line of sight. His hand curled around a second revolver, his index finger hovering dangerously close to the trigger. "It might."

Joseph drew up beside me, his relaxed posture forced as he surveyed this latest arrival. "And I'm Joseph." He raised his hand in a half-wave.

Phenex cut him off. "Yes, Maat, as modest as they might be, the Gods of Water and Air are my companions. You'd do well to remember that, lest you inadvertently play with fire."

I snorted, covering my mouth.

A bark of laughter burst from the nero. "You may call yourselves Gods, but you haven't done anything for anyone." Maat spat at the hooves of my camel. "Until you do more than prance around spouting fancy titles, you're not deserving of my respect. Though if you want to stay at camp, I can't exactly stop you now, can I?"

Coals of hatred burned in his eyes as he shot me another look, then he squeezed the sides of his horse with his knees and galloped back to camp. The two men flanking him followed suit.

"Forgive him," Phenex said. His utter calm confused me. He raised an arm and the caravan advanced. "Maat has had a long a few months on the road and is in dire need of a break. He'll come around."

"Doubtful." Joseph didn't bother whispering despite knowing everyone was listening to us. "Whatever that guy's deal was goes deeper than being sick of work."

"You said it." I patted my camel's head and questions knotted my insides. Maat's words should have ignited my usual fury, but that didn't feel right. In fact, nothing about anything had made sense since we'd arrived in Egypt. From Phenex's motivations to Kaleal's sporadic behavior to understanding my overall mission, even that emerald back at the djinn's home still left a rancid taste in my mouth.

I forced the confusion down and smiled weakly at Joseph. "Since when do you say 'guy?'"

"Since yesterday." He pulled a leather tie from his hair and shook out his mane. "I like its ambiguity." As he blathered on about the underlying meanings of parts of speech, I focused on the sleek tail that was Phenex's hair. He'd wanted me to see that exchange. He'd gotten something out of it, something that he was convinced cost me something in return.

Not even ten minutes later, we arrived at the camp. Roughly a dozen nero gathered around the fire, though they'd put away the musical instruments. As I slid from my camel, grateful to be on solid ground, I smiled at the nero who came over to lead her to a trough filled with water. I watched greedily as the animals drank their fill.

Ryder approached from my left, but before I could so much as call out to him, a cup of warm water knocked against my battered knuckles.

"Here," Phenex said. "Drink up. There's more than enough to go around."

I highly doubted that since we were a handful of days out from any reasonable source of water, but I chilled the glass with a thought and drank deeply. It was barely enough to fill the cracks in the basin that was my soul, but it would have to do. Finished, I smacked my lips and froze, embarrassed when Phenex chuckled.

"Your efforts to conceal your misery have not gone unnoticed." He guided me to his tent that a handful of nero were finishing setting up away from the others. I smiled reassuringly at the pixies, signaling for them that I was alright. I needed to know what Phenex was after, and it seemed that he may finally be willing to open up. "I can hardly imagine how I'd fare surrounded by nothing but sea."

"There's earth beneath the sea," I responded, lowering myself to the red and blue patterned rug. It was a relief to not sit on hardened leather or gritty sand for once. "If necessary, you could reach it."

"Like I'm sure you could tap into the water the earth conceals around these parts if you truly tried." He removed his hat. "Why you don't is astonishing to me."

I had. Repeatedly. I'd sunk my magic deep into the depths of the sand but had come back empty each time. The reservoirs were too far down—not that he needed to know that.

"What do you want, Phenex?" I asked with a sigh. I set my cup on a flat board between us. Someone had charred the intricate pattern of a chessboard on its surface. "I'm tired of playing games. Tell me what you're after."

He settled onto a green mat and poured the same thick, red liquid he'd consumed at his home into a glass. The djinn drank deeply, the purplish shadows beneath his eyes gradually shrinking. He watched the fire as he weighed his thoughts.

"You and she are well-matched," he finally said.

123

I rocked back on my tailbone. Kaleal was one of the last beings I ever wanted to be compared to. Her and maybe Geoffrey. "Me and who?"

"Don't play coy, it doesn't suit you." He swirled his glass and drank again. I reached my magic toward the substance, trying to identify it, but the barrier he'd erected around himself stopped my tendrils short. "Kaleal is hiding inside you." He coughed wryly. "I always knew she'd be back."

My breath caught and, as if her spoken name had summoned her forth, the God in question slipped out of the shadows to take a front-row seat.

"You know who she is?" I asked.

"Of course I do," Phenex scoffed as she preened. "But I don't want to talk about her."

That's not quite true, Kaleal purred as my heart sank. He spoke of her as though he *knew* her, and I badly wanted to know more.

"What would you rather talk about?" I gritted. "You and I aren't exactly friends."

"We could be, in another life maybe." Phenex rolled his neck, and I had the distinct impression that he was alluding to his history with Kaleal. "But, alas, we're stuck with this existence for now, and there's a certain person connecting our lives who you need to understand better."

I frowned, realizing where this was going now. Kaleal's subtle amusement was tangible. "Geoffrey."

"Geoffrey," he repeated, nodding. "He and I have a history. I think it will interest you."

"Let's hear it then." I chewed on the inside of my cheek. "Regale me."

"Don't sound so thrilled." The djinn pulled one of his knees up and braced his forearm on the bone. "About a year after waging war against the Gods and his perception of their fates, Geoffrey visited my palace.

I granted him entry because, I'll admit, I was curious about the first Hand to rise in two-thousand years. I wanted to know more about the person who destroyed my chances of ever getting my magic back again."

Phenex had hinted at his relationship with Geoffrey before, but clearly, their ties ran deeper than he'd let on if he'd known the Hand for the better part of seventeen years.

"I've developed a reputation similar to that incubus you insist on dragging around everywhere," the djinn said and my brows rose. "We're both considered fixers... people who know a little about everyone and everything, using that knowledge to tweak the world as we see fit."

My tension lingered as I wondered whether Phenex and Ryder had ever crossed paths before. They were both entrepreneurs, both apparently well-established. It seemed strange for them to have not talked at least once in their storied histories.

You worry too much about that poor excuse of a fey, Kaleal scoffed. *He's hardly worth your time.*

I don't give a damn about your bias against incubi, I countered. It wasn't the first time she'd made her disdain for the race clear. *Ryder has done nothing to suggest that he would do anything to hurt me.*

But he hasn't done much to help you, either, Kaleal countered slyly, her words striking a chord. That wasn't true... was it?

Phenex was oblivious to my inner sparring. "Geoffrey was well aware of who and what I was. He said he didn't care about any of that. He told me he wanted to talk to someone who may have experienced a few regrets in his life, someone willing to stay out of his way as long as he stayed out of theirs." Phenex's canines flashed in the firelight. "I've had a few regrets."

That actually surprised me. Phenex made a point of being decisive, I couldn't imagine him doing anything that might jeopardize that. I wanted to ask but stopped short at Kaleal's quiet chiding.

Stay on point, we might learn something important, she whispered.

"What was Geoffrey's regret?" I asked instead. He eyed me with a blend of interest and... disappointment.

The djinn brushed sand off his leg. "Killing you." He made it sound so simple, so easy, so absolute. "Or believing he had, rather. He regretted his impulsiveness. He said he wanted to change and become a better person. While I wasn't sure if he meant it, I listened to him and offered what advice I could. After all, he was willing to extend my autonomy for something as trivial as righting his moral wrongs."

Moral? Geoffrey had destroyed his own temples and killed two children. He'd ruined the reputation of his church and disrupted the course of the world. This was so far past the minor moral dilemma that Phenex made it out to be.

And everything you've ever done was with a soul both pure and innocent? Kaleal asked, chuckling when I recoiled. I truly hated having her in my head.

The djinn lifted a shoulder and drained his glass. "I kept an eye on him over the years. True to his word, he changed. He became in what society's eyes is considered a better man. He worked toward fixing corruption within the Order, he sent aid to those in need, he corrected inaccuracies, and yes, he also maintained his vision that the Gods were never supposed to rise again."

I rubbed at my chest, not sure how to interpret the picture he was painting. That didn't seem like the Geoffrey I'd come to know at all.

But you didn't get to know him at all, did you? hissed Kaleal.

Who's side are you on here? I asked, pushing her back when she leaned forward a hair too far. *You don't like him either.*

She clicked her tongue but didn't answer.

"We fell out of touch like people do," Phenex said. "Of course, the Order and I did business together, but he was rarely involved. I only thought of Geoffrey again when, to my surprise, I saw you on the news ripping his troops to shreds from atop a pillar of water." His laughter was quicksilver bright. "I've seen Gods do many things, a great many things in the rise and fall of civilization. I'd never seen anything like that."

I curled away from him. No, Phenex was definitely wrong. We could never be friends, not in this life or any others. I had regrets on how I'd handled things that day, even knowing that I'd done what I'd done to protect myself and my friends. But the djinn seemed to savor my destructive behavior, and I couldn't imagine what other reckless lengths he might push me toward in the name of friendship.

A little recklessness is much more fun, though, wouldn't you agree? Kaleal asked.

"I tapped into my contacts at the Order to understand what was happening," Phenex said, adjusting his seat on the mat. "It was complicated, to say the least, and messy. Geoffrey was moving quickly, making decisions at the behest of himself and his second-in-command. Orders got mixed up, commands given that didn't make sense, and only after you'd vanished off the face of the earth again did a few things come to light."

This is getting good, Kaleal said, inching forward again, only relenting with a small pout when I shoved her back. *Xenith always did appreciate drama.*

Hearing that name for the second time almost derailed me, my curiosity fully peaked, but Phenex's next words snared my attention.

"Geoffrey never wanted you dead. He was still trying to right his wrongs. But his second, a man by the name of *Toren Almasi—*," he spat the name like it rotted in his mouth. I wondered at the vehemence, at the sharp jerk of his chest that was the air moving in and out of his lungs. "—wanted you out of the picture. Not only that, he wanted Geoffrey dead. All because of power. He very nearly succeeded if you hadn't won that battle by the lake, which was nothing short of a miracle."

My skin prickled. The man at the lake, he'd said his name was Toren.

"How do you know about that battle?" I asked. Joseph hadn't mentioned seeing anything about it in the newspapers, and surely that would have been information worth reporting.

And what about Toren? Kaleal asked. *He speaks of this man strangely.*

Phenex's lips curled and he shrugged. "I make it a point to find out things. Like when I found out you'd killed that useless brat, I must say I very nearly extended an invitation to meet you myself. But then you vanished off the face of the planet, and my hopes were dashed." His dark eyes slid over me like oil.

"Who is Toren to you?" I blurted, then cupped my hands over my mouth, wondering if Kaleal had pushed me somehow. Even now, the ancient God was pressing forward eagerly, and the delicate control I held over her nearly snapped.

Phenex stared, assessing. "Toren is… his family is a piece of my past that I'd rather forget." He spoke as if his heart were being ripped from his chest. The djinn scrubbed his wrists so hard I feared he might tear the skin. "Though I do suppose I owe them my freedom."

Ah, Kaleal whispered, *I'd wondered who finally released him from that lamp.*

Phenex's words tripped me up, and I barely heard her. I'd almost forgotten he'd been enslaved once, bound to answer the beck and call of whichever human whose hands he'd happened to fall into. I found myself softening toward him until I remembered his treatment of the nero and the pride he'd radiated admitting he'd devoured his siblings for power.

Power that he'd accused Toren of pursuing as if it were a sin. This fey was such a contradiction.

"How did Toren's family—"

"I will not speak of Toren again," Phenex growled, smacking the chessboard so hard my cup tumbled off. "Nor will I speak of the life sentence I neither deserved nor asked for." He stood and pointed at the campfire, his magic a roar of fury I couldn't ignore

Fix this, Kaleal snarled as I scrambled up. *Fix this now.*

"Will you finish what you started?" I held my hands up while forcing my own magic to not respond to the violence of his. "I won't ask about... *him* again, and I really want to know what you intended to tell me."

"Does it matter? This conversation is over."

"Phenex, please." It almost killed me to plead. "Don't send me away yet. Besides," I closed my eyes wishing I wasn't about to do what I was going to do, "Kaleal wants to know."

I stepped back, allowing Kaleal to fall into my place.

What are you doing, she hissed, but it was too late, he'd glimpsed her shining through.

"Well," he started, then stopped, blinking. If I'd smacked him across the face he wouldn't have looked more surprised. "In that case."

"I'm bored with this," Kaleal said, rubbing her hands together and glancing around as if seeing the tent for the first time. "Why she called me forward, I'll never know. But I don't have time for your temper tantrums, never did and never will."

She turned away when he grabbed her shoulder. "Kaleal—"

"Don't you dare touch me." She brushed him off. "You know better than to say that name out here. You grow too bold."

"You need to be careful," he said, curling his hands behind his back. His voice wasn't steady and he couldn't meet her eye. I'd never seen him so submissive. Whatever history they had, she had clearly held the upper hand. "Geoffrey wants that girl dead. He wants it more badly than he ever wanted anything."

"How do you know this?" she asked. "And why should I believe it?

You always were fond of stories."

The djinn sighed and scrubbed his face. "You don't have to believe me, but what that man did in the years after he destroyed the temples, that was enough to convince me," he said. "Just like I knew he'd changed his skin again when he stopped to see me a week before you conveniently arrived at my doorstep. He knew that Zara, that *you*, were coming or would be coming at some point anyway, and he wanted my help."

"How did he know that?" she asked, her tone flaying him wide open. I hadn't heard so much as a whisper from Geoffrey during my time at Joseph's camp. Even when we had talked, I was certain I hadn't let on to my plans.

"He knew you were after the Earth God, or you would be after you found the God of Fire. Since I'm one of the few who knows how to find that ridiculous temple, it was pretty obvious."

I drew back, wondering if Geoffrey was coming after me right now and if he was, how much time I'd have before he was on me again.

"What you need to know," the djinn said, leaning in, "is that Geoffrey is no longer the calm, collected man I knew him to be. You need to be careful."

"I appreciate the warning," Kaleal said, crossing her arms. "But I already knew that. Don't waste my time like this again. You can't intimidate me."

She thrust me back into my body as she turned to the fire.

That was a clever thing you did, she said, her tone glacial. *It reminds me of something I would have done. But if you catch me by surprise again, you won't like the consequences.*

I'm not afraid of you, I argued.

You should be.

Chapter 20

There was something deeply unsettling about being in the near-constant presence of someone who actively hated me. In swimming, I'd met girls who definitely didn't like me, and there were fey who'd made it clear that my presence irritated them, but Maat's burning gaze was an itch between my shoulders I couldn't scratch. When I pointed that out to Joseph, he'd shrugged and said hatred was the price of power.

Despite saying the nero was badly in need of a day off, Phenex had asked Maat—or rather ordered him—to return to the Lost Temple with us. It was officially two days later and I was going crazy from the tension. The only bonus was it diverted my thoughts from my magic, so I'd let it go right until we stopped to set up camp. Phenex had already pushed us farther and harder than he had the entire journey, and the sun was puncturing the horizon.

As I wrestled with the ties holding my tent to the saddle, struggling with one particularly tight knot, someone snickered. Finn nudged me aside and shifted the bag so he could work it out.

"…useless. What kind of God can't handle her own things?"

My lips drew back. I was sweaty. I was exhausted. I was in pain. And I was done.

"Zara, don't—"

"Stay out of my way," I hissed, drawing my knife from its sheath on my thigh, and marched across the sand. Maat had his back to me, but the flame of his hair was unmistakable. I grabbed his arm and whipped him around.

"Wha—" His mouth snapped shut and his chin went up when my dagger tapped his jugular. I clutched him close, our bodies immobile as our eyes waged war.

"I've never been particularly good at restraining myself, but I'm pretty damn sure I broke my own record after hearing you snipe about me for two days." Despite the threat, he seemed remarkably unaffected. Around us, the nero circled, tall and quiet as specters, as if they held a collective breath. "I've always believed in confronting my problems head-on, so guess what, here we are. What's your deal with me?"

The copper disks of his eyes flashed. "You. You're my problem." Each word oozed with venom. "Cozying up with Phenex like you don't know what he's done. If you actually cared about anyone besides yourself, you would have wiped the desert with the likes of him."

"Finally, you grew a pair." The wind caught some of my tangled hair and whipped it between us. Through my teeth, I hissed, "What exactly has he done?"

The muscles in his back rippled under my hand. Maat glanced over my shoulder, no doubt looking at the djinn himself, since I wasn't picking him up in my periphery. "As if you don't know."

"Try me," I growled.

"Water owes nothing to Earth. It wouldn't matter anyway." Our noses and thighs were practically touching. I'd pulled the knife back as he surged forward. I had only intended to incite him, not actually hurt him. "By aligning with the likes of him you've shown your hand."

"Funny how you claim Earth now." I adjusted my fingers on the grip so the symbol of my temple was visible. "Not one of you bears Earth's mark. It's not on your clothing or your equipment, it certainly wasn't anywhere in Phenex's palace. And none of you bears the badge of loyalty." I dropped his arm and prodded my neck. Maat's face clouded. "In fact, if I had to take a guess, and I'm pretty good at guessing games, I'd say your loyalties lie as little with the temple as they do with Phenex himself. Why?"

It may have been my imagination, but an inkling of hostility leached from his body. His brows drew sharply together, and I nudged him back.

"I'm not your enemy if you don't make me one," I snapped.

Whatever response he'd been working up was lost when the ground trembled. Someone from the outer rim shouted, "Ramalia nest."

Maat growled low in his throat, eyes flashing as he turned toward the voice while simultaneously pushing me behind him. One of the nero racing by tossed him a hooked spear with a serrated edge. He swung it in a low circle, scanning the horizon.

"What's a ramalia?" I asked, stepping around him, trying to figure out what the frantic behavior was all about. Phenex had joined the nero clustered at the north end of camp. Maat glanced at me, his nose wrinkling, then back at his people.

"Sand devils," he muttered, "some of the nastiest monsters you'll meet out here. I thought two millennia in hibernation might have killed them off. Guess I was wrong." He shifted his grip on the staff as the earth bucked again, and tapped me back behind him using the shaft. "How about you stay back there so you don't get hurt."

Flames ignited in my belly and I plunged my hand in my pocket snarling. "Seriously? You're gonna pull that—"

"Your element is water." He spared me another demeaning glance. "You're probably the most useless person in this camp next to the kelpie. Leave the fighting for those who know what to do."

My teeth slammed together so hard I was sure I'd cracked a few when the earth jolted again. Beyond the assembled nero, a fissure formed with a resounding snap. Sun-dried sand rushed over the edges. All was quiet for one second, two, then a dozen dark ribbons rippled over the edges of the crack with a chorus of guttural hissing and spitting that made my stomach turn.

The nero didn't wait. The first dozen ran forward with a yell, spears thrust forward. The creatures rose, black scales flexing around sinewy muscles. One shot forward, its body uncoiling to an eighteen-foot length, fangs flashing as it unfurled a burgundy-tinged fan around its head. The nero nimbly blocked its strike and flipped in an impossible circle to dodge a second attack. The creature hissed again, that awful sizzling spitting sound, and circled the nero as he spun his weapon.

"They're cobras," I gasped.

"They're more than that." Maat's arms tensed as the second wave of nero rushed to engage the snakes. Phenex was among them, glittering gold magic at his fingertips. "The only way to kill them is to remove their heads. But that's not easy. Their blood is acid and their bite is worse. One nick and your muscles will melt." He motioned with his staff at one nero hacking through the thick vane around one ramalia's head, flinching when flecks of blood seared her skin. Someone screamed as metal clanged.

"They're fast and they're precise. The only benefit we have is that they're blind, but they can sense movement through vibrations in the ground and air." As if proving Maat's point, one of my pixies dive-bombing from the skies twisted suddenly, thrown when one of the snakes nearly snagged her leg with its fangs. Sand sprayed when her body hit the ground. Rose had followed closely behind her and whooped when she lopped off its head.

Not far away, Joseph whistled a warning and dropped an invisible pane of air like a guillotine, severing the bodies of several snakes. They continued to flop around as nero rushed in to finish the job.

"That's why you're staying here." Maat's lip curled when he shot me another look. "Because your friends are equipped for this. You're not."

134

He sneered at my dagger. "That's barely thicker than the tips of their tails."

I'd never wanted to drown someone so much in my life. Before I could flick the lighter and ignite my magic, someone smashed down next to me and I dropped it. I whipped around, shielding my eyes as I scoured the earth.

"How about we all get through this alive, then argue about it." Ryder rumbled, leathery wings fanning out behind him. "As good as your mates are at handling blunt weapons, we're about to have bigger problems."

Dozens more snakes spilled over the lip of the hole, slicing through dead bodies like scythes. Several nero fell before our forces could recollect themselves. Phenex unleashed a whirlwind, crushing several in a cocoon of sand. But still, they came. The blunt end of a sword tapped my hand and, with retribution swirling in his red and gold eyes, Ryder winked when he passed it over.

"It's not ice, but it'll do that job." He drew his own sword, one rippling with black and white lightning at the edges. "See you on the other side."

I nearly screamed, my heart shooting to my throat when one snake slipped past the clashing nero and snapped at him. The incubus feinted, sword a blur, and sliced through its underbelly like butter. The creature shuddered, scales smoking, and Ryder lopped off its head. I'd barely released the breath caught in my chest when another snake was on top of him.

I didn't see what happened because Maat, for the third time, shoved me, and I dropped to my knees. Over my head soared a ramalia, and Maat was on it in moments. I went eerily cold, the world felt oddly still as the nero stabbed the snake again and again. Blood soaked the sand and the world seemed to right itself once more.

Determination coursed through me. I needed to fight.

I reared back, my blood heating, scouring the sand for the dropped lighter. There wasn't another source anywhere within reach, and fire was all I had. In my periphery, another beast charged, and my blade swung up in time to meet its foot-long fangs.

I gave up the search for the lighter, and stood, circling the ramalia as it coiled, hissing in warning. The creatures didn't even have eyes I realized, feeling calmer as I focused on the immediate threat. It flattened its hood, a move I recognized, and swung as it reared forward. My sword swiped along the side of its head. The creature released a guttural hiss and slipped back again.

It was far from a death blow, but I drew strength from having actually injured it. The ramalia wasn't invincible. I gripped the sword tighter, pulse pounding when it lashed out again. Its fangs hit the sand and I moved in, swiping at its neck with a yell. My sword went clean through, the blood spraying and burning my hands, but its head came off.

I wiped my hands on my pants, hoping the thick fabric would hold up against the acid. As I turned to find Maat in the mess, I spotted the lighter near the ramalia's tail and darted forward, narrowly snagging it as I raced past, then nearly fumbled it again when I ran into Maat bent over the body of his own ramalia.

He straightened, coppery eyes assessing. Then he nodded. But I didn't have a moment to appreciate our sudden comraderie as another snake shot forward. I yelled, pointing behind him and he whirled, easily deflecting its attack with his spear. I turned my back on Maat, keeping an eye out for danger and squeezed the lighter when I spotted the second snake, but sand was caught in the gears and it wouldn't light.

I shoved it in my pocket and whipped out my sword as the beast attacked, beating it off with short, animalistic yells, ignoring the deep ache in my hands that was my magic. The nero and I fought, back to back, fending off snake after snake. Their bodies mounted and the sand churned black with blood beneath our feet, the acid eating through the soles of our boots.

I finally found my opening when I thrust my sword through one particularly large ramalia's head, barely saving Maat's life when the snake knocked his spear clean away. I grabbed his hand, dragging him from the bodies before we collapsed. No ramalia were in immediate reach, and I pulled out the lighter again, brushing away the sand as fire magic surged. Maat snagged another spear, and when he turned back I snicked the trigger, flames roaring to my hands.

The relief knotting my muscles was glorious and I nearly lost myself in the giddy release of power.

Maat's eyes went comically wide. "You can—you have—"

"Yeah. Handy little trick." I started to grin when I saw the dark shadow rearing up behind him. "Watch out!"

I swung my sword, flames racing up the length of the blade, as Maat flattened against the sand, his trust in me incredible. The snake drew back, ribbon of a tongue flickering, but I swung again and again. It retreated, something about the fiery blade confusing it, and I finally found my opening. I sliced through its neck, the heated metal sealing it the wound.

As it collapsed, dead on the ground, I dropped my sword with a yell. The heat had melted the steel. Maat rose, mouth slightly open, staring at the blade with a mixture of reverence and confusion. I shook with adrenaline, searching for my friends as the battle raged, thankful it seemed that we were finally gaining the upper hand.

The pixies had one ramalia surrounded and were taking turns jabbing at it. Nearby, Ryder and Joseph worked in tandem with a group of nero to take down three others. Phenex braced his hands on his knees as he gasped, his back to the gaping hole in the ground. Filleted bodies littered the ground around him.

A shaggy, dark horse reeking of seawater and dripping with kelp surged up next to me. Finn snuffled my back and shoulders, nosing the holes in my clothing. My hand shook as I patted his remarkably soft hide.

"I'd wondered where you'd gotten off to," I said.

He huffed a weak whinny and thrust his head to our right, where a few of the camels and horses were clustered. Most of our bags were ground to a pulp in the center of the mess, but he'd herded a few of them, including one of the camels laden with precious sacks of water, to safety.

"That was smart," I said, "really, really smart."

Maat was already on his knees, wrapping gauze around a nero's injury as I moved toward one of the pixies who wasn't moving. I bit my lip, ignoring the sick feeling curdling my insides, and called out to her when the earth rocked again. Once. Twice. Three times.

Everything in my guts liquified when the hissing started. This was louder somehow, more sinister. The longer it went, the more power it seemed to possess. I tried to move and found I couldn't. My mind whirled as I struggled, as I watched my friends struggle, their bodies stiff with fear caused by whatever magic this thing possessed.

My head buzzed and nausea churned as it emerged from the hole, one massive scale after another. The dozens of ramalia scattered around us looked like toothpicks compared to this monster. Foot by foot it slid out, body coiling and winding beneath it as it rose high. Its tongue flicked and the rising sun reflected off its scales, blinding me with its luster.

Until I realized that brilliance was magic.

My paralysis broke, my magics bursting forward, when a thundering voice clanged in my head, the vibrations driving me to my knees.

"...MY CHILDREN..."

I gagged on the anger and pain those two words contained, the

138

agony of the monster impossible to ignore. It shook my core and I nearly threw up from the power left zinging through me as it withdrew. When I finally gained control over myself again, I gaped at the creature with its scales glittering with hints of gold, its head sweeping high over the battlefield in a pained frenzy.

I knew that voice. Or at least a version of it.

I threw out my magic, but it slid over the beast like grease. I'd never felt magic like this, like it was warped into some dark version of itself as if time had rotted it away. But the magical part of me that seemed to *know* things, a part of me I'd learned to trust through trial and error, recognized that magic no matter how cold and twisted it felt.

This had to be one of the Great Beasts.

Its sinuous body curled again, hood flaring wide.

"No!" I screamed, ripping Maat's spear from his limp hand.

The hissing subsided and the snake's head whipped around. My outburst seemed to do the trick, shaking everyone from their stricken paralysis. Finn's glowing eyes caught mine, a million messages flowing between us, and I scrambled on his back, my fingers twisting in his thick hair as he jumped forward, sand spraying beneath his backward hooves.

"You don't have to do this," I yelled at the snake as we charged. "Snap out of it!"

Phenex recovered first, his magic uncoiling in a violent burst. I leaned against Finn's neck, streamlining our bodies. I couldn't let the djinn strike. I didn't know what would happen if he did, but I had a feeling that trying to destroy one of the keepers of magic wouldn't go well for anyone.

I drew my arm back, the length of the spear bulky and unnatural in my grip, but I had an idea. Maybe if I hit It with magic, all of my magic, I could snap the Great Beast from this daze. I remembered that water magic had the ability purify, so, with the last dregs of my magic,

I froze blood to the long blade, hoping it would be enough as I heated the metal beneath the ice.

Finn snorted, his sides heaving, as we charged past nero. He knew what I did—I couldn't throw this thing. I could barely keep it up let alone straight.

But I had to.

"Joseph!" I called, "A little help here!"

And I threw it.

Wind whipped around me, catching the weapon and carrying it high. I scrambled for my lighter, using my knees to keep hold of Finn as he charged, the world blurring past us. The snake flexed Its hood, already moving out of its path, but Joseph tapped the spear as I pressed the lighter down, igniting the fire magic as it hit the Beast's body.

It reared back as the powers of three Gods crashed into it.

"...I KNOW THIS MAGIC..."

Its tail lashed, catching Phenex and sending him flying.

Finn skidded and I flew off his back, hitting the sand with a punch that knocked the air from my body. I rolled and smacked into the snake's body. It froze, Its head two stories up swaying as It hissed.

"...GOD?..."

"You got that right," I gasped, dizzy at my proximity to danger and Its immense power. I pressed my palms against a scale the size of a car window. "Time to burn that evil out of you."

And I hit It with everything I had.

Invisible flames of my magic scored through the Beast's trunk, ripping along a line that may as well have been a trail of gasoline, burning away the dregs of icy, dark energy holding It captive. The snake's body coiled around me, squeezing me tight, the near-constant hiss turning to white noise in my ears, but I kept myself open, glorying in the uncurling of vivid, healthy green strands of Earth magic. Only when I was certain the blackness was gone did I extricate myself from

Its being.

The snake's head dipped low, one fang as long as my body brushed my side.

But I wasn't afraid.

Whatever was eating at the Great Beast was gone. It wouldn't hurt me. The connection between us gaped wide and I hovered there, hands flat on Its scales.

"...BEWARE THOSE WHO EMBRACE THE DESERT..."

I blinked, dazed from the thunder of Its voice, and stumbled as It slipped into the crack of the earth once again. I didn't know what to say, didn't know what to feel, even when Finn wrapped his arms around my shoulders, shaking me as he screamed in relief and frustration.

I spun in his hold and met Phenex's hooded gaze, the fury around him hot and potent.

He'd warned me against Geoffrey, but was Phenex really the bigger threat?

Chapter 21

W e have one, maybe two days of water left." Maat flung the broken end of a tent pole away in disgust. "Even if we had horses and we were able to push them harder, we'd still have a good five days ahead of us."

Finn swore and Ryder threw his arms up as he stalked away. I pressed my fingers to my burning eyes and wished this were all some great nightmare I'd wake up from soon. My thirsty veins shriveled up even more.

Behind me, the flames of the funeral pyre lapped hungrily at the broken remnants of our camping supplies. Alongside it lay seven bodies covered in sheets. Six nero had given their lives in the fight against the ramalia. With a pang, I glanced at the smallest sheet and immediately wished I hadn't. Wisp, one of the quieter pixies with a knack for fletching arrows, had died in Briar's arms as she tried to stop the flow of blood from a gaping chest wound.

Rose swiped at the black lines of mascara trickling down her cheeks and clutched at Briar's hand. "Basically we're screwed, yeah? All that for nothing?"

Finn was still wrangling our animals. The ramalia had killed a few, but most had survived. Unfortunately, I couldn't say the same for many of our supplies—of which many had gotten trampled or were missing. Joseph and I had thankfully gotten our bags back, though I really only cared about the copy of *The Word* he still hid.

"Not necessarily." Maat leaned against his staff, the very one that I'd chucked at the Great Beast. He eyed me skeptically, the gem on his forehead flashing in the sun. Something about it drew me in now that I could see it in the daylight. I'd always sensed magic from the stones before, but had dismissed it as part of the powers inherent to the nero. Now I wasn't so certain. Maat wasn't the only one looking to me for answers. The other nero ranged from curious to resentful.

I splayed my fingers wide, shaking my head from my cross-legged position on the ground. I'd felt broken and beaten before the fight, now I was drained of everything except my desire to live. "I can only work with what I'm given. You already know there aren't any tributaries nearby, the air is some of the driest I've ever felt, and while I can sense a reservoir below, I'm not able to reach it."

It itched like mad, too, because I was so close I could practically taste the sweet, cool water.

Maat wasn't giving up the good fight. "Maybe if you tried a little harder, dug a little deeper…"

"Not gonna happen." My spine curved and I stared at my blood-speckled hands, then out over the battlefield where the corpses of the ramalia heated under the desert sun. Before long the stench would grow overwhelming. I hated what I was about to suggest and I met Maat's hard expression head-on. "The only thing I can do is maybe, *maybe* purify what little liquid I can pull from the sand. But something tells me even you would hesitate at drinking the blood of your fallen friends. Even then, most of the blood is mixed with the acidic blood of the snakes… I'm not sure how much I'll be able to filter out."

Behind me, one of the nero coughed wetly and a few others turned their faces away in pain and disgust. To his credit, Maat didn't flinch. He actually appeared to think it over for a few minutes, then shook his head. "No. I don't think that's an option."

143

The emerald, I realized as he turned away. It looked like a fragment of the emerald I'd found at Phenex's home. We mostly traveled at night and the jewelry typically looked like flecks of black on their faces when they weren't covered up by hoods or hats. But here in the daylight...

Ryder's arms tightened around my waist. He'd wrapped himself around me after pulling me from Finn's hold, muttering useless words into my hair about how I would be the death of him someday. In my ear, he whispered, "I can teleport, but with a group this large I wouldn't be able to take everyone. Factor in the distance and the fact I can only take us to somewhere I've already been..."

I squeezed his thigh. He'd admitted to me before we'd left that he'd tried teleporting to the Lost City, but couldn't determine which way to go in whatever weirdness was his magic. "That's not an option. You'd drain yourself dry."

His lips brushed my neck. "Fine, but I will get *you* out of here if it comes to it."

"Which it won't." I snagged some orange-tinted hair from the top of his head, and he allowed me to angle him so I could see his face, ensuring he'd see the intent on mine. "It won't."

His golden eyes narrowed, a lazy smirk quirking his lips, but his attention snagged on the funeral pyre and he swallowed whatever he'd been about to say.

"What about the tunnels?" Briar motioned at the pit in the ground. "Would those help? Do you think they reach all the way to the temple?"

I only saw it because I happened to be looking at him when the flash of panic crossed Phenex's face. He didn't want us going down there. I picked at the blood that had dried on my palm. Interesting.

Maat's mouth dropped open and he smacked his forehead. "Of course! The tunnels. Why didn't I think of that." He rushed to the opening and peered down. "We haven't used them in hundreds of years because the snakes infested them, making them too dangerous. But considering…" He gnawed his lip and crouched, arms angled on his knees. "It might just work. They were a shortcut forever ago."

"Do you know how to navigate them?" Finn asked. "It has been hundreds of years…"

One of the other nero smiled broadly and stood, tapping his temple. "I traveled them before with my dad. There's no way I'd forget that."

"I believe that settles it then." Joseph uncrossed his arms. "We're going down, unless anyone has any objections."

The fey muttered their agreement while I kept my attention fixed on Phenex as he shifted his weight from one foot to the other. He stopped when he realized I was watching. "No objection from me," he said.

Ryder heaved a sigh, his chest pressing against my back. He squeezed me a little tighter, his lips nuzzling my spine. "I suppose we should get going then."

With effort, I stood. The nero were already moving toward the bodies of their friends and the pyre they'd built to consume their remains. Maat told me the flames cleansed their souls and granted them passage to the underworld. The pixies would dispose of their fallen comrade in their own ritual that I wasn't privy to. The green skin of their backs glowed in the harsh sunlight as they each gripped the edge of the sheet and hoisted her high.

We'd move after this because sometimes the rights of the dead mattered more than the needs of the living.

Chapter 22

My thirst diminished in the cool tranquility of the caves. At first, I attributed it to the slight chill in the air, but then considered that I might finally be adapting to the burn of my fire magic. Whatever it was, I was infinitely grateful because I could finally concentrate again.

"I have a question for you," Maat said. He'd joined our group when we'd slipped into the tunnels, yet this was his first time actually speaking.

We'd mostly segregated ourselves into tiny pockets on the walk yesterday, but after stopping for some quick snatches of nervous sleep, we'd started to mingle. Well, everyone but Phenex who led the way with the nero who'd spoken about knowing the tunnels earlier. We'd left the animals behind, but brought scraps from the tents and used them as torches that I intermittently lit to counter the suffocating darkness.

"What's up?" I edged around a hole in the ground while pointing it out to Finn who followed me with Joseph at his side. The tunnels were only wide enough for us to walk two across.

"I didn't know you had fire magic." The nero snapped his fingers unhelpfully.

"Was that a question?"

"How did you get it? I've never heard of that happening before."

It was funny how the true extent of pain had a way of fading the longer time went on. "I burned alive." But I could still remember the sounds of bones cracking, the scent of skin burning. I rubbed my nose as if rubbing away the memory. "I guess I didn't want to die as much as I felt like dying."

Ryder walked alone, he was so tall and broad, and I felt him turn toward me in the near darkness. I nudged his back in warning before he walked into a low shelf of dirt.

Maat went quiet and I wondered if I'd been too blunt. I'd never had to explain what happened that day to anyone else before. It amazed me a little that I was able to speak the words as casually as I had. I felt very different from the girl who'd locked her emotions away for weeks rather than deal with the reality of what had happened. I rolled the lid of my canteen in my fingers, working it almost off then screwing it tight again.

"How did you do that?"

I almost dropped the cap. "Do what? Survive?" I rubbed my brands through my shirt, thinking back to the flashes of light and the blissful black. "I guess... part of me didn't want to be done. I didn't want that to be the end. And I had a ton of help. Ryder and Finn and Joseph and my Great Beast, the Kraken, they all came through for me." I flipped him a half-smile. "They'll deny it, but I owe them."

Joseph squeezed my shoulder in silent support while subtly guiding me around another hole.

"Why do you ask?"

"Just wondering," he said.

Finn rolled his eyes.

"If you say so." I fiddled with a tear in my shirt, thinking about those emeralds again. "Now I have a question for you: Why don't you use magic?"

Maat's nostrils flared, knuckles whitening around his staff. He kept his face straight, fixed on the torch held by the nero alongside Phenex, who directed us down the right shaft of a fork in the tunnel.

"I can sense it inside you, like a powerful cat prowling, ready to pounce." I took a sip of water. A muscle in his jaw fluttered and his biceps flexed around the metal bands clamped around them. "You've had ample opportunity. I saw some of your people use it back in Cairo. But even they're restrained. Why?"

His skin stretched thin, his eyes flinty and brittle, the look of someone preparing to turn tail and run. He raised his staff incrementally, threateningly. I'd pushed too hard, but I'd learned enough. It wasn't a decision he made of his own volition. If it was, he wouldn't have such an issue talking about it. I also had a funny feeling that a certain djinn was the answer to the mystery. I was convinced he was somehow manipulating Maat using that stone.

I bumped the nero with my elbow, making him start.

"Never mind. Don't stress it." I forced lightness into my tone. "There's a bunch of fey who don't use their magic. It's still pretty new to the universe and all. You'll figure it out sometime. Though, if you ever want help tapping into it, give Joseph or me a holler."

"Totally." My fellow God adjusted his glasses. "Even an Earth-sworn like yourself could benefit from my masterful teachings."

Maat stared at Joseph, eyes wide, and a glimmer of a smile appeared on his lips. "If you're saying Air is better than Earth, you've got another thing coming."

The two traded jabs as I faded into my thoughts. Controlling the nero and restricting their access to magic would definitely explain their attitudes toward him. He *was* practically a God in that sense. And while Maat was strong and capable, even he couldn't counter someone holding that kind of power over him. It all made sense.

We walked for what felt like hours before stopping to rest in a cutout of the caves that allowed our group to cluster as one. The nero hauling the sacks of water refilled our canteens with what they could before dropping them on the ground with sorrowful shrugs. We all knew what that meant. Our source of water was almost gone and I was still no closer to tapping into a reservoir.

I eyed Phenex as he met with Maat and a few other nero when a haze of smoke unfurled behind my eyes. Kaleal was finally stirring from her slumber.

There's strong magic nearby, she hissed.

It had prickled my skin for the past hour or so like a splinter I couldn't pick out, but I had attributed it to us getting closer to the Earth Temple. Kaleal was weirdly right about so many things, it was possible she was on to something.

Care to share any other fun tidbits? I asked.

You're such a teenager, she muttered. *If I had my own body this wouldn't be an issue.*

If you had your own body, we probably wouldn't have these wonderfully vague conversations.

Something's not right with it, she said, ignoring me. *It's not the Lost City.*

I thought about the Great Beast and the oily quality of Its power. *Plenty of that going around.*

"Alright, grab your stuff. We're getting close," Phenex called, clapping his hands. "Maybe another twelve hours, twenty-four at the worst, and we'll be there. Let's not waste time now that our water supply is out. And I'd rather not run into any more ramalia that might be lurking."

There was no grumbling like I was used to hearing at swim meets or other group events as everyone formed their dutiful lines once more. We were all eager for this to be over, to get out of these caves. We'd certainly beaten back a large number of the snakes, but the thought there might be more was horrifying. Going sword against fang with them in these close quarters would be more difficult—and likely more deadly.

I allowed the nero to go first this time while lingering at the back of the line. Maat stood beside me, keeping a close eye on the procession.

"Listen, you relied on others to save your life," he said quietly. "I'm choosing to rely on you to save the lives of my people."

I perked up and snapped my fingers at Ryder. When he glanced over, I zipped two fingers over my mouth. He understood my command and his magic went up like a curtain around us, a bubble that allowed us to speak freely.

"Go on. You won't be overheard, but you don't have long before Phenex picks up on it," I cautioned.

"You have to take him down."

"I figured as much," I said dryly, my eyes slitting as Kaleal pressed against them. "But *how?*"

He shifted on his feet. "There's a myth that even once freed, djinn can become bound once more, as long as you know their true name. It's part of the reason they kill their former masters, so they can never release that information."

I blinked and thought back on my conversations with the djinn. I had a funny feeling I already knew exactly what his name was.

"I've been searching for his name for years," Maat said, lowering his voice. "The Earth Temple has the biggest, most selective library in the world. It's slow-going, but I'm making progress. With the help of you and your friends, we could probably get through more books faster. I need help, but I don't have many people I can trust." He heaved a frustrated sigh, and I glanced around the nearly empty cavern, realizing that we were quickly running out of time to talk.

"Phenex... he's got a way of manipulating my people," Maat said. "They're scared of him, of what he can do to them if they go against him. I understand why, but my father was a leader among our kind, and so was his father before him, and his father before him. I owe it to them to break the chains he's wrapped us in, but I don't think I can do it alone anymore."

"You're still sure you don't want to tell me what Phenex has on you?" I asked.

"I can't." He sounded like I was asking him to rip out his heart. Maybe I was. "I can't."

I hummed noncommittally. I understood what it was like to have a secret that I literally couldn't spill. Kaleal chuckled darkly. "Alright then. What do we do once we have his name? How do we bind him?"

"I'm hoping to also find that in the library," he said. "And normally blood is involved in ancient rituals, or so I've been told."

"Time's up," Ryder said, snagging my elbow. Cool air rushed over me as he dropped his magic. "We're already drawing attention."

One of the nero was watching us suspiciously as he held a torch at the opening of the tunnel. When Maat passed by to catch up with the rest of the group, I caught his eye.

"I'll help however I can," I said, then turned to Ryder as if I'd been talking to him all along. The incubus's smile was forced and he wrapped an arm around me protectively until we caught up with Finn and Joseph.

I didn't talk much, trying to figure out what to do with the information I had. Not knowing the binding spell would be tricky. And I wasn't sure I could even perform it. The goosebumps trembling along my arms stiffened the more we walked, and soon it grew impossible to ignore the pull of magic.

Joseph had skirted a particularly deep hole when Phenex called out our next left turn. One of the nero protested, but was cut off sharply. The line started moving again.

"Do you feel that?" I hissed to the God of Air, touching my sternum that ached from the constant pounding of magic. Ryder's golden eyes narrowed at our exchange.

"I thought I was the only one," he said, rubbing the same spot on his chest.

"I don't think it's normal."

"Neither do I," he said. "I'm glad we're on the same page. It's why I like you so much."

We hit the fork in the road.

There was an obvious pull to the right, yet the group had gone left. We traded looks.

"He'll catch us if we're not fast," I said. But Joseph was already gone, a gust of wind marking his departure. I scoffed and scrutinized Ryder who was already grinning saucily and rubbing his hands together.

"Does this mean I get to create a diversion?" he asked.

Chapter 23

We raced through the shrinking tunnel, our way lit by a flame I cupped in my palm, the looming sense of danger chasing our heels as we hurdled toward a mystery begging to be solved. The closer we got, the greater the pounding in my chest grew. Kaleal rode close to the surface, keeping watch as we ran faster.

"It's ahead," Joseph called.

I risked a glance backward in the dark. "No Phenex, yet, though he must know we're gone."

Joseph slowed so I could catch up, our feet pounding in tandem, my braid flopping against my back. In the dark ahead, an arch appeared and we stopped before passing through, panting hard, glancing at one another with trepidation, wondering if this was something we truly wanted to do, a barrier we wanted to cross.

The opening was slightly stooped, low enough that Joseph would have to duck. When I moved my flames closer, we discovered its frame was etched delicately with little flowers and vines. What lay beyond was a void, dark and sucking and ominous. I tried throwing my fire magic through it, but it was no use. An invisible wall prevented the flames from crossing the base.

Joseph's throat bobbed, his eyes bright. "I bet he'll know we're here once we breach whatever that barrier is."

"Probably."

"But he already knows where we're going."

"Probably."

"Time to take a page out of your book, I guess," he said, and before I could process the words, he stepped through the opening.

I released a breath I hadn't known I was holding when he emerged safely on the other side. He looked back. "It feels like stepping through silk." He paused. "I can feel it's a room. It's not particularly large, but definitely closed off."

Even if I wanted to turn back now, the press of magic wouldn't let me. I counted to three, then slipped across the invisible line. Joseph was right, the sensation was like cobwebs brushing against my face, the surface of water sucking at my skin. Subtle yet pleasant. When I opened my eyes, he was right there, hair tangled and mussed and badly in need of washing.

"Light it up."

My lighter clicked and it was as if my magic instinctively knew where to go. I gasped and covered my mouth when the flame filled a trench dug along the four walls, the shimmer it cast burned impossibly bright. The polished gold of the walls and ceiling refracted the light, turning the room to day. Each wall bore a copper shelf at eye level; on each self were a dozen items. The magical aura emanating from them was similar to the aura of Phenex's emerald, and I knew we'd hit jackpot.

Carefully, I approached one wall, my arms wrapped around myself as I greedily drank in the offerings. Two fat, matching vases the size of my fist and the color of newly-blossomed violets were closest, their lids latched closed with clever little hooks concealed in the clay. Next was an Arabic lamp, its brass finish tarnished with age. The list went on: a wooden container the size of a box of cards, a hollowed-out book bound by satin ribbon, a crystal decanter, a sapphire inkwell with a rubber stopper.

At the end, tucked in the corner of the wall, was a slender vial the length of my index finger. Silver caps clasped the top and bottom of the tube, through one was woven a long, brassy chain. The glass played peekaboo through the delicate, swirling pattern of silver encasing it.

I wondered if these were the same containers that had been used in the past to bind Phenex and his brothers. When I reached for one an explosion rocked the tunnel behind us.

"Time's up," Joseph yelled as dust and sand slammed the barrier at the doorway. "Any idea what these might be? Or why they're down here?"

"Remember that story you told Phenex?" Another explosion rocked the tunnel, this one much closer. "I don't think it's only a story."

I snatched up the pendant and slipped the chain over my head, its strange magic dissipating as if it never had been. Hurriedly, I shoved the vial beneath my clothing, and when I looked up I jumped at the shadow darkening the doorstep.

"I knew you Gods would be more trouble than you're worth," Phenex hissed roughly. "And now you've forced my hand."

A booted foot stepped past the barrier and I barely caught a flash of needle-like teeth when the world around me erupted. My body was sucked into a sandstorm, barely able to move as I was pummeled from all sides. It was sheer luck that I'd pulled my arms high to protect my face. I couldn't get a sense of up or down or where I might be going. Fear blanketed me in waves. If this was what it felt like to be buried alive, I wished it would end already. There was so much sand and dust in the air I could barely breathe.

Then the world stopped.

I was buried.

I'd never been more horrified.

I clawed at the sand encasing me, not knowing or caring if I was going in the right direction, a desperate drive to survive pushing me harder and harder. When dizziness hit and I was sure I'd pass out from the lack of oxygen, my fingers punched through the sand and met... open air.

With one last burst of energy, I shoved myself up and out. I clawed at my throat, my knees and legs burning where they met the sun-heated earth, hacking and coughing, choking in sand-soaked oxygen. The black haze cloaking my vision slowly faded as my lungs filled.

Outside.

I'd made it outside.

My limbs trembled with the shock of nearly dying *again* as I scanned the horizon. Had Joseph survived? It certainly felt like I was alone out here. Even Kaleal had vanished. I patted my body, wincing at the bruises already forming, realizing half my clothing was gone and the rest was shredded. To my immense relief, I'd retained my knives and my lighter. My necklaces were still intact.

I was shaking sand from my hair when the earth trembled again.

The gear of the lighter caught when I clicked it. It was filled with sand. I shook it, a cry escaping my lips, trying to dislodge the grains when the ground trembled again. The lever wouldn't depress. I didn't know how else to spark a fire and my water magic was still out of commission...

My hands tingled.

The earth shuddered one more time and a yawning hole opened in front of me. I scrambled backward before the cascading sand could suck me down with it. Quiet moments passed before hands appeared at the rim of the hole, the nero emerging one by one. I'd grown used to their quiet ways, their easy confidence, their laughter around Joseph, so to see their eyes as flat and blank as they were now was more than a little horrifying.

Behind them, on a wave of sand, rose the darkened figure of Phenex wrapped in his dark blue cloak. He floated over the small army, nimbly landing before them, his aura dark in my Iridescence. Though he still appeared relatively human, the creature I'd always sensed lurking beneath his skin had finally emerged: his teeth were sharper, the bones of his face longer, and his eyes glowed with the white heat of the sun.

"You just don't die, do you?" he spat, the sandpaper quality of his voice was grating.

"I am a bit averse to the idea. Though you're certainly welcome to keep trying." My throat ached from taking in sand and I spat. I dropped the useless lighter and drew my dagger. I hoped my friends were alright, though part of me worried that Ryder's distraction hadn't been enough and Phenex had finished them off. Or buried them alive as he had me.

I bit my tongue so hard it bled. No. I couldn't think like that. They had to be in there somewhere. I refused to believe that Phenex had taken them out that easily.

"I intend to do more than try," Phenex said and his cloak billowed in the wind. "I'll even do you the courtesy of killing you myself."

"How thoughtful of you." My palms tingled again, as they did when...

Water.

I could sense water.

No, more than sense it. I latched on to the reservoir with all I had, ripping the water up through the ground as fast as it would go, but it wasn't fast enough. I didn't know how I could reach it this time, maybe this particular reservoir was closer to the surface, maybe Phenex had dislodged something with his blast of magic, but I wasn't about to complain. Behind Phenex, I spotted Maat. Worry twisted his lips before he firmed them and jerked his eyes from mine, his face set and still as his comrades.

"Tell me, did you lock away the nero's magic before or after the last round of Gods died?" I called, wishing the water would move faster, wishing I had *anything* that would end this right here and now.

Phenex pulled the emerald from his pocket and held it high. The power radiating from it nearly blinded me, so I fixated on Maat's face instead.

"They placed their trust in me several thousand years ago," Phenex said. "They asked me for help out of a tricky spot and in exchange, I... took the key to which they bound their magic. Can't blame fools for being fools now, can I?"

He crooked a finger and my friend moved forward, his steps stilted. My stomach bottomed out.

"If they ever want to get their magic back, all they have to do is serve me until I'm through with them—indentured in both body and mind. Simple enough, right?"

"That's slavery," I yelled. "You were a slave once, too, Phenex. How can you live with yourself forcing that on someone else?"

His face flickered and he shrugged. "You mistake me for someone with a conscience. I spent an eternity enslaved after my father tricked me. My sympathy died when he locked me away. When I got out, I wasted no time making sure no one could best me ever again—including my siblings. And in my rise to the top, I picked up a few odds and ends, including a few followers. These ones are a bit more devoted to the cause, I suppose you could say."

"You're not a deity," I snarled, a cry nearly ripping from my chest when Phenex hauled Maat up and pressed a knife, startlingly similar to the one he'd given me, to the nero's throat. "A God may have created you, but that hardly makes you equal, no matter how much power you take by force."

He wasn't listening to me though, the djinn had lost interest in this conversation. He grabbed the top of Maat's fiery hair, jerking his head back. I willed the nero to move, to escape, to do something other than

158

allow this to happen. Why wasn't he fighting back? His magic was gone but his control wasn't.

"Sometimes followers must be taught a lesson. And this one broke the cardinal rule, spilling secrets he wasn't meant to." Phenex knew what Maat had told me, he'd heard through Ryder's barrier. Impossible. "Too bad."

His knife moved and I screamed, surging forward as the tingles in my palm seared painfully. A horn blasted. Once, twice, followed by a third longer tone.

Phenex froze, his eyes moving over my shoulder. His lips twisted, exposing sharp teeth.

"Then again, I'd rather watch this play out first," he said.

Chapter 24

"What did you do?" I screamed. My arms jerked as the full weight of my magic slammed into me. About damn time. "What did you do?"

He pointed with the knife. "Take a look for yourself."

Zipping toward us was the bulging body of some strange cross between a plane and a helicopter. The desert sun winked off its gunmetal gray hide as it made its swift approach. My mouth went dry when it drew close enough to make out the O with a forward slash through its center embossed on the side of the aircraft.

The Order.

And on board... my magic recoiled.

"You called Geoffrey?" I snapped back to the djinn, hating the wild desperation of my question. I redirected the magic skyward, needing to feel my element all around me—especially while caught between two fronts. And where the stars were Finn and Ryder? "You told him where we were? I thought we had a deal!"

"A deal you broke when you deviated from our plan." His smirk ate up his whole face. He'd released Maat who remained on his knees, blood dripping from his wound, his arms hanging limp from their sockets. His glazed eyes were unfocused. "You'll also do well to remember I made a deal with The Order first. It's called playing the field."

The aircraft touched down, appearing more like a bloated ship than a plane. Its wide belly scraped the sand as lights flashed along the hull. A door opened in the side and shouted commands drifted down. From the opening shot a long ramp. Everything in me went cold when a figure appeared at the top of the ramp. The golden cane Geoffrey clutched tapped the thin, red carpet as he stepped forward.

My Hand appeared as he had in our shared dream. Thick, blotchy burns roped around his neck, along his jaw, and up one side of his face, where they vanished in his shortly-shorn hair. The slashes of scars marring his cheeks were twisted on one side, the other side a smooth and painful contrast of normalcy. Across his forehead blazed the signatures of the Gods marking him as theirs.

At the base of the ramp, he paused, drinking in the sight of me in this torn and broken state. Behind him filed twin rows of soldiers, their helmets and black uniforms as familiar to me as my own magic. Speaking of magic... the sky overhead roiled with dark clouds, thunderheads billowing, ready for release.

"Zara." Geoffrey tasted my name, savoring it. I wrinkled my nose. "It's good to see you again."

"I'd say the feeling is mutual," I said, "but then I'd be lying, wouldn't I?"

"Good to know your spirit isn't as battered as the rest of you appears to be." He stepped onto the sand as purple lightning forked across the sky. "I would hate to beat you at anything but at your best."

"What makes you think you're going to beat me?" I had him right where I needed him. If only my friends would find their way to me. Only then would I feel more certain about the outcome of what was about to hit.

"Do you remember what I told you the last time we met?" The soldiers fanned out behind him, guns raised and aimed at me. "I meant every word. Knowing you're powerless, drained of water, and apparently incapable of drawing fire…" He motioned at the lighter at my feet. "It's too perfect an opportunity to carry through. This is where it ends for you, Zara. Phenex, thank you for this… unexpected gift."

I dropped my head submissively while calling my magic to me, wild and fast and free. The torrent flooded me, gushing and churning and clamoring for my attention, *wanting* me to use it. *Demanding* I use it. My arms and legs shook with the force of it.

"Of course," Phenex's drawl was low and smooth. I knew that tone, the deception lurking beneath the surface. "It was too prime an opportunity to pass up."

Geoffrey raised his arm and the soldiers clutched their triggers. "Any last words, Zara? There's no coming back from the dead this time."

"How about five?" I whipped back to Phenex, allowing the blaze of my magic to light my eyes. "Maat, now!"

The nero at his feet sprang to life, ripping the emerald from Phenex's loose grasp, his body blazing with white light before I flung a wall of water around me, a swirling tornado that launched me into the sky and away from the gunfire that erupted from the soldiers. At the top of the waterspout, I nimbly spun, head tipped toward the heavens, arms flung wide, glorying in the sensation of my element flooding me, filling me like it was meant to be…

Then released it in a violent surge, a physical ripple racing the length of the storm clouds.

They burst, releasing their showers as I toppled from the top of the tower, grinning crazily as the rain splattered against my face, remembering another similar fall. I flipped as the ground surged closer, hair streaming behind me. At the last moment, I wrapped myself in a cocoon of water that cushioned my fall and I tumbled to my feet, twin swords of ice sprouting from my palms.

Phenex was back-peddling as the nero charged as a unit, rushing him with all the fury of their unleashed sand magic, uncaring of the storm sweeping over them. Leading the way was Maat, who spun one of those steely spears with vicious intent. Geoffrey only had eyes for me, but before I could engage, a hole opened in the ground and Joseph burst from it, yellow eyes blazing as the rest of my friends followed.

"He's mine," he snarled, skating on the air, rushing for Geoffrey with a pair of spinning balls swirling in his hands. The pixies roared up from the opening, black magic blazing as they darted for the dozens of Order soldiers, hacking and clawing at limbs without care. The kelpie thundered past, hooves churning in the muddy sand, rushing for another cluster of soldiers.

Ryder stopped beside me, muscles flexing in his glossy, black second skin. The horns sprouting from his head curled around his temples and beneath his eyes in a twisted mask of bone. Behind the mask, his eyes swirled red and gold and black. "Sorry for taking so long, glowstick. Phenex apparently knew where to find more of those snakes and they slowed us down." His lips pressed hard against mine in a burning kiss, then he released me. "Glad you found your magic again. Let's crush these hellions."

Then he was gone, sweeping for Geoffrey who flung bolts of fire at Joseph. The God of Air easily blocked them and countered with wide panes of cutting air. With rain streaming from my face, dripping down my chin, I clutched the vial hanging from my neck. It had swung out from beneath my clothing when I fell.

I left my friends to rain retribution down on the Order and turned to the djinn whose crimes were too numerous to count. Phenex had unleashed an army of sand soldiers who the nero were cutting down as quickly as they rose, wielding blades of their own magic. Maat himself squared off against the djinn, his spear a blur of brown and silver as he sparred against the demigod.

I cut down a wave of Phenex's soldiers who rushed at me with swords, relishing in the familiar movement of muscles as I blocked their thrusts and split them up the middle. When they bogged me down, I froze the sand, carving a path in front of me. A path right for Maat and Phenex who clashed in a wild swirl of spinning sand. How they could see let along attack was beyond me, but despite his lack of practice, Maat wielded his magic with an intensity that reminded me of myself.

"You think you can beat me?" Phenex roared, delivering one particularly brutal assault that knocked the nero back a few steps. "You'll never beat me. You're nothing."

He dropped his sand magic and black smoke spilled from his palms. Maat snarled then went still as he inhaled, the smoke seeping in his mouth and nose, soaking into his skin. He twitched, falling forward, still fighting the effects of whatever it was. His copper eyes went wild with fury and panic. The djinn raised his sword, stalking forward.

"You've always been a troublesome brat," he crooned. "But now that you've got your magic back, it will be my true honor to strip it from you again—along with your soul."

"Hey, Phenex." I flung a bolt of water, drilling him in the side, knocking him off-balance. "Forget about me?"

The djinn brushed sand off his shirt and spat. "Ready for me to finish you off?" He threw up a wall of sand that blocked a dozen spears of ice. "So eager for death?"

The ground yawned open under my feet, but this time I was prepared. I ripped a wave of water beneath me, allowing it to push me forward as I crafted arrows, launching them in flashing volleys. Once back on flat ground, I threw a wave at the djinn as his sand creatures attacked. I dodged the first one that looked a little like a bulldog, but the second knocked me flat. I froze the obstacle solid, then shattered it with a thought. I rose, muscles humming, braced for Phenex's next attack.

"Afraid to fight me like a man? Or do you only have fancy tricks up your sleeve?"

He bared his sharpened teeth and swiped rain-slickened hair from his forehead, his chest heaving with exertion. He bent and picked up his sword.

"I'd rather wipe you from this earth from my own hand anyway," he said.

I flattened my palm against the pendant, remembering Maat's vague instructions.

I had the container. I had his name. I now needed his blood.

My arms jarred when our blades connected. My sword buckled, cracking down the center, but miraculously held. The driving rain lashed at my face when I withdrew, then I struck again, aiming for his side. He blocked it and thrust for my chest, forcing me to dance to the side. Again and again, we came together, swords clanging, limbs brushing, equally matched in this war of physical strength.

Until I found my opening.

His sword came down, but rather than block it, I allowed the blow to land. The blade bit deep into my arm, bruising the bone. I dropped my weapon and grabbed his arm, using it to curl *into* his body, while reaching for the small knife he'd given me. I slashed it across his chest, right above his sternum, and slammed my hand to the blood that welled there. He knocked me away, but I had what I needed. My eyes blazed triumphantly.

My own blood slicked down my arm, mingling with his, as I yanked the chain out of my shirt and ripped the cap off the pendant in one move. His eyes went wide as he stumbled, mouth opening in horror.

"You're the one who told me the simplest attack is the most effective." I swiped my hand down the length of the vial. The silver encasing the vial shone bright as starlight, burning so hot I felt the imprint melting into my skin, but still I held on. "I don't know any fancy words, but consider your freedom revoked, Xenith."

The djinn shrieked, his body turning to smoke that was sucked into the opening of the vial with a roaring howl that nearly punctured my eardrums. Then it was gone. My muscles felt weak, my arm burned, as I capped the vial and dropped it against my chest with a thump.

Around me, the rain pounded, clearing away the evidence of the fight.

Chapter 25

Geoffrey escaped.

That information tumbled around my head as I rolled Phenex's cage between my fingers.

"I almost had him trapped in a box, but he did this peculiar thing with the sand," Joseph demonstrated dramatically with his hands, "and he slipped away. I swear I blinked, then the plane jetted off. It was crazy. Bodies everywhere and he turned coward."

Rose tied off a bandage stained black with blood around Briar's forearm. "He's slippery as soap, that one, but we'll get him one of these days when he can't run. Right, Zara?"

I'd sunk into some weird murky part of my mind and couldn't quite claw my away out. I'd only grudgingly responded to my name when Ryder had come for me after the battle and led me back to the group. While Finn filled our canteens in the rapidly shrinking puddles, Rose had talked me into healing my arm. Though it was fixed, the limb still didn't feel connected.

"I think we learned Geoffrey is a problem that will need to be solved sooner rather than later." The words moved like sludge from my mouth. Physically, I was the best I'd felt in weeks, but emotionally... everything felt dark. "He's not going to stop getting in our way. I'm tired of it. I don't see how any of us can focus on figuring out how to stop a nuclear apocalypse with him constantly snapping at our heels.

I can barely think about how to solve that problem already without him launching these attacks."

I pushed some frizzy hair behind my ear and clenched the vial hard. The sun had dried us quickly once I'd banished the storm clouds. The silver warmed beneath the pads of my fingers. I lifted it, watching the smoky substance that was Phenex swirl angrily. He must be furious with me. Gods, I was faintly furious with me.

"You did the right thing." Maat crouched beside me, knees splayed wide for balance. He toyed with the emerald he had yet to put away and scratched his head. "Phenex was a monster. He imprisoned me, he imprisoned my people... for a very long time. He needed to be taken down."

I chewed my tongue and tucked the pendant beneath my clothing once more. It rattled softly against my Water rings.

"Good riddance, I say," echoed Ryder, following the movements with intent. I'd filled him and the others in on how I'd defeated the djinn while patching up other injured members of our party. "If he hadn't betrayed you now, he would have later."

I knew that. I understood that. But it didn't sit right with me, enslaving someone because he'd wrongly enslaved others. Especially someone who'd already escaped his chains before. However, no matter how much I twisted it around in my head, I couldn't figure out another way to take him down, so inside the vial he'd remain until I had a better plan.

"Are you sure you don't want to take him with you?" I asked Maat for the dozenth time.

"Nah, he's all yours. You sealed him in there, you're his new master." Oh yeah. I guessed he was probably back to his wish-granting, soul-stealing ways. "Besides, we need to air out the palace, make it ours again. There's no place for him there anymore, even locked away."

He and the other nero had decided to head back to base after depositing us at the Earth Temple. Now that they finally had their magic back, they were eager to return to the rest of their people and spread the good news. They were ready to reclaim their lives and figure out where to go from here.

I was happy for them. They'd lived with enough evil for too long.

I surveyed our little group. Funny to think how things had changed in a fortnight. Gone were our luxurious digs, our fashionable clothing, even our animals, but in its place lingered a firm sense of unity, one only acquired through hard work and surviving something truly inexplicable together.

Rose, Briar, and Vera had returned from saying goodbye to two more of their sisters. I'd asked to go with them to honor Oak and Laurel's last rites, but they'd told me to stay. Granted, Rose seemed touched I'd asked. A few nero had also perished, and the funeral pyre had already consumed their bodies and souls.

"There's something you should know," Maat said, fiddling with his ripped sleeve. My own clothing was barely clinging together at the seams, reduced to a simple long-sleeve shirt, my hardy gloves, and thick canvas pants. He was confident we were only about four hours out from the temple, or else I'd seriously worry about the implications of staying out in the relentless sun.

"If it's another djinn, I may need you to figure that one out on your own." I cracked my first grin of the day. It felt nice.

"Not another djinn. Gods help us, there's only one out there." He licked his cracked lips. "It's about the Earth Temple. You need to be on your toes there, it's not a particularly pleasant place."

"I'm starting to wonder if there's anything pleasant about having magic." I swatted at the sand with a heady dash of raw bitterness. "Most of the time it seems like more trouble than it's worth."

"That's not true. There's beauty, too." He flicked a hand at the ground where a small cactus at his feet sprouted a single red flower. "But not there. The temple is led by a group called Davos. They're a council originated from the teachings of the original Earth God Davarius—so they claim anyway." He closed his eyes and stroked the scar along his nose.

"They're twisted. You'll understand when you meet them. They don't like me very much, so I try to avoid them most of the time when I'm bartering for supplies." He flashed a wicked smile. "Be careful, ok?"

"Basically, you're telling me I've traded one power-hungry freak for a *bunch* of power-hungry freaks." With effort, I got to my feet. He quirked a brow. "Sounds pretty par for the course."

"One more thing—"

"Someone's coming," Joseph yelled, spurring us all into action. He pointed to the western horizon and the dark specks hovering above the dirt. I could sense their signatures. "Whoever they are, they're coming in fast."

"Sand skiffs." Maat shielded his eyes, squinting. "Must be Earth Temple guards. If that's the case, I would be best served not catching their attention."

I shook my head mournfully as he shoved the emerald in his pocket. He yanked me close in a one-armed hug, then released me all too quickly. "If you need anything, anything at all, I owe you a great debt. Contact me anytime for anything."

I stared at him quizzically, wondering what was happening.

"Say you accept, please?" He clutched my wrist hard, his eyes bright with sincerity.

"I—I accept?" I hissed through my teeth when my arm seared. He, too, grimaced and released my arm. Circling our wrists were identical black tattoos. Great. More magic I didn't know anything about.

"There. Now it's official." When I rubbed the raw skin, gaping, Maat returned to the nero. They discussed something for a half-second, before transforming into small, yellow cats with long legs and even longer black-ringed tails. They wasted no time slinking away, disappearing in the endless waves of sand.

"Did that happen?" asked Finn, scratching his head. "What was their hurry anyway?"

"He didn't say, exactly," I said, scanning our small group. Two Gods, one kelpie, one incubus, and three pixies. "Are you guys ready for this? Whatever it might be?"

Ryder grinned. "Wouldn't have it any other way."

The pixies thudded their chests with their fists, then raised them high in a salute.

Finn and Joseph shook their heads wryly as the long, hovering platforms—what Maat had called sand skiffs—stopped and kicked up sand around us. On each platform stood two burly dudes, arms big as boulders and faces decorated thickly with ink. I wasn't picking up on any magic, but they might be able to do some damage with the spears they gripped.

They also didn't speak, merely stared at us somberly.

One minute bled into two. And then a handful more.

"Would you mind turning off the jets," Ryder yelled over the hum of the engines, circling a finger over his head. "This dust is doing something terrible to my allergies. When I start sneezing it's impossible to—"

"Who are you?" The guy in the nearest skiff spoke first. He'd shaved his eyebrows and red-streaked tattoos fanned out from the corners of his eyes.

I tucked the tips of my fingers into what remained of my pockets. "Who's asking?"

The engines whirred faster, kicking up more sand. Finn elbowed Ryder who held a hand up to shield his eyes. Only about five yards separated us now. The big guy glared at him.

"We are representatives of the Lost City. If you don't answer me now, we're about to have a pretty serious problem on our hands." He shook his spear as the man behind him fingered the trigger of a large gun.

I sketched a bow. "Zara Ramone, God of Water and First of Four at your service. This humble young gentleman beside me is the God of Air, Joseph Windrunner." I pointed around the circle, naming off members of our group until I ran out.

The guy blinked a few times, his face firm and flat and blank.

"What are you doing here?" he asked.

"Believe it or not, we're looking for you."

"Were you responsible for the disturbance we detected this way?"

I scrubbed the back of my neck, grimacing at the fresh layer of sand I found there. I pointed somewhere behind me in the direction of the battlefield we'd abandoned. "If you go maybe one-hundred yards in that direction, you'll find about three dozen bodies. I can't say for certain, but that might be the disturbance you're talking about."

Not-so-big-guy with the gun muttered something too low for me to hear.

"What do you want?"

"A tall glass of ice water would be great," I said, then winced. Rose chortled across from me, barely covering her mouth with her hand, though her eyes danced merrily. I sensed Finn glaring daggers, so I was careful to avoid looking in his direction. I loathed that expression.

Big Guy wasn't impressed either. "I don't like your tone."

"Listen, I'm sorry. I'm hot, I'm tired. I've been through a hell of a lot in these past few days." I toed the sand. "All I want is find your God and give him his magic back, then maybe take a shower and grab a nap if I'm lucky." I mulled that over. "Though it doesn't have to be in that order. The shower can come first, I suppose."

Big Guy blinked again.

172

Sand went down my windpipe and I coughed. Ryder had a point. They could have killed the engines.

It floored me, though, when the guard cracked a smile. "Get on board, *God*. All of you." He swung the spear in a slow circle. "As eager as you are to visit our temple, we'll see if you feel the same once you arrive."

Chapter 26

"You don't look like a God."

"Yeah?" I scrubbed at the underside of my wrist. Nope. The tattoo encircling it wasn't going anywhere. The small sunburst directly over my artery was also new. Maybe bleach would help. "What's a God supposed to look like?"

Big Guy—whose name was actually Adio—surveyed the deck. Rose and Briar flanked me, masking their throaty yawns with the backs of their hands. Joseph was nerding out over the control panel at the front of the skiff while Finn stretched out on a bench beside him, the back of his head cupped in his hands, battered boots swaying with the movement of the ship. Both of them were scruffier than normal, with at least a few day's growth of hair on their faces.

Ryder had managed to stay clean-cut somehow and mimicked my posture across from me: back against the rail, arms braced so his biceps bulged, legs crossed, one toe jabbing a hole in the floorboards.

"Like that guy." Adio thrust his spear at the incubus. Ryder's golden gaze lightened, his grin blinding. Great, an ego boost was just what he needed. "You look at him, you know what you're gonna get. Lots of brawn, lots of power, maybe not a lot of brain."

My jaw dropped in delight as the incubus glowered, feigning indifference by shaking sand from his hair.

Adio wasn't done yet. "You though, you're shifty." I barely restrained the laugh threatening to burst from my chest. "I had a girlfriend once, she was shifty. She ran away with my best friend."

I patted his shoulder companionably. Poor guy. "I'm sorry to hear that. Women are the worst."

If he had eyebrows, they would have furrowed. "But you're a woman."

"Exactly." I winked at him dramatically. "So I have it on good authority."

"Gods," Rose muttered, scrubbing her hand down her face. "Save me now." I jabbed an elbow into her rib cage and she glared from the slit between her fingers. "You really want to go there, Zara?"

I eyed her extra-digited fingers. "Maybe not."

"Didn't think so."

"Yeah, you definitely don't act like a God," Adio repeated, nodding once as if that solidified the deal. Rose and I exchanged glances. "Just like the other one."

"Joseph?" I flipped my thumb at the helm where the God of Air pretended like he wasn't listening. Around us, dunes whizzed by at speeds I couldn't comprehend. It was a marked difference from traveling by camelback. "Don't let him fool you. He's in disguise."

Joseph shifted a long piece of hair out of his face, still bent over the controls the pilot fangirled over. I tugged on my collar. "Most of the time he's a monster to be around. Throwing stuff across the room, slamming doors, raising all kinds of holy hell. He's got this deal where he can create a ghost version of himself, and he'll follow you around without you knowing." I mock shuddered. "It's horrible. Try keeping secrets from someone like that. You can't! You're lucky I made him pinkie swear to behave."

How I said that with a straight face was beyond me.

"Stones and bones," Rose growled. Joseph showed me his back and Ryder snorted. Adio eyed the God with newfound cynicism. He started to say something, but a dark spot along the horizon snagged my attention. Walls of dark stone arched high to the skies, topped with metal spikes and electrified wire and men with guns. Our sand skiff was aimed at a pair of gates garnished with bleached femurs and skulls. Beyond those gates, looming high over those walls, were the distinct triangles of pyramids. Three of them. My head tipped back as we approached the Lost City, trying to fathom their magnificent height.

The doors slowly swung wide with a piercing shriek. Our pilot slowed the skiff, the other two following our lead, and ghosted inside the walls. A small, stoic crowd had gathered, their energy radiating excitement. Like the nero, these people, too, wore brightly colored clothing and laced sandals. The men sported longer hair and thick beards, while the women observed behind wispy black veils that shielded their eyes beneath thick hoods. Bracelets of bleached bones were draped around wrists and ankles, others had strung strands of teeth around their necks and wove broken bits into their hair. One man who stood particularly close to us had what looked like a piece of skull clasped to the cup of his ear and I shivered. I wasn't sure what I'd expected, but this wasn't it.

Near the back of the masses stood a long line of steely-faced soldiers wearing bits of leather armor. Some held swords and bows while others clutched guns. I straightened my spine and lightly touched the blue-bladed dagger in its sheath on my thigh.

Adio had laughed when I'd offered it as we'd boarded, telling me that if we really were Gods, a puny little knife wouldn't matter much. To his credit, my magics were both operating at full blast. A river roared somewhere beyond the pyramids and I sensed flames devouring wood in controlled fire pits and ovens scattered around the city.

The skiff passed easily through the gaping spectators, approaching the nearest pyramid. On its sandstone steps stood thirteen figures in billowing robes white as swan's wings. Each of them wore masks of bones that jutted out from their faces, assembled to look like the skulls of a wide array of animals. Some I recognized, like the horse and the eagle. Other masks were more twisted as if some experiment had gone horribly wrong—like one that bore the unmistakable skull of a deer with a mouth filled with wolfish teeth.

I twisted my hands together, uncomfortable with the combination.

On the top step, standing alone, was a man wearing the skull of a large reptile—maybe a dragon? He raised his bare arms over his head when the skiff rolled to a stop. Adio nudged me with the butt of his spear. I stepped to the ground first.

Out in the desert, I hadn't minded the torn rags that were my clothes or the layer of hard-earned dirt and grime that streaked my face. But here, before this obvious show of power, I belatedly wished Adio had taken me up on my suggestion of stopping to bathe first. For the first time in weeks, in front of all these people, I realized my own odor, the heady stink of sweat and sun.

"Welcome to the Lost City, home of the Earth Temple," Dragon said, his voice carrying to the crowd behind us. It was impossible to make out his eyes through the mask's blackened sockets. He moved down two stairs. "You may not be aware, but you are the first visitors we have welcomed in nearly two decades. We closed our borders to any and all we didn't know, only reopening them recently at the request of a close associate."

I brushed my shirt where the vial burned against my chest.

Two guesses who that was.

They even talked alike: smooth and polished and offensively polite.

"While we are fortunate you not only made the dangerous trek across the Momani Desert, your journey is still not yet complete," Dragon continued. "Two of you claim to be Gods, but we know two of the Gods perished long ago. If you are truly those mighty sovereigns and

177

not mere impostors, you must prove yourselves in the shadows of our sacred pyramids."

"Well this ought to be fun," Joseph said dryly, throwing his voice so only I could hear it. "I love having to prove myself over and over again."

I rolled my eyes, hoping this wouldn't be a repeat of our greeting at Phenex's palace. A headache throbbed in the back of my head.

"We are Davos, the council in command of the Earth Temple, and as per our law, we require a demonstration. Should your demonstration of power and ability prove satisfactory, then, and only then, will you and your guards be permitted to stay within our walls."

Davos. I recalled Maat's warning.

Magic burned in my fingertips and I followed the glowing strands back to the smallish robed figure standing on the lowest step. He wore one of the twisted masks, a creature bearing both the heavy tusks of a boar but also the large, flat eye sockets of an owl. Behind those darkened sockets, I sensed him watching me. The magic flowing between us felt familiar and I eyed the connection. It was kind of green. Could this be the God? If so, why wasn't I certain about it, like I had been when I'd met Joseph?

The God of Air heaved a sigh and stepped forward. I'd missed my cue. "I'm Joseph Windrunner, God of Air. While I'm not sure what you will find satisfactory in terms skill, I sincerely hope you find my demonstration worth your valuable time."

In a small show of theater, he brushed the skin beneath his eyes, muttering lightly, then raised his hand over his head, wrist quirked, and brought his fingers together slowly.

The world went quiet.

The temperature, too, dropped, and I wrapped my arms around myself as I shivered, wondering what he was up to.

A few minutes passed.

Not a grain of sand swirled, not a single person in the considerable crowd whispered.

When I realized what he'd done, a slow smile crawled across my face.

Oh, he was brilliant.

Dragon stepped forward, arms spread wide. His sandals moved silently over the gritty stone steps as he gesticulated. I imagined he was speaking, maybe even shouting, though none of us could hear it. We also couldn't hear the blast of the horn when the soldier next to him raised the polished instrument to her lips.

Joseph had literally silenced the world.

With that realization, the curtain lifted as the lingering note of the horn vaporized like mist.

The hundreds around us sucked in a cumulative breath, eyes wide and mouths parted. Then slowly, oh so incredibly slowly, did they begin clapping. Joseph didn't so much as smile as he stared down Dragon. Only when the jawbone dipped, did he step back beside me.

"That was incredible," I cheered. He sneaked a glance at me out the corner of his eye. "How do you expect me to follow that?"

"I imagine you'll find some terribly, rambunctiously, unnecessarily reckless way to demonstrate your might like you normally do," he replied as the clapping faded. "I'd expect nothing less."

That was encouraging.

I prodded the spot in the back of my mind where Kaleal had taken to hiding lately. Nothing. I wondered if she was guarding the door again, protecting me against Geoffrey's fiery temper. Since she wasn't inclined to answer, I cracked my knuckles and stepped forward, my thoughts tumbling like leaves in the wind. I couldn't settle on one idea until I remembered what Maat had said about the beauty in magic.

Maybe strength wasn't all I was capable of.

"I'm Zara Ramone, God of Water and First of Four." I paused to allow the words time to inflate, to sink in. "I can't claim to possess the poise my partner here does, but I'll try my best nevertheless."

Like Joseph, I didn't need to motion for my magic to work, but the sweeping arm gestures helped me center myself, to draw the magic to me slowly, carefully, allowing it to grow and develop. With one long inhale, I lowered to the ground, my legs barely holding me a mere inch above the earth, and bowed deeply, magic to sweeping over me. I breathed out, and it froze as it touched my lips.

Overhead, feathery clouds gathered, their misty forms exactly what I required. I raised my face and then... let go. As one, rain spilled in a choreographed sheet, but before a single drop so much as touched those assembled, I closed my fist, halting the movement. Sweat streaked down my back and I fought the urge to shake from the exertion it took to hold that kind of power, to control it with immeasurable delicacy.

The next part of my plan was even more complicated.

Slowly, I carefully froze the droplets closest to the ground, crystallizing them in midair. From there, I worked in reverse, focusing intently on the blend of magic straining both my muscles and mind. It wanted to fight, it wanted to destroy... and that's what I'd done with it thus far, but now I *knew* my magic was so much more.

I wanted to be so much more.

I forced back those destructive impulses, freezing the water droplets one by one, all the way up to the clouds. Once the curtain was finished, my hands circled slowly, pushing the droplets into motion, shifting them into an icy pattern, weaving them in and out, around and around.

A spider's web emerged.

I couldn't resist shaking, this was worse than trying to hold up a house with one arm, but I couldn't stop now. I refused to stop despite the headache now thundering away. The wispy sensation of Kaleal even peeked out, drawn by the incredible pull of magic.

With one last thought, I dismissed the clouds and the sun emerged. The crowd gasped, some crying out with wonder, as the light shimmered off the millions of tiny beads, turning the creation to the glistening wonder I'd known it could be. I held it there, relishing those who reached toward the lowest hanging crystals.

When I hit my breaking point, I allowed my masterpiece to evaporate into the wind.

The thunder of applause beat back the torment of my headache and I grinned broadly at the crowd. Joseph hauled me against his side, shaking me with delight, and pressed a kiss against my hair. "That was beautiful," he said. "And not at all reckless."

Part of me wondered what Ryder had thought.

The web and all its tricky implications reminded me of him.

Chapter 27

The bone masks were really starting to piss me off.

Immediately following our displays of power, a guard had led us into the temple. From there, we'd proceeded through a labyrinth of meandering hallways and ended up... here. A boardroom. It boasted soaring ceilings and exposed wooden beams. Four long windows that started at the floor and stretched up and up and up were the only source of light. The skulls of animals hung from pegs on the walls, and the table around which we were seated appeared to be one very long cut of granite.

But it was still a boardroom.

I'd wanted a shower. Even a change of clothing would have been nice.

Nope, that wasn't in the cards.

Ryder snagged my hand and wove my fingers through his.

"Calm down," he whispered, golden eyes glowing with assessment. "If you don't, your headache will return, and then you'll be even more miserable than you are now."

He was probably right. With effort, I'd forced back the headache on the walk here, though I had a feeling if I didn't sleep soon it wouldn't matter because heady waves of exhaustion still hovered in the recesses of my mind.

The Lost City hasn't changed much at all, Kaleal said lazily, leaning

182

against a wall in my head. *Same conniving people, same hideous decor.*

I see you're feeling much better, I snipped. *Was the fight with Phenex not interesting enough for you?*

I knew you'd figure it out, she volleyed back. *You have an uncanny way of getting yourself out of tight spots. Like a mouse.*

The pride that had filled me deflated and I tried to block her out. Twelve of the council members had arrived. Our group was lined up along one side of the table, with Joseph and me at the center, while Davos took up the other side. The boy with the owl mask sat directly opposite me. His stare and creepy mask were already making me twitchy.

He had to be the God. There was no way he wasn't.

I rubbed my fingers together as if it would help me feel the texture of the magic connecting us. That sensation was still there, similar to the one I'd felt with Joseph, but it wasn't anywhere near as strong. I didn't understand what felt off about it, but I didn't like it.

We all turned when a door opened at the far end of the room. The other members of Davos stood, but my party remained seated as Dragon hovered at the entrance.

"Please, no need to get up," he said, and the members of Davos sat once more. Ryder arched a brow as he relinquished his grip on my hand. I immediately missed the casual intimacy, though I was able to focus better as Dragon took his time moving down the line of chairs. I wondered what had taken him so long.

And seriously, what was with the masks? Did they ever take them off? What did they mean?

Once he was seated and had arranged his robes just so, Dragon swung my way. "We appreciate you taking the time to speak with us on such short notice, Gods of Water and Air. We realize you had a long and strenuous journey, and we seek to streamline your stay here."

I folded my hands on the table. "We appreciate it."

"As you heard me say outside, we are Davos. Together we lead the Lost City, providing both protection for the people who live here and all their essential needs." He motioned at himself. "I'm called Seth, I'm what you would consider the head of our group, a president of sorts. To my left is Oron—" the boy in the owl mask—"he's in charge of our security forces…"

As Seth worked his way down the line, I kept my attention on the boy. Why wasn't he in charge? He was the God here, after all. Though, apparently, no one was willing to cop to that yet.

I imagine Davos has wrestled control from the Gods, seeing as they were gone for so long. Kaleal's words were a hush. *The temples of Water and Air are long gone, so it's hard to say how they operated on a day-by-day basis, but it's fascinating how Earth's power dynamic has changed. I wonder if Fire is similar.*

Joseph was introducing the various members of our party, and I inclined my head, continuing my intense scrutiny of the boy. His skin was the color of freshly poured coffee and he sat with a slight hunch. Unlike the bone jewelry most seemed to favor here, he wore eight brass rings emblazoned with the tri-peaked mountaintops of Earth's symbol. His nails were short and trimmed.

"How may we assist you today, Ms. Ramone?" Yeah, Seth definitely was giving me Phenex vibes. The vial seemed to heat against my chest in response.

"The answer is two-fold," I said. "May I speak bluntly?"

You really do remind me of myself, Kaleal mused, and I shushed her.

"I believe you already are, Ms. Ramone." He leaned on his elbows.

An irrational urge to rip the bleached bones from his face and fling them across the room bubbled before I shoved it down.

"How friendly are you with the Order?"

The dragon mask dipped. "We've not had contact since the attacks on the temples," he said.

Joseph shook his head, the movement minuscule. I flattened my palms on the table and selected my words carefully. "I deeply want our temples to not only cooperate with one another but to trust one another, too. There's a rich history there dating back to the dawn of time I'd like to respect and encourage. But I can't do that when you lie to my face. Would you please reconsider your answer."

Going for the jugular, I like it, Kaleal preened, raising her arms in a boxing fashion.

Seth's shoulders stiffened beneath his robe. Other members of Davos shifted in their seats.

"Very well," he said. "We've had correspondence with the Order and its Hand, however, relations haven't been particularly friendly given all that happened seventeen years ago. I will say that in light of recent events, they were keen to inform us about the circumstances surrounding you and the God of Air, here."

"So you're aware the Order is hunting us down, right?" I leaned back in my chair and folded my arms, fixing my attention on the boy. "How does your defense minister feel about all that? For Gods who are wanted by their own church, and who I presume are being painted as reckless magical creatures bent on destruction, you seemed to open the gates easily enough."

The boy didn't so much as twitch a finger.

I frowned and Seth tapped the table twice, reverting my attention back to him. Heat filled my cheeks as I glanced between them, not understanding the power dynamic or the boy's silence.

Seth spoke smoothly, cleanly. "We also understand the true relationship between the Gods and the Order, and are willing to assist as we can, even if it's something as simple as providing temporary shelter."

Temporary. Interesting, Kaleal hissed. *They really don't like you, do they?*

I tried a different peg. "Are you also aware that Geoffrey targeted me and Joseph in another harebrained attack not far from your temple walls?"

A clock in the corner of the room ticked.

"We did locate the bodies of Order soldiers not far from your position, yes. While we weren't fully informed of the circumstances, we drew natural assumptions."

"Allow me to draw another assumption for you. Geoffrey isn't going to stop." My tone brokered no argument. "He will not give up on his twisted crusade until I'm dead. Until Joseph is dead. Until *your* God is dead. Whether or not you've reached that conclusion yet is your business, but as the only God among the four who's had any real contact with him over the past two months, I can guarantee that I speak truthfully."

"Your conviction is noted."

The other members of Davos might as well not be here, not even the God. It was clear that Seth was in control. It was obvious that he might call himself the president, but I had a feeling it was more like a dictator. I wondered if Kaleal was correct, if the temple had, in fact, changed so much over the past two-thousand years that its God would no longer be viewed as the true authority.

"I will be up-front about my intentions." I rubbed my hands together. "I came here seeking the God of Earth, hoping that *he*"—I squinted at the boy who held still, stiff and unbending—"would join me on our fated quest to end an impending nuclear apocalypse. While I'm not sure which role we will all play in averting disaster, I assure you I still intend to accomplish that mission."

I drew myself up, still addressing Oron as Seth seethed. "But before that can happen, we must bring the Order to its knees. I want to remove Geoffrey from his position. I'll do whatever it takes to knock him out as an obstacle because that's what he is right now: a barrier standing between us and success. I simply can't allow that—especially

186

after his display this morning."

"You've spoken plainly until now, Water God." Seth's voice vibrated with an emotion I couldn't pinpoint. "What exactly are you asking of us?"

"I'm asking you to join me in my assault." The legs of my chair screeched on the stone floor as I shot to my feet. Joseph was a step behind. "I'm asking the Earth Temple to stand with Water and Air—and Fire if I have any say in it—in taking down a monster. Geoffrey is incredibly powerful and he's incredibly unstable. Throughout history, we've seen the disastrous consequences of that combination. Stand with me now and I'll remember forever. Help me end his reign so we can proceed as we were meant to."

Well said, Kaleal congratulated, bringing her semblance of hands together in a silent clap. *You are learning, aren't you?*

Seth, too, rose, the motion as sinuous as the dragon whose face he hid behind. He braced his hand on Oron's shoulder when the boy attempted to follow.

"You speak with the ferocity of a lion, Water God," Seth said. "But I wonder if your spirit is as strong. We'll consider your request. You'll have your answer by the week's end." He bowed, the motion mocking, but when he turned I shook my head.

"I wasn't done," I gritted.

Seth stilled, his back to me. "Oh?"

I turned my laser-like focus on the boy across from me. "Where is your God and when can I meet him?"

Infuriatingly, he remained silent, unbending beneath my harsh words.

"Soon," Seth quipped. "We in the Lost City move at a different pace than you may be accustomed, Water God. Patience, here, is a virtue."

"If I were him, I'd be about out of patience by now." I stared down those dark sockets of the boy who lingered, my own eyes burning, glowing, knowing. "Whenever he's ready, I've got something of his."

Chapter 28

"It isn't rooted in Latin, that's for sure," Joseph said.

I peered at him as the wind fluttered the pages of the thick volume open in my lap. My thumbs pressed down harder, securing my place in the text. Joseph flipped the original copy of *The Word* upside down and squinted at the spidery print with one eye closed.

"I am about ninety percent certain it reads like English." He closed the wafer-thin pages and dropped it in the metallic box at his hip. The book, fortunately, had been among our items recovered by Earth scouts when they'd gone to dispose of the soldier's bodies three days ago. "But don't get too excited, I haven't discounted that it reads right to left like Japanese, and that could change everything. I'm finishing up a few keys today that should help."

"You have me on pins and needles over here," I muttered dryly, giving up on my own reading. After the meeting, we were told that we were free to explore the pyramid but to not step foot on the grounds outside. This was the first time I'd been outdoors in days, and it was technically only possible because I was besties with a guy who used the wind to turn the pages of his reading material for him.

Which reminded me... the pads of my fingers went white as I pressed them against the limestone and peered over the ledge and down at the colorful specks I assumed were people milling about hundreds of feet below. The sheer height gave me a tinge of vertigo, and I leaned back again. While the sides of the pyramids were primarily flat, each also possessed three-foot ledges that stuck out at four distinct levels. About an hour ago, after declaring he was going stir crazy, Joseph had whisked us to the highest ledge.

Bonus point: we technically hadn't stepped foot on the grounds to get here.

"Seriously though." I swung my leg up and leaned my cheek on my knee. "I meant what I said, if anyone is going to figure out what it says, it's you."

A dusting of rosiness touched his cheekbones, and he hurried to change the conversation. "How did things go with Seth this morning?"

I dug a nail into a crack in the ledge and worked some of the dirt out. "About the same as it did yesterday and the day before that."

The first full day at the temple, I'd met with Seth and another member of Davos bearing the mask of a large feline, discussing our predicament. After that meeting, when it became clear they were more interested in strategy than anything else, I'd roped Finn into the mix, imploring him to use his military intellect to keep the conversation moving.

To our surprise, Davos didn't seem opposed to a war against the Order. Turns out, they had an abundance of well-trained soldiers champing at the bit for some action, however they wanted more control over the situation than I thought was reasonable. As much as I wanted to dust my hands of the whole affair... I couldn't. Not yet anyway, I reasoned, monitoring a bird coasting on an updraft. Once this was over, I'd step back. But until then, I had to trust my instincts, and those were screaming at me that Davos wasn't the long-term solution we needed.

When we'd parted ways this morning, our stances on the situation hadn't changed much. The sinking feeling in my gut told me we weren't going to find a compromise.

"You and Finn will figure it out," Joseph said. He'd blanched at the idea of negotiation, and, while he offered advice he'd learned from his books, he still had yet to enter the room. "You two are some of the most clever people I know."

I tried to smile but failed. He took pity on me and snatched one of the books in my small pile.

"Where did you get this anyway?" he asked, scratching his chin. He claimed his face felt itchy without the rough beard he'd shaved off the other day. He now seemed a little strange without it. "This doesn't look like anything from the library. It's too old for that."

"I may or may not have discovered a *secret* library."

"And you're only now disclosing this information?"

"I live to keep you in suspense." I plucked a small pouch of pistachios I'd snitched from lunch out of my pocket and tossed them at him. "I also know how to earn your forgiveness."

He cracked a shell and popped the green meat between his lips. "I accept your apology, despite its lack of originality." I couldn't keep the disgust from my face when he chewed two more. I hated pistachios. "Now, stars tell, where did you discover this secret library?"

"The third level of the basement."

He clicked his tongue. "Speaking of lack of original thought."

"I actually found something interesting a few minutes ago." I snagged the book he'd grabbed and opened it to a page I'd dog-eared, then ran my finger down the scribbled text. "Maat gave me an idea out in the desert with this whole binding thing. I know that Phenex is out of the way for now, but what if there were a way to do something similar to Geoffrey?"

"You mean you don't want to kill him?" Joseph asked with surprise.

"I—" I stopped scanning the page, my chest tight. I wanted retribution, I wanted justice, but the more I learned about this world and its inhabitants, the less I was convinced that death was the answer. "No. I really don't. He's done horrible things. Terrible things. And I think he needs to pay for what he's done. But death isn't the answer to that."

In my mind, Kaleal rustled restlessly. I winced at the sensation of claws dragging down the inside of my skull. She wasn't pleased with my reasoning

"I'm proud of you," Joseph said, squeezing my shoulder. "You are not the girl I met back on that dry lakebed anymore. In a good way, of course."

My cheeks warmed. I didn't know how to respond.

"What were you going to show me?" he asked.

"Oh! That." I pointed at a paragraph near the bottom of the page. "You mentioned similar things back at the cabins, about how people were bound by blood promises in ancient times. You know, swearing oaths that were impossible to break? Well, this says the fey used to strip other fey of their magic if they abused it. It was always seen as a last resort but..."

"But if we strip Geoffrey of his magic, he's only a human. He's no longer the Hand," Joseph exclaimed, pulling me in for a quick embrace. "You're a genius, Zara. Seriously. How do we do it? How do we bind him?"

"The answer is probably in the library still." I closed the book. "I only got lucky when I found this earlier."

"What are we waiting for then?" He jumped up in a move so fast I flinched. Factor in how high up we were, and I'd think him crazy if I hadn't known he was incapable of falling.

I tucked the books into my satchel and grabbed his extended hand. "How do we get down?"

"How do you want to get down?"

I glanced up through my lashes. "I have a choice?"

"Flying? Sliding? You say it and I can probably do it."

An idea rose and my whole body buzzed with the possibility. I leaned over the edge, again, considering. "How about diving?"

He shoved his glasses up his nose and moved his head side to side in consideration. "Sure." He grabbed my shoulders and positioned me in front of him so he could see where I was in relation to everything. We were really, really high up.

"Ok. The window is about seventy-five feet straight down. Yes, there, you got it. At this angle, you should drop right through—don't look at me like that, of course I can tell the window is open. Remember, I'll be guiding you, and if something goes horribly wrong I'll be ready to catch you."

"I think I got it." Glorious energy zinged in my veins. I'd never done anything like this before. The idea of putting my entire life in someone else's hands was absolutely crazy, but also so completely *right*. I shuffled forward, my toes poking over the edge, arms raised over my head in a vee.

This was like swimming.

I'd loved diving with my team, even though I wasn't especially talented at it. For the first time, grief didn't swamp me when I remembered the laughter of my friends when one of us would execute a particularly awful dive. Instead, joy fluttered its butterfly wings. With it, I recalled the feeling of weightlessness that came with springing from the board, the sensation of that one, clean moment where the water parted for my hands and then sucked me under. The power that pulsated through me when I touched the smooth bottom and propelled myself to the surface once more.

I'd loved swimming so much.

I needed this.

I jumped.

My stomach bottomed out, but I held position as I sliced through the air, moving faster and faster as I fell. This was nothing like diving, yet absolutely like it all at the same time. Just as I was getting used to the twisting wonderfulness in my gut, it stopped, and I was tumbling, rolling on the floor of the window we'd sneaked out of earlier. Adrenaline pumped hard and fast through my veins, and I realized I was laughing. Real laughter right from my core, the kind that had me curling up as my limbs shook.

Joseph coasted gently through the window and shook his head at me where I rolled around on the plush blue and green rug. "You're an adrenaline junkie, I hope you know. When this is all said and done, I'll make it my mission to find you a specialist to help you handle your urges."

"You do that," I yelled gleefully at his retreating back. "We have to survive whatever 'this' is first."

The thought sobered me and I sucked in a great gulp of air, moving to sit on the cheap, metal frame that supported a thin, twin-size mattress in the corner. That had been fun. I needed a little more fun in my life.

"You can come out now," I said to the empty air when I could no longer sense Joseph's presence. I pretended to examine my short, chipped nails while measuring the push and pull of my water magic, sensing my unwanted shadow crouching on the other side of the wall. "At first I was flattered that I'd captured your attention, but I'm starting to get stalker vibes."

Nothing.

I sighed. "I know who you are. I know you know that, too."

I'd been watching the open doorway, but he must have moved when I blinked because there he was, the boy with the twisted owl-boar mask. He had exchanged the robes for loose, white trousers and a white, silk shirt that hugged his body beneath his vest. A thin cloak the exact shade of moonlight draped from his shoulders. Khaki boots and a bandolier outfitted with finger-length knives provided the only relief in the monotonous attire.

"It's Oron, isn't it?"

His hand went to the short sword at his waist, but he made no move to draw it. The dark hollows of his snarling mask stared me down.

"Why don't you come inside?" I asked when it became clear he wasn't about to answer. I got up and moved to the windowsill to put some extra space between us. He took two steps forward and halted. He held himself eerily still, like a lion with a gazelle in its crosshairs.

"I knew who you were when I saw you outside the pyramid," I said. "It's a weird quirk of being the First. I recognize the signatures of the different Gods. I think it's part of knowing who needs their magic woken up." I waved a hand, scattering dust motes in the hazy air. "Anyway, now that I've got you pinned down, you're greener than a field of daisies in the spring."

Oron sat gingerly on the edge of the chest, every muscle in his body was locked in anticipation. The tips of his fingers touched in his lap, and I'd sparred with the pixies too often to not recognize he was ready to reach for any number of weapons, should I give him reason to.

I cleared my throat and pulled my legs up on the wide ledge, crisscross style. "Would you mind removing the mask?" I circled my face vaguely. "It's a little unnerving speaking to... whatever you're supposed to be."

His head dipped. The tips of his fingers tapped. Then his middle finger and thumb met in a circle and he reached up behind his head. I blinked. It resembled one of the first signs Rose had taught me. The pixies pressed their thumbs and forefingers together all the time in quiet displays of agreement or the affirmative.

Metal clicked as he pulled apart the buckles at the base of his skull holding the mask tight around his head. Oron hesitated, gripping the muzzle of the snarling beast, and lowered it to his lap. The stretchy, black material that I'd first thought was his shirt was actually a secondary cloth mask, one that covered his whole head and neck, rendering him faceless.

I tugged on the edges of my sleeves. This somehow felt even weirder, more intimate, almost as if he'd stripped to his underwear instead of remove a simple headpiece.

"How about the other mask?" I asked uncertainly.

This index and middle finger drew straight and slashed right to left. No.

Another pixie sign.

"How do you know pixie?" I asked, leaning against the frame. "Do you talk?"

He flicked a few more signs: *I prefer it this way.*

I was intrigued. "What's with the masks?"

They represent spirits that protect the temples, he signed, the movements tight and precise. *Each member of Davos serves as a representative of their spirit until the day they either step down or are dismissed.*

"Does anyone ever step down?" I definitely wasn't getting that kind of vibe from this place. Judging by his hesitation, it was more of a 'till death do us part' type of gig. "That's fine, you don't have to answer. But does that mean you always have to wear the... skull thing?"

Out in public, yes.

"But with me it's ok?"

We're technically equals, he said as if that answered everything. He held himself eerily still as if extra movement would cost him something he didn't have to spend.

"No 'technically' about it, Oron. We are equal." I pressed back to the window frame, tracing the water band around my wrist as I stared up at the ceiling. A long crack stretched diagonally from one corner to the other. "Do you want to hear a story? About how this all started? For me anyway?"

He offered an affirmative.

"Great." I thought back on those days, remembering the good and the bad and all the ugly. It was strange, but I felt ready to face it, to talk about it. Something about Oron and the mystery he exuded spoke to me. "You might not guess it by looking at me, but I used to be this crazy awesome swimmer with a whole bunch of dreams I wanted to achieve. Then I fell off a boat in the middle of a storm created by a devious Kraken and everything thought I knew about the world changed…"

"No kidding? You guys train by hunting ramalia?" I asked with genuine amazement. That sounded terrifying and totally awesome. The heels of my feet tapped the wall as I dangled them from the windowsill.

Oron's index fingers circled one another rapidly. Laughter.

I braced my chin on my fist. "Your Great Beast is pretty scary, you know. Scary in an awe-inspiring way—like the Kraken and the Thunderbird." I shook my head in wonder.

"I wish you could meet them. But the Kraken doesn't do very well in deserts and the Thunderbird is protecting Joseph's family." I ran my fingers through my hair. I wondered when Ryder would insist on weaving his pattern into the locks once again. "Joseph managed to call them here, I guess. Apparently, the Order tried attacking again not long after we left, but the T-bird headed them off. Fortunately, they're doing fine now."

I hopped off the windowsill and dusted off my pants. "Alright, Oron. What will it be?" I reached out, palm upward and flat. "I'm not asking you to join us, but do you want to taste the full extent of your power? I won't force you—" even though I desperately wanted to because the magic was zinging this way and that inside of me, making me mildly nauseous, "—it's totally your call."

He appeared frozen on the trunk, trapped in indecision.

Then slowly, oh so slowly, he stood, his hand pressed against his middle. Taking my cues from him, like squaring off with a wary predator, I held still, allowing him to come to me. Inside, though, his Earth magic spun faster and faster, frothing riotously, demanding release I couldn't give it. If it kept up much longer, I might hurl. To distract myself, I remembered what Joseph had told me after he'd connected with his magic.

"I'm told it hurts a bit, but it's a good kind of hurt. Like if you've ever wrapped a rubber band around your finger to watch the tip turn purple. That feeling when you remove the band. Or when you suck in that first gasp of air after trying to see how long you can hold your breath with your friends." I flicked a half-smile. "Then again, you could also be like me and not even realize you have it until you do something with it. Either way, it's pretty awesome."

His eyes bored into me from behind the veil of black. His whip-like body was tense, uncertain. Smoothly, his hand flung out and wrapped around mine, his grip sure.

My palm tingled and then it was gone. The chaos swirling in my stomach subsided, and I swallowed back a frown. The boy gave absolutely no reaction, either, but his hand remained locked around mine, hard as stone. It was the exact opposite of what had happened with Joseph when the power had flooded me with electricity and heat and energy. It had overwhelmed the God of Air, who had been bedridden a full day while recovering.

"Do you feel any—" I started to ask when through the open window blared the bleats of horns. Three short bursts followed by a longer bellow. Oron's grip closed impossibly harder around mine, turning me around with him as he went to the window, peering out.

The same pattern sounded and I looked over his shoulder at the view across the city. Along the top of the western wall clustered soldiers, rushing to and fro. Below them, civilians raced away, ducking into shelters at the base of the pyramid. I gasped when flames erupted from one large, black basin on top of the wall. It was quickly followed by another and another until fire ringed the city.

With uncanny speed, Oron pulled the bone-mask over his head and smoothly buckled it in place as he climbed on the windowsill. At the last second, he seemed to remember my presence and glanced back. He pointed first at the western wall, then his hands worked together in the slashing motions for "approaching enemy."

My gut knotted, the magic swirling faster again.

The Order. It had to be.

I scanned the darkening horizon, not seeing anything, yet believing something must be there.

I'd given Geoffrey more than enough time to plan another attack.

"Take me with you," I begged, snagging his cloak as he prepared to leap. His shoulders jerked, and the tusks swung my way. "Whatever it is, I'm better served on the front lines than back here."

A million unspoken moments seemed to pass between us.

The horns blasted a third time and he latched on to my forearm. I eagerly hopped up next to him and he...

Jumped.

My stomach dropped as we fell. I scrambled in midair, completely out my element, when a column of sandstone carved from the pyramid itself shot upward and caught us. My ankles screamed when I crashed into it, but I didn't have time to ruminate over the pain before Oron dragged me upright and hurtled down the path rising up before us. Faster and faster our feet churned, the ground falling away at my heels.

"How are you doing this?" I yelled into the wind. "You haven't had any training."

He didn't look back, his grip unchanging as he focused on the wall.

I hit it with a gasp, wrenching away from Oron to cling to the iron bars with all I was worth. As I recovered, wiping away sweat streaming down my face, the God of Earth sketched a short bow and marched the length of the wall toward a helmeted officer with a cloak of gold.

A strong blast of wind nearly bowled me over, but I clutched the bars firmly.

"I see you and Oron are bonding," Joseph murmured, nimbly dropping beside me. I narrowed my eyes, wondering how it was he kept his long hair so impeccable, even when flying. "You know, I didn't think I'd actually *feel* it when you gave him his magic or whatever it is you did."

"You did?" I asked, scanning the desert but only finding waves and waves of dunes. The soldier beside me was pale as he fumbled with a contraption that looked like a cannon. He kept spilling dark powder all over the ground. "That's strange. I didn't feel much at all."

"Like a hook in my intestines," Joseph said, rubbing the spot.

I'd only felt... relief. Relief to not have that magic inside me any longer.

"I'm a little surprised I haven't seen Finn—oh, there he is." A broad grin lit Joseph's face. I swung around to find a shaggy, black horse shoving its way down the line opposite the direction Oron had gone, snapping at any soul unfortunate to stumble into his path.

I released the iron bars, firm on my feet once more. "What's the deal with you two, anyway?"

"I haven't the faintest idea of what you speak."

"Sure, and I'm comatose." I stretched to the tips of my toes, struggling to see over the larger, bulkier bodies. "Listen, I'm going to find Oron and see what's going on."

Nimbly, I wove and ducked through the crowd of soldiers fortifying the wall. The sun was quickly fading and the chill of evening had set in. I coaxed the flames in the basins higher as I raced along. Hopefully, the extra light would help. The tension was thick as mud as everyone readied for a threat I still had yet to actually sense.

"...asked to identify for a fourth time, sir," I heard the guy in the gold cloak say as I dodged a woman rolling a barrel of oil. "No answer. But the scouts confirm there are three of them coming in fast."

Oron nodded once, his hand flying too quick for me to comprehend, but it apparently was enough for the officer, who grabbed hold of a woman with a gold-toned Earth symbol patch on her shoulder and snapped something in her ear. The God turned to the wall and I edged up beside him, peering through the cutout between the spiked pillars.

"Three people?" I asked. That didn't sound like the Order. Geoffrey was more likely to bring tanks and nukes at this point. "Are you sure they're a threat?"

He merely pointed, identifying a tiny blur along the horizon. I rubbed my eyes and squinted, trying to make out more than the indistinct form it was. I still wasn't sensing anything. I scrambled up on the ledge as if that extra three feet would bring them into focus. As I did, the ground buckled and I slipped. The only thing preventing me from falling was my grip on a pike embedded in the wall.

The earth grumbled again, and a thin crack formed directly in front of us.

A crack I remembered with awful clarity.

I swung to Oron. "What are you doing?"

He clenched his fist and the earth unleashed another groan as the crack widened. My pulse raced as I looked back over the desert, switching to use my Iridescence to gauge the magical signature of the approaching figures.

The one in the middle lit up a bright and fiery red.

The exact shade as the magic lighting up my own veins.

Understanding dawned and I reached down to stop Oron. "Don't do it!" I yelled as the hooded head of his Great Beast rose from the ground. Around me, people screamed as It hovered there, red eyes burning like coals as It awaited orders. Its scales flexed as It stretched and swayed, the movement strangely hypnotizing. "You don't know who that is. But I do! That's the Fire God. I can sense—"

The earth buckled again. This time I wasn't holding on.

Bright lights flashed before my eyes as I flailed, toppling over the edge. My mind went blank as I hurtled to the ground. I reached for my magic but didn't know what to do with it. I was eerily out of ideas. Then the earth rose, a moving, shifting, *very much alive* thing, and strong arms wrapped around my middle. The hard stop knocked the wind from my lungs, keeping me from yelling as wings beat hard and fast on either side of me.

"Once, just once, could you pretend to be the obedient, demure creature you very much are not?" The frustrated amusement in Ryder's voice calmed the wild fluttering inside of me. Simultaneously, a swarm of butterflies swarmed my chest. Must be the dizzying height. "One of these days it would be nice to see you running *away* from danger instead of swan diving into it."

I gulped as the incubus barrel-rolled, closing my eyes against the flipping horizon.

Definitely the dizzying height. Ryder made me feel nothing but nausea.

"On second thought, that was more of a belly flop of epic proportions," he cackled. "I'm also not sure I'd be as attracted to you if you weren't so headstrong. Forget what I said."

"Could you be serious?" I shouted when the world stopped spinning. "I need to get to those figures. It's the Fire God. I can feel it. But I'm not sure what will happen if Oron unleashes his Great Beast first."

"I'm not sure I understand this term 'serious,'" he said, snagging my earlobe with his teeth. I smacked him even though wild, wonderful emotions flooded my chest, making me jump. He adjusted his grip, snuggling me closer as we rocketed across the sand. "Your heart is beating so fast, glowstick. Fear? Or maybe something else…"

"Ryder," I growled.

"Oh fine. Though you should know, that snake never moved. Oron called It off," he said. Our forward momentum slowed. We touched the ground and I could finally breathe again. He snagged me when I tried to move away, humming into my hair. "I expect payment later since you so kindly used me as a personal, flying Uber. I know what I want."

I snorted and struggled from his hold, making a rude gesture as I swiveled to keep my body between him and the threat. His rumble of laughter shook me. The incubus might not need my protection, but he was definitely getting it.

The three incoming figures pulled up on skiffs the size of skateboards about eight yards from Ryder and me. The roaring inferno of red that was the pint-sized girl in the middle approached first. Two other humans with the slender hilts of katanas sprouting from their shoulders held back.

Kaleal eased forward, eager to get a look at the final God of our quartet.

The wisp of a girl stood barely four and a half feet tall and one-hundred pounds dripping wet. Her lithe body was encased in olive leather, and a samurai sword hung at her side. Hair dyed the exact shade of Hot Tamales framed her smooth, round face. Eyebrows drawn by hand arched severely over eyes so dark they were practically black. When she grinned, her pearls of teeth glowed against her black lipstick.

"Meetcha!" she called, holding out her gloved hand. I grabbed it, wincing when she nearly crushed my bones. "I know who you are."

"You do?" I asked, resisting the urge to shake out my limb when she released it.

"Sure do. You're all over the television," she said, bouncing on the balls of her feet. "I'm Pyra, your fourth and final counterpart if I've done my math correctly." She peered past me at the fortress that was the Earth Temple. "I gotta say, I'm a little miffed you didn't come visit me before these old bores. The Castle of Glass is way cooler than this."

She's not exactly wrong, Kaleal intoned.

"How did you find me, anyway?" I asked, ignoring the ancient God. "And why?"

"I got tired of waiting around for you, of course. And, well, Ren over here—" she jabbed her thumb over her shoulder at the man with a mask covering the lower half of his face. "He came here as a child, so I kinda needed him to find the place. Stimpy, however, couldn't be parted with him for even one day."

My eyebrows lifted.

"As for why, that's obvious. I wanted to join the fun. Kicking butt, saving the world, wielding magic." She executed a series of elaborate punches. "It's like stuff out of my books. Couldn't keep me away even if you wanted to. Now gimme." She flung her gloves to the ground and held out her hand again, voice crackling like a bonfire. "You've got something that's mine."

"I'm not sure if you're ready for this," I joked. "You seem a little hesitant. I want to give you a moment to wrap your head around this."

She smirked. "I like you. Now hurry up."

I snagged her hand and our bodies snapped together, a blast of light and power and energy surging outward, bowing reality. A roaring filled my ears, my blood sparking and blistering my veins, my bones rattling and shaking as I melted our hands together, forcing my counterpart to absorb all I was offering. Her head was thrown back, eyes open and glowing red as embers danced in her skin. I was breaking and shattering and splintering and reforming and congealing and binding all at once.

This must have been what it felt like when the universe had formed.

Wild and hot and vibrant and *utterly insane.*

It was laughter that brought me back down from the enormous high.

Pyra's hot, brash laughter. She folded one arm over her gut and threw her head back, the column of her neck exposed as she brayed.

Ryder appeared at my side, chuckling along with her.

"That was *wild!*" she cried and pulled me in for another hug. "Absolutely wild! I'm so freaking glad I didn't listen to the temple masters. Imagine missing out a moment more of *this*." The God of Fire literally glowed in the dark, her skin flickering as if embers cooled beneath her skin. She squeezed a lighter and cupped a small bundle of flames that burst forth, already easing into her element.

I bit my lip. She and Oron seemed to fit so well in this world. Even Joseph had adapted to his magic pretty quickly. But me? I'd barely known what to think of magic, let alone wield it. I felt inadequate when faced with their apparent easy mastery.

Good thing you have me, then, isn't it, Kaleal whispered, peering with glee at the newly reborn God. It stung, realizing she was right to some extent. Without her showing me the way, who knows how long it would have taken me to figure it out.

This is why the Gods grow up in temples, Kaleal said with a shrug. *They master things like patience and control as children. It allows them to adapt almost instantaneously when they finally do acquire their magic.*

I rubbed at the ache in my chest and the small hole there that nothing seemed to fill.

I hated that Kaleal made me doubt myself.

I tried to shut the ancient God out as Pyra scrolled fire over her shoulders and down her legs in one seamless motion. She slipped a cigarette between her lips and lit it once the flames returned to her palm, the gesture familiar and practiced. She blew out a stream of smoke and laughed at the question on my face. "What's it gonna do? Kill me? I'm made of smoke and ash, aren't I?"

Ryder roared with laughter, finally unable to hold himself back as he introduced himself to the little firecracker.

She flicked her cigarette at the temple, suddenly somber. "So what's the plan?"

Her whiplash mood swings seemed to fit her element. "You familiar with the Order?"

She hawked a loogie and spat.

"Good," I said. "The plan is to take them down."

"Thank us," Pyra crowed. "Geoffrey is a pain."

"You know him?"

"You mean the guy who wiped out two temples and turned the other two against one another?" She stubbed out her cigarette on one of the black throwing stars sewn to her belt. The lipstick-stained butt vanished into a pouch at her hip. "The guy who picked off each and every search party we attempted to send out and look for survivors from Air and Water? Yeah, I know him. We all do. No one likes him."

I exchanged a look with Ryder. He nodded slowly.

"I didn't know you did that," I breathed, amazed to discover that Water's allies hadn't entirely abandoned the temple after all.

"Well, you were an infant and technically everyone thought you were dead, so that doesn't surprise me," Pyra said, stretching her back with a groan. "Your temple warned mine about the danger just in time. They wanted to do you a solid in return. Didn't quite work out in the end, but they tried." She extricated a tube of lipstick from her pocket and touched up her lips. "So how do we wipe out the jerkwad?"

"That's why I'm here. I mean, I came here to partner with Earth, and then found out that they have a pretty impressive little army built up." My head swayed in a so-so kind of way. "I'm waiting to hear if they'll support a plan to take him out."

"I bet that isn't going well." She fiddled with her belt. "Earth has only ever looked out for Earth, so you'll need to appeal to their desires."

"I'm starting to see what you mean," I said, looking over my shoulder. I could only make out the fires burning on the far-away walls. "Our

206

welcome was lukewarm at best."

"That's why you should have come to Fire first." She swatted my shoulder. "They know how to throw a party." She clicked her lighter a few more times in thought, brushing away the sparks that flew. "But if you insist on starting here, I might be able to help you out."

"Seriously?" I asked. "Because we're getting nowhere."

"Yeah, seriously." Her answering grin was wolfish. "Come on, I'll show you how it's done."

Chapter 29

"I'm bored," Pyra proclaimed. She was picking at dirt underneath a nail with a knife. I curled my own fingers safely against my palms, wondering how she didn't cut herself.

"You're the one who insisted we arrive thirty minutes early," Joseph reminded her, crunching on some trail mix. "I was perfectly content with getting extra sleep."

It was irritating how quickly Davos granted Pyra access to the city. She'd flourished a dragon of fire in the air as she passed beneath its gates and boom, she was in. She wasn't even confined to the pyramid as we'd been. After eating a quick meal, we three Gods had stayed up late strategizing how to approach this meeting with Davos. Now we hovered outside the conference room doors.

"I was bored then, too," the Fire God sneered, slipping her knife back into a sheath inside her vest. "You sleep too much as it is."

"And you're a pain in my—"

"Would you two knock it off." Finn clapped his hands from the floor where he sat, playing hangman with me on a spare scrap of paper. His facial piercings winked as he stretched to glare at the pair of them. "We have enough problems *without* adding infighting to the mix. We've only been here for ten minutes, Pyra, you can be patient a little while longer."

The God pursed her lips, eyes glowing red as she snagged a cigarette and lit it up. Her shoulders slumped when the nicotine hit her bloodstream. "Yeah, yeah. You know, you remind me of my teachers back home. My *least* favorite teachers."

Unphased, Finn scratched a letter into one of the slots beneath the poor stick-guy, who was just a head and torso at this point. "I'm glad you—"

"Nope," she interrupted, a bundle of flames appearing in her palm. Around the cigarette, she continued, "Can't do it. Won't do it. I have to know what they're talking about. They owe it to us."

"What are you going to do?" Joseph asked with alarm. "Burn down the door? It's locked."

"I like how you think," she said with a wink as Finn and I scrambled to our feet, recognizing the dangerous glint in her eye for what it was. Flames lapped at the edges of the formerly gorgeous oak door, and Pyra kicked in what remained of the barrier. She grabbed my hand and strode inside the room I was beginning to loathe. I couldn't think in boardrooms. They were so… boring.

As they had for the past few days, thirteen people bearing masks of bone stared at us. Oron moved away from the table around which they were assembled, peering down at a wide array of paperwork spread across its surface. His fingers twisted into a sign I didn't recognize.

"This is an unseemly display, Ms. Zhang," Seth drawled from his standard spot at the head of the table. "Though it's not wholly unexpected from someone associated with the Fire Temple."

"I'm happy to uphold your preconceived notions," she snarked, sidling up beside Oron. "Because you're holding up your end of that stick, too."

"Ms. Ramone, I'm more surprised to find you joining these antics," Seth said, his tone betraying his annoyance. "I thought you and I had an understanding."

I crossed my arms while scrutinizing the orbital bones that made up his dragon's skull. I bet they knew the masks made newcomers uneasy. That was the real reason they insisted on wearing them everywhere. Across from me, Oron surveyed the volley of our conversation, and he deigned to make that sign again.

"We *had* an understanding, but I'm tired of waiting," I drawled. "All we're doing is wasting time and giving the Order opportunity to launch a counterattack. If you aren't interested in joining us, then say so."

"I'm amazed she's waited this long for you schmucks to make a decision," Pyra added, tugging a document out of a woman's hands. The page charred around her fingertips. "But that's ok, because she's got me now, and I know how you operate. It's time to make a decision."

She stared hard at Oron as if daring him to say something. Anything.

He didn't so much as twitch and she snorted. "Figures you guys would lock away your God, too, with all the other radical changes you've made. You've turned him into little more than a puppet. I hope you're pleased with yourselves."

Seth drew himself up and I imagined the beast he wore spewing flames as his anger flared. "You know nothing of how this temple has survived the past two-thousand years," he snarled. "Sacrifices were made in the name of protecting the people of the Gods. That meant certain old-fashioned ways of life had to go."

"Fine. Fire tried something similar, too," Pyra snapped back, brushing ashes onto Oron's white robes with a sneer. "They failed."

Finn and I exchange a glance. The room pulsed with waves of tension.

"Ms. Ramone," Seth began, "since you insist on associating with this—"

"Before you say something you really don't want to, to my friend over there—" Pyra interrupted, hooking her thumbs in her belt loops and swaying, "—you'll want to hear me out. If you decide to not aide our First in her greatest hour of need, the Castle of Glass is prepared to declare war between our two temples." Her sneer was downright sinister as hushed whispers surged around the table.

Never in recorded history had two temples attacked one another.

"Believe me when I say this is seventeen years coming, and we've done little else but prepare in that time." Pyra slammed her hands on the table. Even though I knew what was coming, a shiver ran down my spine at her vehemence. "Not once did you answer our requests to communicate. Not once did you extend help to the survivors of Water and Air, the ones persecuted for little other than their loyalty. Not once did you publicly break from the Order."

Flames licked Pyra's heels as she advanced on Seth. Smoke spilled from her fingertips and rose from her shoulders as she continued, "Your support for the cause is long overdue. I demand your answer now, as head and God of the Temple of Fire, what will it be, Davos? Which war will you choose?"

Seth seemed frozen, his chest barely rising.

I flicked a look at Joseph and together we moved behind the smaller, but equally, mighty God. In my hands, I spun a wheel of water and Joseph used skates of wind to glide along.

"I may be the sole remaining member of Air," Joseph said, tone steely, "but I, too, will throw my support behind Fire. Should you choose war with them, you choose war with me. I warn you, my lack of followers doesn't make me any less frightening a foe."

The dragon mask shifted my way. I inclined my head.

"We will fight the Order," Seth said, seething. "However, I make one request before we deploy all our troops on a whim."

Chapter 30

Seth's agreement shattered the tension. I dissolved my magic and dropped into a chair, ready to hear him out. None of us really wanted a war between temples anyway. Joseph slid down beside me, and, after a beat, Pyra backed off, though she continued to pace the space between the chairs and the rows of windows at our backs.

"What would that be, Seth?" I asked. "You've made so many requests over these past few days that I'm having trouble keeping up."

At some unseen signal, Oron walked over to the wall and propped a shoulder against it, his owl mask following Pyra's constant motion with steady patience. The other members of Davos stood and exited, seemingly unconcerned now that a deal was basically brokered.

"I have a contact within the Order." Seth shuffled some papers until he came up with a page so dense with layers of writing I wondered how anyone could interpret the scribbles. "She has expressed discontent among the councilmembers regarding the actions Geoffrey has taken. I'd like to reach out to her and see if there might be a way to negotiate an end to this all—peacefully."

Finn scratched his scruffy jaw and shrugged at me. That actually wasn't a terrible idea.

"How can we trust your contact?" I asked.

"She used to sit at this very table, an esteemed member of Davos from decades ago," he said with force. "She transitioned to Order headquarters for this very reason, to monitor the Council as a spy for us. When she's done in Rome, she will return to the Lost City. With Geoffrey gone and the Gods restored, her job would be complete."

Pyra grumbled as she passed behind me, but I couldn't make out the words.

"What could it hurt?" asked Joseph. "Geoffrey already wants to kill us all. If we reach out to the Council and they want nothing to do with us, it's a scratch for everyone and we move forward with our plans. I bet Geoffrey is even anticipating we contact the Council, just so we can all pretend to abide by diplomacy."

"Call her up." I motioned at a state-of-the-art computer at the other end of the room. A projector screen was draped along the length of the wall. It hadn't been there before, and I wondered exactly what it was Davos discussed in my absence.

"Now?" Seth asked, startled.

"I want to see with my own eyes that you aren't trying to trick us in some way," Pyra said, collapsing into a chair and throwing her feet up on the edge of the table. "Call it an act of faith. We're giving you a chance to do things your way, as long as you're willing to meet us halfway."

My attention remained fixed on Oron. I understood that he didn't speak, but he should play a larger role in all of this. However, he seemed content hanging on the edges and staying out of the drama. I wondered about his upbringing at the Earth Temple and realized it must have been a very lonely existence.

"Alright," Seth said, drawing out the word. He rose to grab the laptop and tapped a few buttons. A program launched on the projector. I didn't recognize the name of the video conferencing app, but the set-up was familiar enough. "Please allow me to speak with her first. We'll bring all of you in if it appears this is something the Council will seriously consider."

I had no problem with that. I elbowed Pyra when she opened her mouth.

The computer hummed a few times in the soft trill of a ringing phone. There was a click and a woman's face filled the screen. Long, blonde hair tangled with tight curls bracketed her face, setting off her soft, blue eyes. She wet her lips as she tapped something on her screen, then smiled broadly.

"Seth, it's so good to see you," she said. "Did I forget a meeting? I didn't think we were supposed to touch base for another month."

"No, you're right, Lydia. This is completely unplanned," he assured her while adjusting the angle of the camera pointed at his face. "I have an interesting idea I'd like for you to consider."

The screen shook and she raised one elegant brow. "This wouldn't have anything to do with three Gods showing up at your doorstep, now would it?"

Pyra snorted.

"You always were astute," Seth said. "They're actually with me now, all four of them."

"Oh?" Her grin tightened, becoming more sinister as he spun the laptop around to show our faces. "Yes, so I see. They are all there, aren't they? What exactly is the nature of this call?"

"We'd like to negotiate removing Geoffrey from his position as Hand," I said, despite what I'd told Seth about leaving this to him. "We hear you may be interested in making that happen."

Lydia ran a slow finger down the column of her neck, her expression distant as she stared off-camera. When she finally glanced back at her phone, her expression was intense and direct.

"Yes, I believe we can reach an agreement on that accord," she said.

Chapter 31

The office chair squeaked as Ryder spun a slow circle with his toes.

"Would you knock it off?" Pyra snapped. She was applying another layer of crimson polish to her blade-like nails. "You're obliterating my concentration."

"And I'm tired of waiting," he replied, increasing his speed defiantly. "What'cha gonna do about it?"

She blew on the backs of her hands. "I'm sure I'll think of something."

I scratched my arm and rolled my own chair back and forth, shrugging off the creepy stares of the animal heads mounted on the walls. I was starting to wonder if Earth had any other conference rooms in this massive pyramid. I glanced at the analog clock on the wall again, while trying to avoid the heavy gaze of the predatory animal nailed next to it—one with lots of black fur and large fangs.

Across from me sat Seth, Oron, and a third member of Davos named Lim who handled community relations. He bore the mask of a hawk with an extended beak. They neither spoke nor fidgeted. It seemed to be a trait the temple valued highly.

"I still don't understand why we're wasting time negotiating with the Order anyway," Pyra said to no one in particular and removed a roll of black tape from her pouch. It was probably the twentieth time she'd asked that question in the past two weeks. "You know the

Council doesn't mean it, there's no way this is actually going to work. So why give them more time to plan an attack? We could be raining ash and lava down on their heads instead."

"Because I'm tired of killing people," I answered for the twentieth time. "They've also been pretty amicable up to this point, they seem to want him gone. I think we'll be able to find some common ground."

Pyra snorted and wound tape around her thumb.

This was supposed to be our third meeting with the Council. True to Lydia's word, they were definitely interested in negotiating a resolution. Half of the members seemed tired of Geoffrey's reckless behavior and the other half... I had a feeling wanted him out of the way so they could go about their nefarious deeds without his interruptions.

For the first time, though, the Council was late to our teleconference. I glanced at the gold-rimmed clock again. Eighteen minutes late.

My stomach curdled.

"You and Joseph may have a solid plan," Pyra muttered, "but they're definitely about to back out. I guarantee it."

She finished winding the tape around her middle finger, snipped it off, and snapped experimentally. A small flame sprouted from the tip of her thumb. She'd done something similar yesterday and informed me the tape was a Fire Temple secret. Its sandpapery texture created the right friction to create flame whenever she wanted.

I envied her the ingenuity and vowed to create my own clever devices once this whole mess was over. Though I still had yet to reveal to her or the Earth Temple that I could also manipulate fire, so I still had that little trump card handy.

I flinched when sparks danced across my vision. Kaleal was rarely so aggressive with her entrances, choosing stealth over flashbangs. The ugly twisting of my insides increased. *What are you—*

Something's wrong, she panted uncharacteristically. *Geoffrey isn't there, his assaults have stopped. It's the first time he's deviated in—*

I nearly jumped out of my skin at the tinfoil crackle of the speakers starting to life. Pyra grumbled and Joseph's frown deepened as he stared at the blank, black screen of the projector. Seth rose to check on it when the image flickered to life. I'd grown so used to the bland conference room in which the dozen or so councilmembers normally congregated, that the Robin's egg blue of the sky outside startled me. The horizon bobbed, the wispy clouds and reaching fingers of pine trees blurring. Whoever carried the camera stopped and set it down, the sudden stillness jarring.

Geoffrey stepped into view and a roaring filled my ears.

Too late, Kaleal shrieked, as highly strung as me.

"Good afternoon, Gods." He squinted over the camera at what I assumed was some sort of monitor. His body filled the screen and it was difficult to make out much behind him. "Yes, it appears that you are all there, assuming the one in the mask is Oron. I'd like to start this official meeting with a quick word of thanks for making this easy for me. It's much easier to talk to you all when you're in the same location."

He paused, his head twitching as he wrung his hands. I hadn't so much as spoken to or seen my Hand since I'd blocked him from my mind, and it was incredible how these past few weeks had treated him. Geoffrey had never been a particularly handsome man, given the scars on his cheeks and brands on his brow, but his newly healed burns added a monstrous, mottled quality to his ashen skin. His bi-colored eyes were wide and bloodshot, possessing the unfocused, glassy quality of someone on the fringes of insanity. His curly, dark hair was shiny with grease and tousled by unsteady hands.

I leaned forward. "Geoffrey, what's happened to you?"

My words seemed to ground him again, and he flashed a quick grin. "Zara, how wonderful to hear your voice. I'd so hoped we could resolve our differences peacefully, between the two of us, but when you locked me out, you forced me to take more drastic measures."

I sensed Pyra and Oron turning to look at me, but my attention was riveted on the man on the screen. "What measures would those be?"

"Ah, ah, ah." He wagged a finger. "Not so fast, wouldn't want to skip the pleasantries. Joseph, how are you faring?"

Joseph ran a hand over the table. "I was fine until you showed up."

Geoffrey nodded. "My sources tell me you're the most intuitive of the four Gods. Would you agree with that assessment?"

"I believe that to be accurate," Joseph said unapologetically.

I flipped my Iridescence and bit back a gasp at the riot of colors exploding from Geoffrey. Magic swirled around him, hot and fast and uncontrolled, a chaotic mosaic I didn't understand. As the Hand of the Gods, he was supposed to possess some of our magics. It helped him connect with us and, to some extent, control us, but this seemed like the opposite of control.

He's gone insane, Kaleal reasoned, shrugging as she relaxed into the wall of my mind as if that made all of this somehow ok. *Sometimes it happens.*

"Very good," Geoffrey said to Joseph. "Have you realized what the others likely haven't?"

Joseph's eyes narrowed and he drew a long breath in through his nose. "You're broadcasting this signal. We're hardly alone."

My limbs locked and I swore I heard my knees and elbows crackle with ice.

"Very good," Geoffrey repeated. "When I realized the treachery going on beneath my very nose, I thought it best to take my case before the people themselves. I felt it was the best option, because—Zara, you'll want to listen closely to this in particular—*people*," he punctuated the word with a jab of his hand, "aren't terribly pleased with you all."

Here we go, Kaleal rasped. I wanted to strangle her with my bare hands.

218

"You aren't supposed to exist and yet somehow you do," Geoffrey said. "And you do so unchecked and unaccounted for. You operate under your own set of rules without the guidance of your leaders or the Order. You run rampant through cities and neighborhoods, destroying homes, businesses... and lives. Turn on the news now, if you dare. I know if I were a teenage God with unlimited powers, I probably wouldn't have checked the networks once."

I bristled. His one green and one gray eye seemed to bore into my soul. Things I'd wanted to forget, people I'd hoped to bury in my past, all rising to the surface.

Lim located a remote and a panel opened beside the projector. On the television screen revealed behind it was a news station I didn't recognize playing footage of me wiping out an entire city block. The next clip was of a house—my house—up in flames, the fire spreading down the street as people ran screaming. In quick succession came any number of natural disasters: the devastation from a hurricane, rescue crews scouring the wreckage left by an earthquake, firefighters battling intense forest fires, and a trio of tornadoes roaring through a downtown area at night.

Slowly, I stood. By juxtaposing those images, Geoffrey was creating a damning case against me and the other Gods. It didn't help that we'd remained silent for so long because there wasn't much we could do to save face. To deny it would be futile, no matter how insane Geoffrey appeared.

Oh this is tricky, isn't it? Kaleal said with glee. *What to do, what to do? How do you respond, knowing the world is watching?*

"And now, after my multiple attempts at contacting you and the other Gods, trying to reach peace and understanding, to call you in to account for your crimes, I discovered you'd turned my Council against me." His face twisted sorrowfully. "You not only conspired against me but sought to bring me down."

I moved toward the screen. "What did you do, Geoffrey? Where are they?"

"Oh, the Council is safe, for now. But they won't be. The consequences for treason are harsh." He locked his hands behind his back, appearing for the first time sane and absolutely serious. "Speaking of consequences, do you have any idea what happened to Phenex Allard? You know, the man the world better knows as the mastermind behind the investment firm Senet."

His name was like a punch to my gut, completely out of left field.

Nope, I didn't see that one coming either, Kaleal said, spinning smoke between her hands. *Denial is your best bet.*

"I don't know who that is," I said, pressing my lips into a firm line.

Geoffrey clicked his tongue. "Don't lie, Zara, you're not very good at it. Besides, there's footage I'll release to the media shortly showing you entering his home, then leaving it again with him. After that, he was never seen again. Ring any bells?"

He could be bluffing, Kaleal said, almost to herself.

"Nope, no clue." I realized the vial containing the djinn was in my hand as if it had moved there of its own volition.

"How peculiar. Because little fey sources of mine tell me that you, Zara Ramone, destroyed him in a storm of your making."

I'd gone stiff. Maat. The other nero. My pulse throbbed in my ears, but I couldn't ask, didn't dare ask about their well-being. If Geoffrey were talking about them, they were already in grave danger. And if he weren't, bringing them up would only land them there.

"That's not true," yelled Pyra, launching herself up as Joseph yanked her back down. "She didn't destroy him, she—" He silenced her before she could dig us all into an even deeper hole. What I'd done to the djinn was basically destruction, and even though he wasn't dead, I couldn't risk letting him out.

My knuckles went white around the vial that I couldn't seem to release. Geoffrey smiled coyly.

"That's what I thought," he said. "Time is up, Zara. You and the other Gods have had your fun… and your destruction. Now it's time to account for your crimes and atone for your sins."

Joseph moved to stand beside me, his hand curling around mine.

"For their treason, my entire Council is sentenced to death. Before you protest, that is the punishment spelled out by the charter of the Order." Geoffrey stepped back, nearly out of the shot. "But there are a few friends of yours that you might still be able to save, should you make the correct choice."

He had the nero. If he didn't have Maat, he had some of them. *How* he'd apprehended the fey, I had no idea. But I was certain that Geoffrey wasn't bluffing.

"Turn yourselves in, Gods. All of you." He moved out of frame. "You have seventy-two hours. You don't want to find out what happens one minute past that."

The screen went blank and Lim severed our connection, his mask bowed.

I clenched my teeth so hard I thought they might shatter.

"I told you we should have gone in and wiped him out," Pyra said after a beat. "Can we do that now?"

Chapter 32

Ryder's hand circled the small of my back as we waited for the other Gods on the limestone stairs of the pyramid. He was preparing to teleport us to Rome where we would meet with Geoffrey.

"I can't believe he executed them," I whispered. I felt strangely detached from my body as if my spirit weren't fully connected. "No jury, no trial. None of it. It's…"

"Horrific," Ryder finished for me, gripping my side and tugging me flush against him. His cheek rested on the top of my head. "And that's why he needs to be stopped for good."

You can't allow that evil to fester and rot any longer, Kaleal said tightly. *You know what you have to do, and that isn't stripping him of his powers. He deserves to die.*

A cord in my chest panged and I closed my eyes against the hazy, purple hue of dawn. The executions of the Order's full Council yesterday had not been publicly broadcast, but Geoffrey had allowed five neutral people—some government leaders and others reporters—to witness their deaths and share what they saw with the various news networks. I didn't understand how the world couldn't see him for the monster that he was. Why weren't people calling for an investigation? Why were they ok with this?

They're waiting for the Gods, said Kaleal. *This is your responsibility if you're truly ready to bear the mantle of your birth. Geoffrey is your responsibility. His actions reflect on you.*

I rubbed my sheathed dagger. As much as I'd preached about finding another way to solve this dilemma, I didn't know what it said about me anymore that I was seriously considering the idea of slitting his throat. Kaleal was right. He didn't deserve to live for all the atrocities that he'd committed.

What was almost worse than the executions, was seeing the network helicopter footage of Phenex's compound reduced to rubble in an earthquake. It was something Geoffrey was quick to blame us for as well, claiming the God of Earth had returned to destroy the evidence of my wrongdoings on my behalf—no matter that the footage of me and Phenex had already been released to the media. Seeing the once-gorgeous castle in ruins had rattled me to my core. I still couldn't figure out how Geoffrey had done it, but I was convinced he had at least a few of the nero in his grip.

I traced the band that bound me and Maat together. Ryder had shown me how to use my blood to activate the trigger that would signal to the nero I was ready to cash in on what he owed me. He said it would hurt Maat if he didn't respond, but in the two and a half days since Geoffrey's threat, I still had yet to hear so much as a whisper.

A door behind us opened and I turned as Pyra clattered down the stairs, her twin shadows in tow. The hilts of the katanas crossed at her back jutted over her shoulders as she adjusted one of her wrist guards. Her red eyes glowed in the early morning light.

"Glad to see I'm not the last one here," she said around the cigarette tucked in the corner of her mouth. The Fire God had grown quieter, her expressions harder in the hours following the execution. In fact, she'd only spoken to me when we headed for our bedrooms, telling me with callous sincerity that war was about sacrifice and we'd all learned something very valuable that day.

I'd stayed up most of the night thinking about that, wondering about the strangers I'd chosen to surround myself with.

Ryder stroked my braided crown, carefully tucking a loose strand back into place. I hadn't told him as much, but I was glad he was here with me. I'd come to rely heavily on his unwavering support.

"There was nothing you could have done," he whispered against my head as if listening to my chain of thoughts. It was also an echo of what he'd told me yesterday. "You could not have anticipated that he would take such extreme actions. Taking the diplomatic approach was the smartest thing you could have done. It shows the world that you tried to reason with him and counters his claims that you act with violence first and ask questions later."

"As much as I hate to admit it, he's right." Rose folded her dragonfly wings behind her as she landed on the outside wall of the stairs. Last night, Briar had carefully shaved the fuzz growing on half of her scalp. Her tattooed skin gleamed brightly in the torchlight.

"Thanks, guys," I said, soaking in their strength. "Let's get through today."

"Speaking of," the pixie said, hooking her thumb around the whip wrapped around her waist, "I have a slight change in plans."

"Why would you mess with the plan?" Joseph demanded, hopping up the stairs two at a time. He'd gone for a walk earlier, claiming he needed to clear his head. "We carefully laid everything out last night. Everyone agreed on the strategy, and now you're calling shenanigans?"

"It's not shenanigans since I'm telling you about it," she retorted. Briar and Vera dropped beside her, flashing signs that they were ready to go. I frowned. "We need more firepower and I'm going to get some. Three pixies, a handful of Gods, and two weirdos aren't going to be enough to take on the entire Order."

"I suppose there's no stopping you, is there?" I asked, lifting a brow.

Rose swallowed, inky eyes intent. "If you order me to stay, I will.

But I'm telling you, as my God, that I have a feeling about this fight. And that feeling is screaming at me to bring backup."

Ryder removed his arm from around my shoulders and I stood. She crouched on the stone railing to bring us to eye level.

"You know there's only one way in through the main gate, right? I can't promise the forcefield they've erected over the compound won't drop down and cut off that channel, too." I braced my hands on my hips and glanced up at the temple where Oron hovered at the door and then down at the city below, its people getting started with their days. "We hadn't planned on touching the towers, but —"

"But it will be fine," the pixie said, flashing her pointed teeth. "You guys will figure it out, bring them down. Have a little faith here. You are a God, after all."

I shook my head, feeling wildly out of my depth given the extremity of our circumstances. However, I couldn't say that, not right now, not when everyone was looking to me to lead this assault. Which meant—

"You get your allies, and you get to Rome as fast as you can," I demanded, gripping her shoulders. "That's an order."

"*Promedis ad.*" She raised her palm and lanced a straight line from the heel to the tip of her middle finger, the sign for commander, and one of weighty respect I didn't feel like I'd earned.

"You heard the lady," Rose called to her mates who let out whoops as they launched into the air, wings humming. She tipped a salute with two fingers. "I promise, we'll be there at noon."

She better, because that's when we'd agreed to meet with Geoffrey and turn ourselves over.

The pixie didn't look back as they vanished into the sky.

When I turned, I shrugged at Joseph who seemed downright thunderous, his chest heaving. He really didn't like having his carefully laid plans messed with. Finn had emerged at some point and hovered at his side, tugging on his lip ring. As the God of Air collected himself,

225

our small group drew together.

"Would you mind reviewing the plan again?" I asked him. "This time, taking into account that the pixies might not be with us until after we've started negotiations?"

He shot me another look, slashing his fingers through his hair, but withdrew a folded document from his bag. We knelt in a circle on the stairs as he flattened the page and started talking.

I snagged Finn's hand and drew him close as we poured over the map. The steady warmth of his skin and the familiar pulse of his water magic soothed my nerves. The Order headquarters was large and sprawling, built in seclusion on the far outskirts of Rome. The Order owned the land in a one-hundred-mile radius around the facility, ensuring no homes or businesses would be built that could threaten its intense desire for privacy.

The headquarters itself was surrounded on three sides by a cliff that stretched several thousand feet in the air and ended in a long, sheer drop-off. The only way through the cliff was to take a narrow, winding path that ended with a pair of iron gates. Caging in the fourth side was a heavily fortified wall that butted up against the banks of a river that whirred and churned with whitewater rapids. Seven towers that loomed high over the dozens of other buildings that composed the campus. Three of them controlled the magical barrier that formed a forcefield around the city.

"It's imperative that we bring that forcefield down." I pointed at the towers in question. "I know we hadn't planned on destroying the forcefield, but that's Rose's only way in if she's not there when we enter."

"It's also our way out if things go badly," Ryder chimed in. Pyra scoffed. "Not that things will go badly, but you need to consider it as a possibility."

Oron raised his hand, drawing our attention. With quick, sure signs, he offered to destroy the towers. He figured it would be a simple matter since the structures themselves were likely made of some kind of stone or earth material.

"That works for me," Joseph said after I translated for Pyra. "It seems like our easiest option right now, and you won't necessarily need to get close to them to bring them down. That brings us to the center of the compound. I assume that's where Geoffrey will meet us."

In the center of those buildings was one tower that loomed taller than the rest, the main headquarters that used to house the Council and Geoffrey himself. It was situated next to the training facility and barracks that housed the bulk of the Order army.

The campus was sure to be heavily armed, heavily staffed, and one-hundred percent prepared for us. And we were about to walk in like we owned the place. Granted, we kind of did.

"Everyone clear? I don't want any mistakes," Joseph said as he folded the map up again. We collectively nodded, a sense of resolve binding us together.

"You all should be prepared, though," Pyra said, stubbing out her second cigarette while fixing her intense gaze on me. "There is a possibility that your nero friends could die, or may very well be dead already."

Tightness clenched in my chest as I brought the branded bracelet to my lips.

I refused to think of that as a possibility.

There was no way Maat's oath would linger if he were gone.

You need to be ready for anything, Zara, Kaleal chided. *This is the biggest battle you've fought yet. I guarantee things won't go as planned.*

I shut her out as best I could, though she continued to mutter in the background.

Everyone double-checked their weapons stashes while Ryder prepared himself to teleport. The sensation of his magic buzzed against

227

my skin like static. He'd told me he could handle a group as large as ours since he'd had two months to relearn how to use his magic, and I trusted his abilities. I felt in my pocket for my lighter and Phenex's knife, then hesitantly squeezed the vial through my shirt.

"Zara?" I blinked at the sound of my name from Ryder's lips. He was holding out his hand, the unbroken link in our circle of arms and hands. "Are you ready?"

"Yes." No. The answer was a large, resounding no, that I'd never be ready for what was coming. Rather than cave to my doubts, I laced my fingers through his. "Let's go destroy an empire."

Chapter 33

The animals and insects knew what was coming.

Our feet kicked up dust on the red-rock path of the canyon. Not a branch stirred, not a single bird chirped. The world had fallen eerily silent, the tension a palpable thing that pressed hard on our inner ears. I tapped first my water bracelet then the brand above it: one a promise to someone else, the other a promise to myself.

Ahead, iron gates rose from the earth like fierce defenders. Emblazoned on the front were the twisted tentacles of the Kraken, the scaly hide of what could be a dragon, the sleek feathers of an eagle, the curved fangs of a ramalia, and other representations of the Great Beasts who'd come before and would long survive our demise. When our toes touched the reaching shadows of the twisted tops of the iron spires, we halted.

"This is it." I eyed the outpost on top of the cliff and the figures veiled behind the tinted glass. Geoffrey would know we were here. Pyra snapped her fingers, encouraging flames to run down her arms and around her heels. Joseph spun a mass of air around him, kicking up dirt and debris.

At our flank, Finn had already adopted his true form, and smoke curled from his nostrils as he scraped at the ground with his hooves. Ryder flexed his wings as he waited for me. I scanned the skies. No sign of the pixies in the clear, blue expansion.

"I'm not one for fancy speeches," I said, calling my ice sword to my side, "so I'll keep it simple: save our allies, take down Geoffrey, and whatever you do, don't die."

Pyra grinned toothily, the intensity of her flames growing exponentially as she pulled forth a crown of embers. Oron raised his hand, his twisted mask firmly in place as he examined the gates. The hair on my neck rose when he whistled three somber notes.

With a groan that echoed down the canyon, the cliffs holding the gates upright on their massive hinges shifted, bowing outward. The gates creaked as they took on more of their own weight, but the earth didn't stop moving, rolling and rumbling as it retreated. Oron's hand fisted and a screech screamed down the pass as the gates ripped away, their bases hitting the earth with a thud. At first, they stood there, held up by nothing, perfectly balanced, before Joseph hit them with a strong gust of wind. Slowly, they fell away from us and crashed in the compound, a plume of dirt and dust mushrooming up around them.

We moved forward as one before the ground stopped grumbling. Our boots rang out with every step as they crossed the broken doors. Joseph flicked the dust away with a sweep of his hand, revealing a street lined with soldiers on both sides. The black-clad, heavily armored figures clutched guns and swords and crossbows. They stood at attention, and the path they created led right to the core of the complex and the obsidian tower spearing the sky. I spun my sword loosely as the soldiers closed rank behind us. The little display didn't matter. I could sense the magical barrier closing behind us.

There was no way out.

In the reflective visors of the soldiers' helmets, I saw my own glowing eyes and those of my companions. Despite what Ryder had cautioned earlier, we all knew there was no leaving this place without a victory.

When we finally reached a clearing at the center of the small city, Pyra was burning so bright it hurt to look at her, and Joseph shook with the force of the tornado he kept contained inside. My eyes narrowed as I took in Geoffrey standing at the center of the clearing.

The man I'd once thought dead—and wished he'd stayed that way.

Behind him, as I'd expected, knelt Maat and three other nero hostages. Cuffs wrapped around their wrists and ankles, chaining them to the ground. Beside them stood a helmeted figure clutching a sword. Maat's eyes widened as he surveyed us, though the others offered little reaction. Their faces and arms were speckled with blossoming bruises and long, bleeding cuts that made my own blood boil. I still didn't understand how Geoffrey had captured them. Surely they would have put up a fight that, even with the massive amount of resources at his disposal, he would have had a difficult time countering.

As my fellow Gods lined up shoulder to shoulder, slow clapping filled the square, reverberating off the cobblestoned streets and glossy glass walls of the buildings.

"I knew you wouldn't let me down, Zara," Geoffrey called, his hands meeting twice more before lifting toward us in greeting. Behind him, the twisted, spidery column of the primary tower loomed impossibly tall, maybe fifty stories or more. "All of you, in fact. It's a glorious day in history: the day the Gods surrendered."

His words had the effect of throwing gasoline on coals.

Not yet, Kaleal whispered, twining herself around my mind in a smoky haze. *Not yet.*

I choked back the burning sensation and made a show of scanning the buildings and skies. "I can't help but notice that you didn't invite any reporters or camera crews to witness such a monumental occasion." I tapped my chin. "Convenient."

"Some things are best left for the historians to sort out," Geoffrey said. "I had a feeling things might get a little... messy."

"It doesn't have to." I took a calculated risk and moved toward my enemy, wicked glee slashed across his scarred face as he matched my

231

strides. "Give us our friends first and I'll happily turn myself over."

We stopped mere yards from one another, close enough for me to see how much he'd aged in these past few weeks. Thin lines fanned from his lips and eyes, wrinkling his forehead underneath a thick swatch of dark hair. His back arched, spine slightly twisted from an injury I didn't remember doling out.

"No," he spoke with quiet finality, nodding toward the dozens of soldiers surrounding us, weapons at the ready. "I don't think I'll be doing that. I don't trust you and you don't trust me, but I've got something you want, and to get it back, you'll give me what I need." He stepped back. Behind him, four figures strode through an opening left between a few of the Order soldiers. These beings weren't human, nor were they soldiers, if their blue and silver uniforms were any indication.

Elves, Kaleal snarled as a woman with milky skin stepped up beside Geoffrey. She hooked her hand in her belt as she examined us. The God inside me recoiled.

But the elves serve no one, she spat furiously, *and rarely make themselves known. Take care, Zara, elves are particularly nasty creatures. They can—*

"Consider these wonderful individuals my highly specialized, extremely adept special police force," Geoffrey said, cutting off the voice in my head. "I think you'll find they're uniquely situated to counter your own magnificent abilities."

I glanced at Joseph who lifted his brows a centimeter. He was as in the dark as me.

"It's truly in your best interest to cooperate. You see those shackles your friends are wearing?" Geoffrey moved toward the nero, leaving me with the cluster of fey that made my skin crawl. "Those are specially crafted by the elves, unique creations designed to bind magic to the user. Once in place, they're immobilized, their magic harnessed. The cuffs are powerful enough to even hold back the torrents of power inherent to, well, *you.*"

The woman I'd noticed before tugged a set of cuffs from a pouch at her hip. My magic recoiled from the metal as if burned. The three other fey removed similar cuffs, eyes fixed on the Gods lined up behind me.

"Time to put this ordeal behind us, Zara," Geoffrey said, waving at the figure standing with the nero. He removed his helmet, revealing a fifth elf who drew the gleaming rapier at his side. Without hesitation, he wrapped his fingers deep in Maat's hair, tugging his head back and pressing his blade against the sun-darkened skin. I barely contained a snarl as the woman unraveled the cuffs before me and dangled them tauntingly. "Surrender peacefully and I'll let them go. You have my word."

The steel in my spine hardened as I calculated the situation, taking in all the players, their motives, even the addition of the elves who we certainly hadn't expected. I turned to my fellow Gods, the bravado stark on Pyra's hungry face and the quiet resolve on Joseph's. As one, they inclined their heads and a small tremble trickled through me.

"Alright, Geoffrey." I held up my arms, my sleeves falling down and exposing my wrists.

His smile slipped, eyes narrowing as they moved from me to the other Gods to the elf reaching for my arm. He opened his mouth. "Wait, don't—"

"Sorry about this," I said and snapped out with a long tendril of water that wrapped around the woman's neck, slamming her to the ground. The handcuffs skittered away as the other fey drew their swords. Joseph raced past me, a blast of air throwing the elf holding our friends hostage backward as he jumped on one of his handy panes of air.

"Get Geoffrey," I screamed at Pyra, not daring to take my eyes off the foe I didn't know or understand. "I'll get these guys."

"Way past you, hombre." The Fire God unleashed a volley of flame at the Hand who countered with a shield of air. It wasn't as strong as Joseph's, but the barrier gave him enough time to duck out of the way before it shattered. Delighted laughter ripped from Pyra's lungs as she darted forward.

The earth quaked and I steadied myself. One glance at Oron crouched on the ground, a wall of earth rising up before him, and I realized he was already deviating from the plan as he attempted to nullify the threat of the other Order soldiers. The elves circled me, faces eerily blank as if they'd prepared for this moment all their lives.

"I'll bring down the towers," Joseph yelled, realizing what I had. As he rocketed away, a dark figure swooped low overhead, bat wings spread wide as dark mists shot toward the Order soldiers on the perimeter, their nightmarish shrieks rose above the shaking of the earth.

Ryder.

I'd watched him for a moment too long and nearly missed the swoops of three swords closing in on me. The ice of my sword rang out as I countered two and dropped to my knees to dodge the third.

Don't engage them, Kaleal yelled. As I straightened, a second sword spilled into my free hand as I swung wildly, countering the quick parries and jabs of the elves. *You don't understand what they can do. If you use your magic—*

A little busy here, Kaleal, I screamed back, the sweep of a blade zinging past my ear kicked my pulse into hyper speed. They were so much faster than Rose had ever been in training. Furiously, I shoved Kaleal back in the recesses of my mind, throwing up walls and magic and barriers to hold her back until I couldn't hear her shrieks of outrage.

"You want me?" I hollered when one of my swords shattered under the onslaught. "Then you'll have to take me at my worst."

A cyclone of water spun up around us, knocking the elves off their feet, then immediately froze it, locking them into place. As they struggled on the ground, a fireball erupted ahead of me and I started toward it. I didn't want to kill these guys, not unless I had to, and Geoffrey was the primary concern—

"Not so fast."

I tripped, a quick tuck and roll preventing me from face-planting. On the ground, I whirled, confused when I spotted the whip of *my* water retreating toward the fourth fey—the one I'd knocked out when I'd whipped her to the ground. "We're far from done, Godling."

She clenched her fist, drawing a spinning wall of water around her feet. Her smile grew. "Did you not know what we can do?" At my back, ice splintered and cracked. The frost on the grass around my fingers melted away. "We're magical mimics." I gritted my teeth and my head spun as she clenched her fist, the water around her weaving into the elegant shape of the dragon that had taken me weeks to perfect. "I'd never sampled the power of the Gods before. It's simply decadent. Thank you."

The dragon attacked.

The world blurred as I reacted blindly, spinning up water and ice in a frenzy, doing all that I could to stay alive. My breath burst harshly from my lungs as I spun and swirled, freezing and thawing and boiling in intervals as I worked from one opponent to the next. Their instantaneous mastery of my element was as equally awe-inspiring as it was infuriating.

I leaped on a sheet of ice when the puddle of water around my feet rose to boiling and flung hundreds of icy darts at my attacker while simultaneously drawing a whip of water to smack back the other three closing in.

"You're good," the first fey cried. "But you lack creativity."

Through the fog I saw her slash her bicep, then draw the blood out in long, stringy ropes. My stomach churned as I knelt in the grass, panting. Blood was made of water, but after reading about a Water

God who specialized in using it as a torture technique thousands of years ago, I'd vowed to never draw it into my repertoire.

The sky over her head exploded. At least one of the towers had crumbled.

"Blood is better than the most powerful river any day," she said, flinging long spikes of scarlet ice at me. One sliced a long gash in my thigh and I felt the power surge in my own veins. Her throws were more accurate, her creations more precise. In defense, I threw up yet another icy barrier while simultaneously setting my stance in a vicious clash of swords.

I considered using fire but didn't dare call it forward. To do so was a death wish. It would add another powerful tool to their already incredible arsenal.

One of the elves went flying when a horse the size of a tank shot through the fog. Finn whinnied, rearing back, his hooves flying as he kicked another one of them in the face. Overhead, someone whooped and whistled, but I didn't have time to watch as the woman snarled and increased her flurry of attacks. It was getting more difficult to keep up, her icy blade somehow heavier and stronger than mine, her footwork a hair quicker.

I screamed when I missed a block and her sword bit deep into my upper arm, driving me to my knees. My blade melted as I scrambled back, ignoring the roaring pain, trying to get away as she advanced, her movements rife with triumph. I didn't know where Finn had gone and for some reason, the dregs of my water magic evaded me. My defenses were gone.

I threw up a hand when she thrust, aiming for my chest. Out of nowhere, a blur dropped from the skies and ripped the woman right off the ground. Her eyes went wide as the green-skinned fey slashed her throat with a tiny, black dagger, then dropped her to the ground in front of me. The light in the elf's eyes died as I stared, trembling with adrenaline.

Rose slammed beside the body and spat. "I hate elves. Hate 'em with a fiery passion tantamount to your flaming friend over there." She shot her thumb at the inferno I now noticed. "But you're alright, yeah? No life-threatening injuries?"

I shook my head, numb and in shock at yet another near-death experience, and she drew me to my feet with a pat. I couldn't stop staring at the elf, at the blood soaking the ground around her. Other pixies descended, engaging the remaining two elves in a dangerous dance of black magic and weapons. Rose's cornrows snapped, one of the braids catching me in the cheek as she shook me.

"Wake up, Zara," she yelled. "It's another dead body. That's it. You have bigger things to do."

A scream ripped through the fog, receding now that the clash of elementals had drawn to a halt. The fire magic raging inside me drew taut.

Pyra.

I knocked Rose aside as the Fire God toppled, her body smoking as it hit the dirt. Beyond her, a figure raced for the tower, the chaos that was his particular blend of elemental magic whirling hot and bright around him.

"Get him," Rose yelled needlessly as I took off, stopping to scoop up one of the handcuffs the elves had dropped. Pyra's tiny frame was peppered with cuts and bruises and burns as I slid to a halt, pulling her into my lap. Her mouth gaped, her glassy eyes wide as she pressed her hand to a gaping wound in her side. I forced what little water magic I had left into healing her, my worry only abating when her tightly strung body relaxed as the injury sealed over.

She struggled when her strength returned but didn't try to stand. She was drained.

"He's a crafty one," she said. "I only hope I wore him down enough."

Chapter 34

I hovered at the entrance, eyes adjusting to the lack of light, scanning the foyer of the tower. It was nearly empty, save for a row of chairs along the back wall. Everything was still, silent, cryptically cool. Then, to my left, a rock cracked on the stone of a narrow staircase. My legs were already moving when as sent my magic out, sensing Geoffrey's in return.

The passageway was narrow and without landings, so I threw my entire focus on staying upright as I wove higher and higher. Only once did I risk a glance out one of the archer-cut windows at the smoking and bloodied grounds far below, but didn't stop to think about who may be alive or dead. I had to keep going. I didn't want Geoffrey to have too much time to plan his counterattack.

Faster, Kaleal pushed. *Harder.*

Around and around I went, my breath coming in short bursts, my fire magic pulsing hard in my neck and wrists, building for a release I couldn't be sure I'd have the strength to contain.

I stopped abruptly when my foot smacked the last step, surveying the wide room from the doorway cut into one corner. Geoffrey stood across from me, hands cupped around the tall back of a chair. His magic swirled manically around him, and I again wondered how he didn't register the chaos. Or maybe he could and that was what finally tipped him over the edge.

The scarred half of his lips twitched in what might have been a smirk as I pressed my hand to my chest, struggling to draw oxygen. The chair he stood behind was one of two dozen running the length of an empty, iron table. The other three corners of the room were composed of floor-to-ceiling, stained glass windows: mosaics of reds, golds, greens, and blues. The walls surrounding us were carved from obsidian and deeply scarred with large inlets.

I edged closer to the wall at my left, keeping a close eye on Geoffrey who seemed to crave my reaction, and ran a hand over the smooth carving, ignoring the ache in my arm. I'd only had enough power left to stem the bleeding. It took me a minute to understand what I was seeing, and when I finally made sense of it all, I clicked my lighter. Flames spilled across the bottom of the inner part of the wall, revealing the arrow that underscored the gust of Air's wind brand.

"This was a room where the Council used to meet with the Gods and discuss battle plans, draw treaties, and generally congregate. Flames enchanted to never go out burned in the walls. All of them." Geoffrey motioned at the other walls where I could now make out the other elemental symbols cut into them. "They were quite pretty."

He paused, taking in the room himself as if seeing it for the first time.

"I had them doused."

He's an insult to the entire Order, Kaleal snarled in disgust, wispy fingers curling into claws. *He's degraded everything this institution stood for, a religion created in my name.*

The flames vanished and I ground my teeth together.

"This ends today, Geoffrey," I said, steady as the ground beneath my feet. Flames flickered up my arms with renewed strength. "You've taken and you've taken and you've taken, but enough is enough. You've destroyed so much of my life, the lives of the other Gods, the lives of those who depended on them, I won't let you wreck them any longer."

239

Flames black as oil spilled from his palms in response, a mutated version of my own fiery abilities. He possessed powers roughly the quarter the strength of each of our own, and I could tell because the fire lacked my intensity. However, I wasn't sure how his twisted, cruel mind could change things in his favor.

"You're right," he said. "This does end today."

We released our inner infernos simultaneously. My orange fire met his black in a combustion that rattled the room. I went flying. My head cracked against the wall. I shook away the dizziness as flame and smoke and fury raged around me.

Geoffrey had fallen too, his body bent awkwardly where his elbow hooked in the bottom of one of the mountain's valleys, holding himself upright. His cheek bled where a sliver of the demolished table had slashed it. I launched another volley of flames, my spirits rising when one hit him and he screamed.

I raced forward, flames pouring from my palms, when a sharp piece of the table flew at my head. It sliced my neck when I threw myself sideways, but I didn't stop my onslaught. The flames filling the chamber burned with sweltering heat. I remembered watching another inferno, the one that destroyed my parents, and my entire body went cold. I choked back a sob as I remembered Kaz, my best friend, dead at Geoffrey's hands. My teammates, my life, all gone.

All because of him.

Don't stop, ordered Kaleal, clinging to the edges of my vision. *Keep going.*

I threw everything I had into my blaze, the roaring heat stifling as I forced it out, not sure if Geoffrey still lived. I couldn't stop, my rage and pain finally unleashed, too great to be tamed. I allowed it to burn, to fester, to cleanse. And finally, when I was certain nothing remained, I tapered it off.

I gaped at what I'd done.

The walls were blackened, the colorful, glassy stones once contained inside the walls reduced to ash. The wooden chairs were gone and most of the table had liquified.

Geoffrey was nowhere to be found. Not even a charred chunk of bone remained.

I spun in a slow circle, dazed, and more than a little wary.

Was that it? Was it truly over?

A whisper of shoes in the stairwell was the only thing that saved me from being run through. I threw myself to the ground as Geoffrey charged past, a jagged chunk of the table held in his hands like a spear. His bi-colored eyes were wild when he turned back to me, tapping the makeshift weapon on his bloodied palm. His clothing was charred, parts of his skin shiny with fresh blisters. I'd hurt him, but he was still very much alive.

I backed up until I hit one of the corner windows, drawing the blue blade from my thigh as I went. I'd used up most of my magic in the attack, but Rose had trained me well.

Kaleal had gone silent, though I sensed her watching.

"That was impressive, Zara," Geoffrey said. I hated how he said my name. I hated his very existence. But when I opened my mouth, to respond. I stopped. My head felt light on my shoulders, my vision wavering. Why did I feel so faint? The battle couldn't have taken that much of a toll. Fighting Phenex had been more difficult.

I shook my head savagely to clear it while breathing deeply to force more oxygen into my veins. Geoffrey inched closer and I gripped my knife harder, thrusting at him threateningly.

"In another life, you may have beaten me," he said, his tone pitying.

I blinked, his words reminding me faintly of something Phenex had said. Why couldn't I remember what he'd said? I drew in another shuddering breath, suddenly nauseous. Black spots flickered in the edges of my vision.

Why did I feel so sick?

I blinked again, jerking back when I realized Geoffrey had moved closer without me even realizing it. What was going on? My mouth went dry. Violent coughs rattled my chest. I couldn't feel Kaleal anymore. I was barely connected to my body. The dagger slipped from my fingers and hit the ground with a clatter. I couldn't bring myself to care.

I couldn't remember why holding it was so important.

My knees locked and I slipped down the stained glass window. I struggled for my magic, struggled to *move*, struggled to *feel*, but my limbs were made of lead.

Geoffrey knelt beside me, the wild light of his eyes extinguished as he surveyed me. Air rattled into my chest, the motion pitching me sideways, and something metallic fell out of my pocket with a rattle, bumping against my limp hand.

He rested the staff across his thighs and brushed some of my silvery hair, now stained with dirt and blood, out of my face. My skin would have surely crawled if I could have felt it.

"It will be over soon," he whispered. "And you fought so valiantly. It's almost too bad it has to end like this."

The air, I realized, the air was toxic. A memory tingled to life, an itch needing to be scratched. Joseph had told me once that he pressed oxygen together to form his panes of glass, but to do so, he had to pull oxygen from the surrounding area. My lightheadedness, the difficulty breathing. If Joseph could pull oxygen from the air, then surely Geoffrey could *increase* it, too.

He was literally poisoning me.

The jagged edge of the spear pressed against my chest, right below my collarbone. I closed my eyes against the hate reflected in Geoffrey's. I didn't want to die like this. Well, I didn't want to die at all. But I especially didn't want to die alone, at the hands of my one, true enemy.

You're not alone. Kaleal finally forced her way through the gaze. Her words made me jerk, a strange surge of energy coursing through me. My hand fell on the lighter I'd dropped. I recognized its shape.

"With you gone, the other Gods will be easy enough to pick off," Geoffrey was saying.

You're not alone! Kaleal yelled, the force of her voice giving me enough strength to push past the dizziness, to think. Too much oxygen… I remembered something about the high density of oxygen from school. My thumb slipped on the trigger of the lighter and I painstakingly moved it back.

YOU'RE NOT ALONE, she roared.

The staff descended as my thumb finally found purchase, and I depressed the switch.

I flew back as the world exploded.

Chapter 35

There comes a moment, one crystalline clear moment that comes with falling where the body is suspended in midair, waiting for gravity to catch up and bring it crashing back down. The world becomes almost painfully clear, more in focus than ever before.

That's what I experienced as my body launched out the shattered window, thrown with the force of the explosion. Shards of glass rained down with me as gravity finally took hold. Below was a battlefield packed with friends and foe. In a blink, I saw my triumphs and my losses reflected in painful clarity. I saw my fears fly and my dreams recede. For one moment I was only me.

A girl pushed to the edges of her limits.

A girl who'd done everything she could when faced with impossible odds.

A girl who never gave up even when magic and energy had fled.

A girl capable of saving the world.

I was a fool for ever doubting that, even in the beginning.

The wall of the tower blurred as I fell, the wind whipping around me. Even knowing I faced true death this time, I realized the element felt strangely wonderful. Too bad I'd never had a chance to...

You are worthy of air, came a disembodied voice, a voice that had rattled through me twice before, at two incredibly pivotal moments of my life. I'd understood one of them when I'd finally embraced my given element of water. But unlocking my fire abilities had been more troubling, more… difficult to comprehend.

However, I'd survived an impossible inferno, battling back something that would have killed a lesser person for who knows what reasons why.

And I'd done it again somehow—unlocked a third element.

Warmth oozed through my chest as I plunged, the healing power of my water magic surging as it embraced the energy, pulling sustenance from the newly discovered magic. Despite the fall, it felt as if I were moving in slow motion as the world around me collapsed, the enormity of what had happened catching me wildly unprepared. As the heat blazed and the scene of ozone filled my nose, I reached out… barely understanding how to use the gift I'd been given.

The sharp stop in midair nearly gave me whiplash.

I hovered there, suspended high above the battlefield as blue and red and green glass sprinkled down around me. I swallowed hard, my heart beating a fast and harsh tempo in my chest as I flung myself *upward*, through the falling steel and glass *toward* the flaming inferno that used to be the top story of the tower… now blown to smithereens.

Half the roof had all but vaporized, the extent of the damage we'd caused was humbling.

Among the ruin I found Geoffrey. He'd been flung backward and now lay slumped against the smoking remains of one wall. A large, sleek shard of glass impaled the center of his chest. I landed beside him, glass crunching beneath my boots as I knelt. His chest rose and fell. His strange, bi-colored eyes opened when I touched his shoulder.

"You… survived," he ground out.

Kill him, Kaleal raged, and I rocked back, stunned. The intensity of her emotions was more powerful than ever before. *Remember what he did? Remember who he killed? Remember what he's taken from you?*

I clenched my fist, transfixed in the clarity I now found in Geoffrey's eyes. For the first time in weeks, the glaze of hatred and insanity was gone. What remained was the man who'd first visited me in a dream, asking me if there was a way for hi to find me so he could learn more about who I was. I scanned his aura, finding only traces of the magic lingering around him.

"You survived, too," I pointed out. I glanced around, realizing I had no idea where my turquoise dagger was in all this mess, and drew the knife Phenex had given me instead. I pressed the point to his heart, my grip on the weapon steady.

Why do you hesitate you worthless girl, Kaleal screamed, pushing at me, trying to shove me aside. I fought back and held my ground, barely resisting the waves of black anger radiating from her form. *He's abhorrent. The man is unhinged. He was going to kill you, remember that? He would have ripped you from this world without a single thought. Kill him!*

I tore myself away from her, everything inside me quaking with the tumultuousness of my emotions. Kaleal was right. I wanted to hate him. I wanted to destroy him in retribution for all the destruction for which he was responsible. But seeing him like this, seeing him free from the shackles of the magic that blinded him from both morals and good sense…

I couldn't.

KILL HIM! KILL HIM NOW!

I flung the knife away, flinching when it hit the wall. Geoffrey peered up at me in puzzlement, relief, amazement. I closed my eyes against it all, incapable of thinking with his focus on me, and slammed my hands to the sides of my head to keep it from exploding.

You don't command me, Kaleal, I snarled, gripping the front of her dress. *You don't tell me what to do. This is* my *body, this is* my *life, this is* my *destiny. I'm so sick and tired of everyone thinking they are in control of that!*

I flung her into the recesses of the shadows, throwing up bars as she rocked back, amethyst eyes huge with shock. That wouldn't hold her for long, but I'd bought some time.

"Why didn't you do it?" Geoffrey asked when I blinked back into reality. I rocked back on my heels, biting my lip as I surveyed him. Blood soaked his shirt, pooling around the edges of the glass. With each inhale, he grew paler, but he still jumped when I pressed a hand to his chest and grabbed the glass, ignoring the way it sliced through my own skin.

"This will hurt," I warned. He screamed when I ripped the shard out. I chucked it away and forced magic into him, enough to prevent him from bleeding out. That little bit of magic was enough to bolster own, and it writhed like an injured octopus.

"You should end it all," he gasped, his voice a hair louder than a whisper. "You should end me. I've caused you so much pain. I didn't want to, but the magic… it does something. It twists me, it twists my wants, and I can't…"

He stopped and struggled to find the words as he slumped again.

Kaleal had said as much. Magic wasn't meant for everyone.

"I know," I said, peering up at the crystal-clear sky. For the first time in a long time I savored the warmth of the sun on my shoulders, the softness of the breeze in my hair.

I was alive.

Somehow, I was still alive.

"I want to hate you," I admitted. "I want to end it all, end *you* for it all. But killing you does nothing. You pay for nothing. All it does is make you a twisted sort of martyr in the eyes of the rest of the world." I looked down, surprised to see his green and gray eyes open, fixed on me intently.

"You made sure of that, you know. Even insane, you knew how to drive us into a corner. So no, killing you isn't the answer here." I lifted my shoulders. "But I can't let you continue going like this, unchecked. I don't think you want to continue living that life, anyway."

"You can take my magic?" He phrased it like a question, but it was really a statement. A granting of permission.

"Joseph figured out the details," I admitted. "It's basically a blood ceremony, but it's easier if you're willing." He nodded as if he'd expected as much. "Unfortunately, I need the others here since you're technically connected to us all." I waved a hand at the magic snarled around him. It wouldn't be long before it engulfed his good senses once more.

"Then it's a good thing we're here." Joseph's voice came from one corner of the destroyed roof. He hopped down into the wreckage with an impressed whistle, then turned to help Pyra as Oron lowered her by the armpits. Her sharp face was washed out with pain and blood loss and she could scarcely bear her own weight. Once his arm was hooked steadily around her waist, Oron smoothly dropped beside the God of Air.

The Earth God held his arm funny as if it hurt to move it and blood dripped from one tusk of his mask. His clothing was stained thickly with crimson and black, so much gore that even bleach wouldn't get it out, but he held himself higher, stronger.

Joseph, too, was covered in mottled bruises, as if he'd slammed into a brick wall and somehow pushed *through* it. I wondered if he'd gotten caught beneath falling rubble when the towers collapsed. His long hair was snarled and ratty, but his hazel eyes glimmered brightly.

I glanced down at myself, at the dozens of healing cuts inflicted by the glass. My back still felt like a chef had smashed it repeatedly with a meat tenderizer, yet I was here.

We all were.

We'd won.

Now we could start a new world, a world that began here, with a bit of mercy.

"So you got him after all," Pyra wheezed when they drew up next to me. Joseph lowered her and sat beside her. "And yet he's still alive."

I looked into the darkness behind Oron's mask, unable to decipher anything from his stance. His hands didn't offer any insight into his thoughts. Joseph nudged my shoulder, his face soft with sympathy. He alone understood what it took for me to do this, to hold myself back.

"Yes, but he'll never be the same again," I told Pyra.

The coals that were Pyra's eyes burned into mine, and I forced every feeling of remorse and forgiveness and understanding into them as I could. Finally, her jaw set hard, she nodded, the motion short and choppy.

"So how do we do this, then?" she asked, working one of her knives out her bandolier.

"It starts with a prayer and some blood," Joseph said.

And together, as one, we entered the new world.

Chapter 36

"You're stronger now. Why?" I demanded of the ancient God pacing the length of this small room. It was one I'd discovered inadvertently when I'd come looking for her in my dreams. On the gilded walls hung lush, colorful fabrics. The carpet was soft and dark. A dozen dresses of all designs hung from a rack beside a wide, four-poster bed.

Whatever this room was actually meant for was a mystery to me, but clearly, Kaleal had made it her home within my mind.

The God tossed a lancing glare at me but didn't answer.

Her figure was more substantial now, lacking the wispiness I'd grown used to. Turned out I was right, we were about the same height and build, but that's where the similarities ended. She now possessed actual hair the color of chestnuts that hung to the middle of her back. Her nose was slender, her violet eyes oval, and her skin smooth.

The God was beautiful in the vaguely unreal way that many fey seemed to have.

"Is it because I have Air now?" I asked, folding my arms. "When I only had Water, you were more of an idea than a person. When I gained Fire, you started to acquire a shape. And now you're here, kind of see-through, I guess, but you now look like a person. Is this what you looked like when you were alive?"

Kaleal bared her teeth.

She'd refused to speak to me since I'd asserted myself against her.

"Why do I have Air anyway?" I asked, uncaring that I was basically talking to myself. "Why do I have Fire? Why do I keep gaining these abilities? What do they mean?"

The God flung herself on the bed and draped herself with a glossy, silver scarf.

"I know you know what's going on. You're too clever not to. And I know that it's part of whatever twisted plan you have for me." I moved to the door, which I'd left open. "But until you can tell me, don't expect to come back out."

I slammed it shut and slumped against it, wondering if, despite my bravado, I would truly be able to keep that promise.

Chapter 37

Ryder squeezed my thigh as the engines of the jet fired. My hand found his, our fingers weaving together in a gesture that was quickly becoming a habit.

"Are you flattered the head of the United Nations Security Council wants to meet you?" he asked, lips a whisper from my ear as our sides smashed together on the sofa. My stomach twisted as I gazed down at the dozens of buildings and hundreds of people that made up Order headquarters. *Former* Order headquarters, I reminded myself for the dozenth time.

"I've put them off for a week," I said, dodging the question. In front of me, a purple recliner swallowed Pyra's tiny form as she flipped the glossy pages of a fashion magazine. She'd drawn her legs beneath her, her head resting on her open palm with straight, red hair spilling like blood between her fingers. She'd made a fully recovery, though she'd later warned me against healing her ever again. She and the pixies seemed to have similar sentiments regarding injuries.

Across the aisle, Oron perched uncomfortably at the edge of his recliner, fingers curled around his knees. His bone mask and new, nondescript white attire remained a fixture he refused to leave behind.

While only an eight-seater, this plane was yet another acquisition Ryder had called up with a favor and a moment's notice. From the white leather seats to the champagne chilling in a refrigerator to the carpet so thick it left indentations of footsteps, everything about it screamed money. I idly wondered if he counted it among is fleet.

"Yes, but they didn't hesitate to draw you all up on war crimes, first, yeah?" Rose drawled from a bench seat where she played Black Jack with Briar. Beside them, a pixie with short, purple-tipped hair curled up against the armrest. A dribble of drool trickled from the corner of her mouth as she slumbered. "It was only after all that footage came out exonerating you that they finally pulled back on that plan."

Choosing to spare Geoffrey's life had turned out to be a good idea in more ways than one. Immediately following the battle, and before the ambassadors and politicians from the Earth and Fire temples had arrived with supervisors and administrative assistants and peons in tow, we'd ransacked Geoffrey's chambers in search of proof that we hadn't been behind the crimes of which he accused us.

I'd been particularly keen to be cleared of my parent's deaths.

After two days of searching, we'd come up with a big fat zero. That forced me to go to our former Hand in his jail cell in a tower at the top of the barracks that housed the soldiers. The battle and surviving his near-fatal injury had seemingly sapped Geoffrey of everything that had once made him so vibrant. His skin had taken on a grayish pallor and his eyes were bloodshot and vacant. As he'd perched on the edge of the thin mattress, he'd silently counted the bars across the front of the cell over and over again. My chest had tightened watching him rock back and forth, eyebrows drawn in confused agony.

"I know why you're here," he'd said through lips that barely moved.

"Did you destroy the evidence?" I'd asked, the bars chilled under my fingers.

"In my office, there's a bookshelf with a row of legal texts. They aren't actually books. Inside you'll find what you're looking for." He'd proceeded to rattle off a series of numbers I'd rushed to scribble on my palm. I'd left without another word.

Sure enough, we'd found all the material we needed inside a concealed safe, and, with the strategic help of the temples, distributed evidence of Geoffrey's deception to news networks from around the world. I hoped that people received it positively, while realizing that we still had two decades of deliberate misconceptions to overcome. We hadn't had a chance to gauge the initial reaction of people before the second summons from the U.N. had come.

The press of lips to my temple brought me back from my musings and I quirked a smile at Ryder as he drew back. To Rose, I said, "Think they'll arrest us at the security checkpoint?"

The pixie chuckled throatily and scratched at the bandage over her upper arm. A well-placed swing of one of the elves swords had nearly removed it.

"I'd love to see them try," she said. "We'd bust you out in no time flat."

"I am surprised you let Finn and Joseph stay," Pyra piped up, tactlessly jabbing a sore spot of mine with a very sharp stick. "Between my people and Davos, there's more than enough administrative oversight. They could have come with us." She cast a hooded gaze at the shadows of her bodyguards that took up the remaining two seats at the back of the plane. "Then Lilo and Stitch could have stayed behind."

My grip on Ryder's hand tightened to a point that must have been painful, but he didn't complain and continued stroking the side of my hand with his thumb. Only when I was sure I wouldn't break down sobbing did I open my mouth. I was pleased that my voice didn't even crack.

"Rebuilding the Order… or whatever they want to call it now… is something right up Joseph's alley. He's read so much about everything, he's got all these opinions about how to do things right, it would have been cruel to bring him."

It was true, too. He'd chattered my ears off for days until the mere

254

hint of his voice made a particularly annoying muscle in my eye twitch. "Finn's agreed to go-between the two camps. I couldn't leave Joseph alone there, could I?"

I may have had a personal reason for leaving those two behind, as well. I wanted to know exactly what might become of their relationship if left alone for a while.

Pyra's eyebrows winged up and she tugged a silver box of cigarettes from her vest pocket. "Fire would have made sure Davos didn't take advantage of him."

I bit my tongue and pressed my face to Ryder's shoulder, inhaling his warm, cinnamony scent. Her promise was well and good, but I didn't know Fire. I barely knew Davos. And I wasn't about to send one of my best friends to the wolves, not until we had a better grasp on exactly what was happening in Geneva, anyway. At least Finn was loyal and well-versed with politics. He would be able to get him out of danger if necessary.

No one else bothered to pick up Pyra's barb-laced gauntlet and silence settled heavily around us. Ryder pulled his hand from mine gently and pressed it to the back of my head, adjusting me so I was cradled against his side. I sighed contentedly. It felt good to have someone look after me for a change.

As his fingers carded through my hair, I snuggled into him and closed my eyes. Out of habit, I reached for the shadows at the back of my mind, relieved when I didn't find Kaleal lurking.

Chapter 38

My heel tapped a sharp tempo on the waxed floors.

"If you don't stop fidgeting, I'll be forced to find another way to get you to relax," Ryder called from across the hall where he sat on a wooden bench. The illuminated face of his cell phone reflected off the Ray Bans he insisted on wearing for this single trip. They made him look weird. "I could use a jolt myself if you catch my drift."

My lip curled and, with real effort, I stopped the bouncing of my knees. I ran my hands over the black fabric of the dress covering my thighs. This morning, Rose had picked out everything from the six-inch, scarlet stilettos to the red, leather belt that wrapped from the top of my hips to the underside of my rib cage. She'd sliced a good six inches off my silvery hair and artfully crafted waves through the locks. However, the moment we'd slid behind the tinted windows of the limo, Ryder had mussed the entire effect by spiraling the strands into one of his increasingly complex braids.

I'd barely paid attention to their ministrations. I was too focused on meeting with the members of the U.N. Security Council. It was more than only the head I was meeting with; representatives of the Big Five would also be in attendance. I wasn't entirely sure what to expect.

"I can see the doubts swirling around that beautiful brain of yours," Ryder drawled. "I'll have you know that you're the most badass woman

I've ever met. Whatever they've got in store for you in there, you'll handle it as well as you have everything else."

I heard the words, but they didn't process.

He'd put his phone away, his attention riveted on me. From the shine of his dress shoes to the sandalwood-scented gel barely holding his unruly hair in place, the incubus was dressed as sharply as I was. When he'd shrugged on his suit jacket, I'd caught the name of the most exclusive designer in the world, and remembered again that there was a whole side of him I didn't know.

"How about a distraction?" His head tipped and he leaned forward, elbows braced on his thighs. The incubus tapped the tips of his fingers together in thought. "It's been a while since we played the truth game. I'll start." He pushed his glasses to the edge of his nose to peer over the frame, and I relaxed marginally at the sight of his amber irises.

"I got it." His dimple deepened and he snapped his fingers. "I don't know how to swim."

"You what?" I couldn't stop the smile that creased my cheeks.

"I know, right?" He clicked his tongue and shook his head. His sandalwood-scented hair gel finally surrendered its valiant fight against the unruliness of his hair and green-tinted locks went flying. "At my age, too? It's abhorrent. Even taking baths can be tricky if I'm not careful."

My laughter surprised me and his teeth flashed brightly as he shoved his glasses back up the bridge of his nose.

"Your turn," he said, radiating self-satisfaction.

I hummed and cracked my knuckles one at a time. "Ok. Brace yourself." I fanned out my fingers and paused to the count of five. His smile stretched wider. "I've never been on a real date."

Ryder's face went slack. "You're kidding."

"Nope." My braid flopped over my shoulder. "Never had time for it. Between early morning training, midday classes, and cramming at nights—not to mention all the swim competitions, I never had the patience for that kind of drama."

It was like watching a powerful panther uncurl from a nap when he slid to his feet and prowled over to me. I was forced to stand, too, when it hurt to angle my head to keep his eyes within sight. Ryder pushed his glasses up, heat swirling in his eyes as he stroked the line of my jaw.

"I guess we'll have to remedy that, won't we, glowstick?"

"I—"

"Ms. Ramone, they're ready for you," came the crisp, cool voice of the woman who'd brought us to this particular door. Ryder held me steady, his eyes never leaving mine as he ran his finger down my nose tenderly.

"Go get 'em," he encouraged, nudging me toward the open door.

With effort, my feet led me away, but as I went through the door held open by the woman with horn-rimmed glasses, blood-red lips, and a chin so sharp she could write with it, I couldn't help but wish she'd given me a chance to answer.

Chapter 39

"Good afternoon, Ms. Ramone. I trust you're well?"

I resisted scratching the itch that had seemingly developed on every surface of my body. Sitting here in a single chair before six of the most powerful people on the planet wasn't exactly something I'd ever considered doing, and my efforts at preparing for such a moment now proved futile.

"I am, thank you," I said to the president of the U.N. Security Council. "It's an honor to be here, Mr. Agard." Placards before the other three men and two women identified them as ambassadors. "I trust you all are doing well, too."

"As well as can be." Mr. Agard spoke for the group, his thick French accent giving the simple words an air of sophistication. "I'll get right to it since time is tight for all of us. The Gods have become something of an international sensation, my dear. You in particular, as the self-proclaimed leader of your renegade group, have drawn keen interest." He steepled his fingers and his perfectly coiffed hair reflected the fluorescent light. Behind him, an array of flags from around the world hung from a wall. "Additionally, do we understand correctly that the four of you have taken control of the Order?"

"That is correct." Ryder's efforts to put me at ease had vaporized the moment I'd entered this stiff, stark room. My knees were locked, but I was careful to keep my hands from clenching.

"And Geoffrey Marcuzzo has been removed as the head of the church?" This came from the representative from the United States: a slender woman with curled blonde hair and intelligent, cornflower blue eyes.

"He made numerous attempts on our lives, including the demolition of his own temples," I said carefully. "We attempted to negotiate with both him and his Council on multiple occasions, but those discussions were unfruitful. You probably saw for yourself that he forced our hand."

"He forced you to destroy half the campus of the headquarters of the world's oldest religion?" demanded the Russian ambassador. His nose was entirely too big for his face, giving him a bit of a pug-like demeanor. "He forced you to kill twenty-five men, women, and fey in a hostile takeover?"

I met his dark gaze without flinching. "We did everything in our power to limit casualties. Considering hundreds of Order soldiers took on a dozen members of my own team, it's astounding that we were able to keep the loss of life so low. On top of that, records show the majority of those killed were standing inside a building that the Order itself detonated in a poor attempt at taking out my kelpie."

"You possess magic." He sniffed as if the term offended his very senses. "Surely there was a more peaceful resolution considering, as we've learned, that magic often trumps guns."

"Not when hundreds of them are pointed in your direction and the leader of those soldiers holding them is insane," I countered.

"Please, Mr. Petrov." Mr. Agard held up a hand. "We're getting off course." When he was satisfied that things were under control once more, he continued by addressing me this time. "My understanding is that you gained your... magical abilities roughly three months ago, correct?"

I straightened. "Yes."

"And you acquired them in Norway?"

"Off the coast actually, in waters that still belong to the Water Temple."

"The temple that's under the ocean?"

I didn't understand his tone. "We both know our world history."

"But you made your way back to Norway, Ms. Ramone. And once there you failed to notify the proper authorities about your discovery."

That threw me and I nearly laughed in confusion. "The Order did everything in its power to convince everyone magic didn't exist. If I was supposed to report to an authority regarding evidence to the contrary, then yes, I was unaware of such a law."

"Since you brought them up, what about the Order?" The man from the United Kingdom bore none of the hostility of his fellow members, and was, by far the most laid back. His suit jacket was unbuttoned and his navy tie wrinkled. "Why didn't you report to them?"

"They killed nearly everyone I knew," I said softly, quelling the tears threatening to rise when I thought about Kaz. It was getting easier to talk about her, but I didn't know if I'd ever get used to the grief. "And they tried to kill me. I was a little hysterical."

They followed that line of questioning for an absurd amount of time, picking apart my actions and the actions of the Gods up through the battle at the Order headquarters. When they stopped to converse quietly, I resisted the urge to rub my temples. My head ached, and I wondered exactly what the point of this was, and where they were going with it all.

Deep down I knew it didn't mean anything good for me.

After ten minutes of whispered discussion I couldn't even attempt to hear because my grasp on Air magic was nowhere near Joseph's mastery, they turned back, pinning me with the pointed gazes of birds of prey sighting a rabbit.

"Ms. Ramone, we'd like to make sure that we properly understand

261

a few key moments in all of this," Mr. Agard said. I nodded stiffly, curling my fingers in my lap. "It was your decision to lead an attack on Order soldiers in Kansas City, an attack that ultimately left five dead and wiped out a city block with a resulting flood and explosion."

My heart thudded painfully in my chest. "Yes."

"And it was your decision to command a charge in the territory of the northern United States that resulted in even more fatalities, as well as the creation of a lake that has caused significant strain on other, more significant bodies of water in the area? A change that has had a drastic impact on people living in those areas?"

I felt numb. "Yes."

"And it was you who killed the leader of one of the largest companies in the world, a man who was an ally to the Order and many of our nations?"

"Yes, but—"

"And it was you, Ms. Ramone, who decided to lead a war to not only remove the head of the Order, but to also dismantle its global operations, heedless of the effects it would have on society as a whole?"

"Well, that's not—"

"And nowhere along the lines did you decide to consult with or appeal to any local, national, or international governmental body about your potentially catastrophic abilities or your intentions toward individuals or other organizations?"

"I did not—"

"What exactly are the intentions of the Gods?"

I was stiff with petrified restraint. My magic jackhammered at my pulse points. "We want to stop a global apocalypse. Nuclear war is on the horizon. You all are aware of that fact. Geoffrey said it as much, too, though he misinterpreted his vision, we believe. We're tasked with preventing that apocalypse from happening."

Five of the six nodded sagely as if it were the answer they were anticipating.

"Do you wish harm on any sovereign nations?"

"No."

"Do you seek murder of any kind?"

"No. I never did."

"And do you, as a group, agree to follow international law in your pursuits?"

"Yes."

Mr. Agard peered down the row of his cohorts, his lips flattening. "In that case, we are willing to work with the Gods in a diplomatic fashion. You understand, nuclear war is something we all seek to prevent. Since we understand your roles here on this earth are ones that you have no control over, we readily accept that, especially considering your roles as representatives of the magic communities that we are... working on ingraining into our societies once more." He paused. The tip of his pen tapped on the table ominously. My chest was so tight it hurt, despite the burst of good news.

"But you, Ms. Ramone, you have proven to be both reckless and inconsiderate in your pursuit of the greater good." Tears pricked the corners of my eyes, but I blinked them back. "You were offered any number of opportunities to take the correct action and work with the international communities to achieve your goals, and any number of times you failed to take that action. As such, your impulsiveness is not something we believe we can trust, let alone work with."

My ribs were a vice preventing my lungs from filling.

This couldn't be happening.

"Today, the Gods of Fire, Earth, and Air temples will be granted seats at the table of conversation and peaceful mitigation. However, we will not be extending that invitation to you or to any representatives of the Water Temple."

Everything inside me hurt. Emotionally and physically I was

destroyed.

I wanted to scream, to rage, to lash out, but that would only prove their point.

This pain was almost worse than drowning and being burned alive at the same time. Realizing that everything I'd done to do what I felt was right, to fulfill my fated duties, was ultimately what was keeping me from doing that at such a pivotal moment was cracking my chest open from the inside out. It was a wonder my dress wasn't soaked in blood.

"You have considerable growing up to do, Ms. Ramone," said Mr. Agard as he stood, cradling a ledger under his arm. "You know nothing of this world or of the intricacies necessary to navigate it. But should you learn, we may reconsider your case one day."

Chapter 40

Y ou know nothing of this world or of the intricacies necessary to navigate it.

The words haunted me, revolving in an endless carousel around my mind. The lasagna the pixies had scared up from somewhere turned to glue in my mouth, and I struggled to chew through the mass. Ryder had commandeered our new, Geneva headquarters from yet another of his many contacts, and I vaguely wondered if anyone was missing the three-story house with all its crown moldings, spiral staircases, and delicate gold finishes.

"Who wants to sit through all those meetings, anyway?" Pyra asked, waving her cigarette. She glared at Rose who mimed dropping the stick in a glass of water. "You should consider yourself fortunate that you don't have to interpret archaic legal jargon."

I cut another triangle of cold noodles from the watery sauce and shoveled it between my lips. If my mood weren't bitter as black coffee I would have hugged her. At least she was trying to make me feel better. Everyone else had hovered anxiously as if waiting for me to explode.

"Besides, you can run recon back here," Pyra continued through a plume of smoke. "Like some sort of insane chess master maneuvering all the pieces around the board. It'll be awesome."

You know nothing of this world or of the intricacies necessary to navigate it.

Ryder tapped his knuckles against mine, and my fork screeched across the plate.

"Thank you," I managed through numb lips. "We'll figure something out."

The God of Fire gave a satisfied head-bob and turned to patronize Oron who had yet to touch his food. He'd set aside the bone mask, but the cloth bit still remained. I dropped my fork and stared into my lap. I'd explained the gist of our conversation with everyone, but I hadn't shared Mr. Agard's parting words. The ones that brought all my insecurities roaring to the forefront, the pointed statement that emphasized everything I found lacking in myself.

I even hesitated to tell Ryder, partly afraid that he might agree with their assessment.

"Zara and I are going upstairs," the incubus said, pushing back from the table. Pyra waved absently, more interested in trying to convince Oron to reveal his face. Rose offered a warm smile before returning to a heated pixie debate about the merits of swords over guns. I allowed Ryder to drag me to my room upstairs where he lightly knocked me to the bed. My legs dangled over the side, limp.

"Talk to me, glowstick," he pleaded, falling to his knees, keeping my hands folded within his. "What's going through your head right now?"

His beautiful, amber eyes overflowed with care and concern I didn't deserve, and I turned to the blue-black night sky visible through the window rather than acknowledge it. My silence lingered, and, after a few long minutes, he lowered his head to my lap, his strong arms wrapping tight around my waist. We stayed like that, the minutes bleeding into one another, our steady breathing filling the void.

"I never wanted to hurt anyone." Ryder kept his cheek against my jean-covered thigh, though I felt his attention perk at my measured words. "I never came into this wanting retribution or violence or destruction. I was pushed in any number of directions very quickly and I reacted. I was trying to protect people, but I see now how, from the outside, that could be viewed as aggression, carelessness, recklessness."

Ryder rocked back on his heels, his thumbs working circles on the juts of my hipbones. His face was pinched, his eyes squinted.

"I know the face of every person who's died at my hands." I flexed the very digits of which I spoke, knowing the dark stains of blood marring the skin weren't really there. "I don't regret any of the actions I made. I take full responsibility for my decisions, but I feel incredibly lost right now." I drew a shuddering breath. "In the end, it doesn't matter what I did or why I did it. I'm a boat without a harbor. A God without a temple."

"Enough of that." The incubus clasped my head in his hands. His thumbs traced my cheekbones before he leaned in, pressing his lips softly to mine. After a moment's hesitation, I sank into the comfort he offered, the lack of judgement, the acceptance. My arms wove around his neck, the long hair there tickling my arms, and drew him closer, our bodies drawing flush. One kiss led to two more until he hummed low in his throat and pulled back, eyes closed. His forehead rested against mine.

"You are a person in a very difficult position, with very difficult choices to make," he said, the minty scent of his breath filling my nose. "I know for a fact that every single choice you made—even the ones that made me want to wrap you in plastic wrap forever and ever because of your impulsiveness—was made with the greater good in mind. Those people are not in your shoes, they haven't faced your challenges, and it's impossible to know how they would have reacted."

"Ryder—" I started, but he pressed another soft kiss to my lips.

"You probably won't believe me, but I know exactly how you're feeling right now." His eyes burned hot as the sun, mercurial and liquid. "That doesn't matter right now, how I felt, but I want you to know that every person in this house cares about you, even that weird Oron kid. We all want to see you succeed."

"What about you?" The question slipped past my lips before I could stop it.

He smoothed some loose strands of my hair behind my ear. "Me most of all."

"Will you always feel that way?"

He searched my face with a desperation I didn't understand. "What are you asking?"

"I don't know," I backtracked, my heart sinking to my feet.

"Hey." He nudged my chin until I looked at him again. "You have my support. I might not always agree with your decisions, but I'm always in your corner. Always."

"Thank you." I managed a small smile when I truly felt like crying—not out of pain but out of gratitude. That would make my impeding decision a little easier. I cleared my throat, the headache pounding at the back of my head transforming into something I couldn't ignore. "I think I need a little time for myself."

"I get that." He pulled me close so my nose pressed into his shoulder. I inhaled deeply, appreciating his familiar scent, wishing I could bottle it. I hugged him back hard, infusing everything I felt for him in that one, tiny gesture.

"But one more thing before I leave." He rubbed my arm as if loathe to let me go, vulnerability bleeding from his pores, soft as the glow of the moon spilling across the floor. "A truth that I'm not asking for anything in exchange." His throat worked around a swallow. "I fear getting close to anyone. No, I'm *terrified* of getting close to anyone. I've been burned before, and nearly lost myself because of it. Hell, I *did* lose myself because of it. But Zara, for the first time in a very, very long time, you make that terror manageable. You make me want to be something better, something more, something worthy." He brushed

268

at the tears streaking along my nose, my soul aching at his confession. "I thought you should know that."

He stood.

Then he was gone.

It wasn't long before tears saturated my pillow.

Chapter 41

With one foot braced on the shingles, I cast one last lingering look around the room.

On my pillow rested two letters: one to Ryder, another to the other Gods explaining my decision. A few shirts and dresses hung in the closet, mostly Rose's new acquisitions for me. Everything else of value was either on my back or shoved in my pockets.

As much as I didn't want to do this, I had to.

Something about leaving felt absolutely, one-hundred percent right.

Straddling the window ledge, I pinned my braid in its now-familiar crown around my head and pulled my dark hood over it, concealing my face. The rings now back on my fingers flashed in the light of an outdoor lamp before I tugged fingerless black gloves over them. I measured the distance to the ground from the third story, and jumped using the wind to guide me to the ground.

My breath misted in the chilled air. Winter was coming.

It was almost too easy to walk out the black gates barring the house from the rest of the city, and my thumbs looped under the straps of my backpack. Ahead, the dark and silent street beckoned. A few more steps and I'd be free.

"You know, everything is difficult at first. But if you keep at it, it becomes easy." Pyra's rasp was like a gunshot, but somehow, I'd expected her. I waited as a shadow peeled away from an alcove I'd missed earlier. The cherry tip of her cigarette glowed white as she sucked in a deep, reviving puff of nicotine.

She moved slowly, holding her breath as if savoring the taste of the smoke. When we were toe-to-toe, she blew a long stream right in my face. I smiled. "That sounded almost wise."

"You have no idea how wise I can be," she said. "Now tell me why you're running away right as things are getting difficult."

"I'm not running away," I argued.

Her irises flared red as she raised her eyebrows. She made a show of looking me up and down as she took another drag of her cancer-stick and finally cocked her head in challenge. "That's not what it looks like to me."

"Things don't always look like they seem."

"Convince me."

I shrugged, confident in my answer. "It's not running away if you're running *to* something. I'm running to find *myself*. Today I was faced with my own ignorance, and I didn't like how it felt. I'm going to rectify that."

Pyra closed one eye and leaned against the wall. The spent cigarette dropped from her fingers. Sparks flew as it hit the pavement and she scrubbed it out with the heel of one black, high-heeled combat boot.

"I need a little time to figure all this out *by myself*," I said, the confession like a weight dropping from my shoulders. "Ever since the beginning, I've been surrounded by people trying to help, trying to show me the *right* way to proceed, trying to influence my decisions. Even you have an agenda." She flipped her lighter in the air but didn't comment. "I need to find my own way and to do that I need to understand what's going on. That begins with knowing this world and the people in it."

The Fire God opened her mouth, then closed it with a peculiar smile.

"I get it," she said. "That's how I wrestled control of my temple back

271

from my High Priestess." There was so much about her I didn't know. Maybe in time, I'd find out. "But why not tell everyone what you're planning? This is going to upset them."

I shifted my weight. "You really think they'll let me walk?"

"Not really. Can I come with?"

"No."

She barked laughter, short and sharp. "Had to ask."

"Are we good?"

"You do know there's one person in that mansion who isn't going to rest until he tracks you down, right?" Her smile turned wolfish. "We both know that person isn't about to let you go without a fight, and I'm pretty sure he's going to be pissed as hell when he finds you gone."

I knew that. I'd accounted for that. I was betting on that.

"I'd be disappointed otherwise."

"You're playing with fire, Zara." She sighed. "And I don't only mean metaphorically. Don't think I've forgotten how you concealed your second element from me."

"Are we about to throw down?"

The lines on her face flattened. "Nah. But I do need to know: how much time are you asking for? We might actually need you at some point."

"Six months."

"And what are we doing until then?"

"Exactly what you were going to do before you knew I was leaving. Solve the crisis."

"You make it sound so simple." Her fingers danced around the silver container of her cigarettes. "How do we get a hold of you if we need you?"

Good question. My rings snagged on my gloves as I twisted my hands together. Wait. I rolled my sleeve up and unstrapped the turquoise knife sheathed there and handed it over. Finn had grudgingly recovered it from the wreckage of the tower for me.

"It's gorgeous," Pyra stuttered, wide-eyed with wonder. "Are you sure you want to leave this with me?"

No. Not really.

"Consider it a bartering chip. I have to come back for it because it's one of the few things I have left of my temple." I ran a hand over my hood, thinking. "If you need me, say as much to the sea. The Kraken will find me. I'm not vanishing, but I am buying myself breathing room."

The Fire God nodded and slipped the knife into her jacket, then surprised me by plowing into me with the force of a freight train. My arms wrapped around her and I realized I counted this girl among the handful I trusted. It shook me to the core.

"Alright, Water. Six months starting now. Not a day longer or I'll hunt you down myself." I smiled at the threat. "Try to stay in touch somehow, or at least let us know that you're still alive occasionally." She cleared her throat. "And we'll hold down the front here." She flicked her fingers dismissively.

I shouldered my bag, a sense of finality settling firmly on my back. I looked past her one last time at the darkened windows of those I cared about and started my long march toward my future.

If you enjoyed part two of The Elemental Gods series, I kindly ask that you leave a review. Reviews are the lifeblood of every author's career and every star counts.

THE ELEMENTAL GODS BOOK THREE

WIND
AND
REIGN

ONE SPELL MAY END MAGIC FOR ALL

SEPTEMBER THOMAS

To pick up your copy on Amazon now, click here:
https://bit.ly/ElementalGods3

Books by September Thomas

To stay up-to-date with the latest release information, sign up for my monthly newsletter. There, you'll also find free and other exclusive content related to both The Elemental Gods series and my other work (including a free prequel novella told from Finn's POV!)

For more information, head to www.septemberthomas.com.

Acknowledgement

A heartfelt thanks to everyone who helped me on my journey toward self-publication.

For starters – this book wouldn't be anywhere near as amazing or as well-rounded without the assistance of my fabulous editor, Fiona McLaren. I wouldn't be where I am today if it weren't for your encouragement and your critiques! I knew from our first Skype conversation that we would get along splendidly, and it makes me incredibly happy to know how right I was. I can't tell you how much I appreciate your input on this series and for your assistance in everything from marketing to creative development. Publishing isn't an easy realm to navigate, but you've helped make it that much more approachable. And, most of all, I love seeing your joy at following Zara's journey. I think you may be her biggest fan.

Also, a huge thanks to my brilliant cover artist Natasha MacKenzie! Yet again, you astound me with your creative ability. I didn't think I could love a cover more than the first one you created (I mean come on! That Kraken!!), and you proved me wrong. Thank you for bearing with my constant questions and requests, you patience is saintly.

I have to send this one out to my brother, David, too. I was a little nervous when you started reading Walk on Water because I wasn't sure if the genre was up your alley. But you dove into the series with the dedication and love of the most avid YA reader. Hearing you talk about Ryder and Zara and Finn and all their awesome encounters was a huge motivator. I hope book two surpasses your expectations—I know they're high.

Josh, my writing career may have never seen the light of day without your encouragement. From listening to my rambling plotting sessions to proofreading to discussing weird character traits, you've been there for me every step of the way. You've helped dissuade my every doubt. Your support never goes unappreciated. I love you.

To my doggy twin. Sydney, I don't know how you tolerate all the skipped walks and late lunches because I was too wrapped up in my fictional world to take the smallest break. You are the fuzzy bumble fluff that's always by my side on the best and worst of days.

And finally, to all of you who believe in magic—don't ever stop.

I know it's there.

Now it needs someone to wake it up.

About the Author

September Thomas is the author of the Elemental Gods series. She lives in Nebraska with her boyfriend and rescued Australian Cattle Dog. She also boasts a large collection of (fake) owls that some consider amusingly ridiculous.

You can connect with me on:

- https://www.septemberthomas.com
- https://twitter.com/SeptemberAuthor
- https://www.facebook.com/SeptemberThomasAuthor
- https://www.instagram.com/september.thomas

Subscribe to my newsletter:

- https://www.septemberthomas.com